WITH LOVE, MADDIE

Amber cotterell

1st Edition

ALL RIGHTS RESERVED

Copyright 2022 Lilymoore Publishing

ISBN:

All rights reserved. No part of this book may be reproduced in any form or by any electronic or mechanical means, including information storage and retrieval systems, without permission in writing from the publisher, except by A reviewer who may quote brief passages in a review.

With the exception of quotes used in reviews, this book may not be reproduced or used in whole or part by any means existing without written permission from the publisher, Lilymoore Publishing, Contact: lilymoorepublishing@gmail.com

Warning: The unauthorised reproduction of this copyrighted work is illegal. No part of this book may be scanned, uploaded, or distributed via the internet or any other means, electronic or print, without the publisher's permission. Criminal copyright infringement without monetary gain, is investigated by the FBI and is punishable by up to five years in federal prison and fine of up to $250,000.

DEDICATION

Bampy was my main inspiration for this book, he always told me I'd be the next J.K Rowling (in terms of success) and I hope he will be looking down on me, proud of my achievement. He is one of the main characters who is based on a real person.

I want to thank Holly, my publisher and editor, who worked to make my books possible, if it wasn't for Holly I wouldn't have written my books, or gotten them published.

Also, a thanks to my mum, dad, and brother, all of whom helped me when I needed synonyms, character traits, editing, or just general criticism. I couldn't have done this without your help as well.

I also want to give a shout out to Miss Grainger, my year 10 English Teacher. She may have only taught me for one year, but her kindness and support left a lasting effect. It's surprising how much you did in such a short amount of time. Thank you.

With Love, Maddie is a book that may hit home to a lot of you reading it. The book depicts mental health and how the signs aren't always as prominent as seen on TV shows or films. This book is a fictional story however this subject is something that the author, Amber, has experienced herself. Amber spent a couple of her teenage years suffering with depression and anxiety and is now wanting to write about it in hopes it helps someone reading this to open up if they're struggling.

In this book there will be scenes that may be distressing to some readers.

If you or anyone you know is suffering with mental health problems and/or wants to talk to someone you can contact the people below to receive any help you may need;

Samaritans - For all ages

Phone: 116 123 (free 24-hour helpline)

Childline - For children and adolescents aged 18 and under)

Phone: 0800 1111 (7.30am and 3.30am every day)

CALM - For men aged 15 to 35

Phone: 0800 58 58 58 (daily, 5pm to midnight)

Mind - For all ages

Phone: 0300 123 3393 (Monday to Friday, 9am to 6pm)

Crisis Text Line - For all ages

Text: SHOUT to 85258 (24 hours a day 7 days a week)

100 DAYS LEFT

Dear Diary,

In 100 days, it's going to be September 24th, my 23rd birthday. It's also going to be the day I die, because in 100 days, I'm going to kill myself.

This is the first time I have ever written a diary. It seems strange, but my psychiatrist suggested it to me a couple of months ago. I laughed when he initially told me to do it; but I decided to start one now as a parting gift for my family. One day they will find it, and then they can have closure. Take this diary as my suicide note, a long, detailed suicide note with the last 100 days of my life on the record. Everything from my feelings to my final meals. It's also going to be a great way to look back at my life, the good and the bad.

I'm Maddie, I'm 22 years old, I have curly, dark brown hair, I wear glasses, and I'm what doctors would call 'overweight'. I work in a coffee shop 30 hours a week, and I wouldn't say I like it. Honestly, if I was able to, I would become an artist. Unfortunately, I came to realise that most artists only ever become famous after they die.

Like most people in the world, I opted for an incredibly dull job that pays minimum wage but allows me to continue making art in my free time. I gave my artistic dream up two months ago when the thoughts became worse.

I call these thoughts, The Void; they start small like an itch that you can't scratch but gradually become worse and worse. Most of the time, my fix for the void includes drinking, smoking pot, or cutting myself. I know it's not the right way to deal with it, but after having five psychiatrists in four years, I decided that the only person who could help me was me.

For my whole life, I've struggled with depression. In my teens, everyone said it was down to puberty, they said I would grow out of it. When I turned 14, I stopped talking to family, friends, and teachers about my feelings and kept it quiet. Most of the time, I can ignore the negative thoughts that come up, and I can swipe them away by distracting myself, but this time is different. In the last two months, I haven't enjoyed doing anything; even my drawings no longer please me. I feel nothing. I enjoy nothing. Food, which used to be my comfort, doesn't interest me anymore. Usually, anytime I get depressed, I happily help myself to the contents of the fridge or go to the shops and buy £20 worth of food, just to eat it within two days, and then feel completely disgusted with myself. But this is different. Nothing brings me comfort.

The thoughts have become stronger, and they won't leave this time. I spoke to my psychiatrist about it, who has suggested that I talk to the doctor about changing my meds, but to be honest, I don't see the point. I've tried so many different meds, Sertraline (which made me feel sick all the time), Fluoxetine (which gave me insomnia), and Citalopram (which made me constantly tired and weak). Finally, they put me on Duloxetine (which doesn't seem to be working). I preferred not taking meds at all because despite having so many highs and lows, at least I felt something. Since I've been on these meds, all they've done is make me emotionless. I told my psychiatrist this. He explained that it was normal and should improve in a couple of weeks. That was six weeks ago, and it doesn't seem to be improving.

There's one thought that keeps coming back, and it's troubling me; it keeps me up at night, eats away at me during the day and stops me from functioning. It stops me from laughing with my only mate, Becks. Stops me from enjoying time with my family. It has taken over my whole world. This thought is eating me up from inside.

Kill yourself. you're worthless

And I have to agree.

That's why I've decided to take my own life. I can't fight it any longer. I have the perfect plan; I've thought about it constantly for such a long time. I guess I should be scared about how much I have planned this, but the void stays vacant when I plan my death as if we have a mutual agreement for it to be quiet when I am giving it what it wants.

Of course, There's a part of me that wonders about my family. What they'll do when I'm gone, which is why I've been saving all of my extra money from work. I've saved up roughly five grand, which isn't enough to thank them for everything they've done but, hey, at least they'll be able to afford to go to Disneyworld.

The thing is my family is pretty amazing. I wish I at least had a terrible upbringing that I could pin my depression on. Perhaps I could have had a father that was an alcoholic or a mother that beat me. But in all honesty, it was nothing like that. My family has worked so damn hard to give my brother (David) and I the best life we could possibly have.

When I was a child, I remember my dad working 12-hour days, six days a week, to have enough money to put food on the table. My mum worked three jobs to buy all of the Christmas and birthday presents that David and I could dream of. They gave us the best childhood we could ask for, and we were most certainly spoiled. But we weren't brats. They brought us up with good values. Taught us how to be respectful. Once we got to a certain age, we worked to earn money. I remember cutting the grass or washing the car to earn pocket money and then mum would take us to Woolworths where we would buy a pick-a-mix or Top Trumps.

Then, when we both turned 13, we got our first job. We did the paper round, which gave us a bit of money to buy our parents Christmas and birthday gifts. So, we knew the value of money from a young age. We never once took for granted the things our parents gave us.

I wouldn't do anything to change the upbringing I had. I just wish I could bring Bampy back. Bampy is what my brother and I called our Grandad (mum's dad); he passed away when I was 13. 13 was a terrible age, mix the increased hormones from turning into a teenager and then the death of a loved one, and you will have a shitty time. I hated everyone, and everything, all I wanted was for Bampy to come back. We called him Bampy because when my brother was younger, he couldn't pronounce his G's, so instead of grampy, it was Bampy. Instead of grandma, it was momma, granny; it was nanny, and our other grandad was called DanDan. Bampy loved having his nickname, I guess it made him feel special, but he didn't need a specific name to feel exceptional because he already was.

David and I adored him; we would build Lego houses, and Bampy would insist on a tour of the houses with lots of detail. We would watch films together, our favourite being Disney's Robin Hood. Bampy would whistle along to the beginning, and anytime we were at his house, he would make us check on the "snakes" at the top of the garden. He said that they kept getting into his compost. Only somehow, they were always "on holiday" when we looked.

As I've gotten older, I've realised how much David and I are like our Bampy. My brother has Bampy's determination, he's good with his money, he works hard to get what he wants, and he gets it. In comparison, I have more of the useless parts, like being short-sighted, being left-handed and not being able to put a book down once I've started it.

I miss him every day. Despite my thoughts and problems being there before Bampy passed away, they became more prominent after. Bampy and I shared a lot in common so when he passed away, I felt like the odd one out of the family.

I don't know how often I will write to you Diary, but I promise to keep writing. My goal is plain and simple. This will be the self-portrayal and confessions of Maddie Miller.

With Love,

Maddie x

99 DAYS LEFT

Dear Diary,

It's weird to think that all of my planning will become a reality in 99 days. I guess I should actually explain my plan for taking my own life.

On my birthday, everyone in my house is working, 23 isn't a big celebration date so I convinced everyone not to take the day off and do something in the evening instead. I made sure that I didn't ask for anything but money for my birthday, this would make it easier for them to take back once I had passed rather than having presents lying around. While everyone was at work, I would walk up to Bennetts Castle, watch the sunset, drink, smoke and then overdose. I would rather have a random stranger find me than my family. I would never put them through that.

I am determined to follow through with my plan, and nothing can change that; but I would never wish for my family to find me in that state, it would ruin them, and that's not part of the plan.

Why on my birthday?

You may wonder why my birthday? The answer is simple; the people who know me will only have to celebrate me for one day a year. I don't like being the centre of attention, actually the exact opposite. So not only do I not want too many days revolving around me, but I also don't want my family to have to commemorate my life and death on two separate days. I only want them to feel the pain of losing me once a year.

I don't want my family to suffer; I don't want them to feel what I feel, to go through what I'm dealing with mentally, and by sticking to my plan and doing everything I need to, this is the best way to ensure I succeed. Not only will it be the best way for me to take my life but also the least traumatising for my family.

Today was not a good day. I stopped taking my medication; it doesn't work anyway. I think my mind is playing tricks on me because they seem to have instantly stopped working. Which shouldn't happen, the thoughts were horrible, some of them were intrusive and dark, they would tell me to hurt people and then myself. They wouldn't stop.

This is the thing with my thoughts. I don't know what I'm thinking about and what depression is thinking about. It's hard to differentiate. I don't want to think of those thoughts, but I must be a bad person if I do. Good people don't think of doing horrible things to people.

Depression is a constant war between the two sides of your brain, and I'm becoming too tired to put up a fight anymore. I have lost every interest in living. If this is what living is for me. I'm ready to meet the grim reaper, and yet I still have 99 days. I have a meeting with my therapist tomorrow; I'm wondering if I should talk to him about it. I'm not worried he will do or say anything because I've mentioned it before, and he simply gave me "coping mechanisms".

Before the age of 18, if I mentioned anything about self-harm or harming others, it would be reported. To keep myself and everyone else safe. Thing is there's a difference between having suicidal thoughts and being suicidal. The difference between the two is the impulse to do something. The first time I mentioned having suicidal thoughts to my therapist, she called my parents and told them to keep an eye on me in case I did anything "stupid". That's when I realised that I couldn't talk about my deepest, darkest secrets without them being shared with my parents. I asked to change therapists. I was too angry and too awkward to go back. When I realised that I could only honestly explain my thoughts and feelings after 18, I waited. I kept going to the therapist under my parents orders, then when I turned 18, I chose another therapist.

His name was Dr Williams. He was amazing. For the first time since beginning counselling, I began to feel better. He talked to me as though everything I said was the first time he'd ever heard it, and whenever he tried to make sense of something to me, he would use questions in a way that would make my thoughts seem more normal.

For example, when I was having a particularly hard time of it. I told him "Sometimes I will be walking, and my brain will tell me to jump into the road. I don't do it but it's calming to know I have the option." I remember him looking at me and thinking how sad he looked.

"Maddie, that's a sombre thought. It makes me a little concerned." He began, much like the other therapists. "Have you ever actually thought of doing it? Or was it just the internal void that made you think of it?"

I smiled, I never knew why I smiled, but I guess it was because he didn't automatically jump to 'I have to tell your parents' Like the previous therapists did.

"The void?" I asked.

"I call these thoughts the void. It means nothing or empty. The void is the thoughts that make you feel nothing; they consume you so much that you feel like there's nothing left to do except listen to them." He explained it in a way that instantly made sense to me. I understood what he meant or what he was trying to say at least. That's when I started using the phrase.

"99% of the time I would never do it, but some days it's so hard to get out of bed like there's a brick on my chest. Sometimes I think it would be easier if I were to simply disappear." I confessed. I remember that look as well. I remember all of these things he said and did and didn't do, because he was the therapist that listened, he didn't judge, and he never once told my parents about the sessions.

"Maddie, it seems like you have a battlefield in your mind. Most of the time, you can fight the opponents and win; however, the next day, the battle continues. Most of the time you win, and you still feel bad because it's a battlefield there's nothing good about it. Then sometimes you lose, and it feels like you're on the brink of death. The important thing to remember is it's okay to pick yourself up and continue fighting, but it's also okay to take a rest. To have a reset day where you focus on yourself and your own wellbeing." He told me.

"I don't know how long I can keep going fighting this war" I voiced aloud. Something about the way he explained things resonated within me. He was the first person who had made sense of the way I was feeling.

"Sometimes the battle will last for years, sometimes there will be days where you don't see an end in sight, sometimes there will be great days, and you think the war is over. It's all about allowing the good days to happen and preparing for the bad days." Although his advice made sense to me, it also brought up a feeling of sadness. I began to imagine being on an actual battlefield. They had it so much worse, and here I was complaining about my comfortable life.

"There are things you can do to make bad days better or to keep your mind busy. I know you love art; why not draw your bad thoughts. Draw your feelings. They can be as obvious or subliminal as you like." He continued. And that's what I did. I started drawing, I drew all the time, anytime I felt like the world was crumbling around me, I drew.

After a year of sessions with Dr Williams, he moved to another city. He found his dream job of being a councillor in a college to help teens going through hard times. He said he was sad the sessions would stop but gave me a book, he said it was a book from when he was having a difficult time. The book was all about Mindfulness and how to cope when you aren't able to. It had a few activities to do and also spoke about the scientific facts about depression, anxiety, and stress.

It used to help but, nothing helps anymore.

With Love,

Maddie x

96 DAYS LEFT

Dear Diary,

The last couple of days have been rough. I went to see my therapist, Dr Goodall, I told him about how I was struggling, but I didn't exactly say everything I wanted to. I froze. I tried to tell him about the thoughts and the plan, but that didn't come out, what came out instead was.

"How have you been this last week?"

"I've been fine." NO. Why was I like this? Why would I say I'm fine when in 98 days I was going to die? Why couldn't I just say it? It's not like it was going to make a difference. "Have you had any bad thoughts this week?" He asked first to like he did in every session. When you first go to see a therapist, they like to know why you're there and I said 'bad thoughts' so at the beginning of every session he asks.

"They've been a bit more prominent this week, but I'm coping." I've always been good at hiding what's on the inside. He smiled. Dr Goodall was a slim man with black hair and a small stubble. He spoke professionally all the time, there was no friendly nature, which I didn't mind as having a friendly therapist was the last thing I wanted after having so many. He wasn't rude or stern, he sat and listened, and asked questions, so instead of counselling me, I would counsel myself. It worked, for the most part.

"How are you coping?" He asked. "I've been drawing a lot. It's a good way for me to cope." He sat back in his chair "It's good, drawing is a good alternative. Have you spoken to anyone? Tried expressing your feelings to friends or family?" Dr Goodall has been trying to get me to express my feelings more, as I internalise them too much, which doesn't help. The problem is I can't just vocalise my troubles; I don't trust anyone enough. I worry about how they'll react.

"I can't. I have one friend who has a boyfriend and her own life. She doesn't have time to listen to me moan about mine." I spoke, thinking about Becks. "My family, they're not talking types, that's why I'm here. We're not a mushy family. We talk about work, films, that kind of thing but we don't talk about feelings or emotions."

I think that might be part of my problem; I don't like talking about my feelings because I don't want to upset anyone or make them believe they're the reason for why I feel like this. "It must be hard for you not to be able to talk to anyone about your feelings."

It is every day.

"I'm used to it, it's been like that my whole life, it's not a new thing." He moved back around in his seat and put his pen down. "Okay, I want you to do something next week. I want you to talk about your feelings. In one way or another, I want you to tell a friend or family member what's going on in your mind, not everything but one thing." I nodded, I don't see why I can't try, it's not going to make a difference to my plan either way.

When I finished my session, I headed straight to work, which was only a 15-minute walk from Dr Goodall's office. I told my manager when I started that I couldn't work at specific hours because of 'prior engagements'. I'm happy she never asked more and just accepted it, putting me in for 30 minutes after the session. Which always gave me enough time to come in, get changed and sign in.

My manager's name is Sophie. She is the sweetest person ever. She wants to help everyone. No matter how nasty a customer is, she never gets angry or mean. She always calms the situation down and then asks if the employees were okay as well.

Sophie was the person I aspired to be. She was one of those people that others envied because of how nice she was. I didn't envy her in a bad way. I just wanted to be her best friend. I remember when she finally found out I was having counselling sessions and that's why I couldn't come in early, she hugged me and said she hoped I felt more of myself soon. I liked that. I liked the way she didn't say "When you feel better." She just wanted me to feel more of me. That's when I realised why Sophie is so lovely. She is always so happy and wants everyone else to be because she understands the way that emotions and feelings are different things and how the lack of one can result in a cascade of the other. That the simplest things such as a smile or a hug can be the biggest difference of all. She got it. She got it and she never asked directly. She would sit and listen and hope for the best. She would make a great therapist, she's the best non-therapist therapist that there is.

Work was, how work always is, busy and tiring. Our coffee shop is the only one in a couple of miles, so before people go to work, they always come in for coffee, and when the same people finish work or go for lunch, they come to us. That often means we're the target of stress abuse; this is what I call it for those people who are stressed and want to take it out on someone. They take it out on someone who they believe is a lesser person than themselves. These people who stress abuse usually look the same, they have posh suits, a phone always in their hands and a briefcase. Sophie has become great at lowering a bad situation; however, I don't react well. I wouldn't say I'm rude, but I like to give them the attitude they give me. That results in some sticky situations. On the flip side of that, if someone is nice and friendly, I will sometimes treat them to an extra shot of coffee or syrup for free. I don't tell anyone about it; I just like the idea of brightening someone's day.

Yesterday started as a typical day. I went to work and dealt with the same abhorrent businessmen and women, but within them, was one of the most delightful elderly ladies that I've had the pleasure to serve in the last two weeks. She came up to me and gave me a piece of paper, on which she had written her order of a small cappuccino with a caramel shortbread to have in. I have never seen her before, but I'm guessing that she wrote it down because she was deaf. I know basic sign language, so I signed 'okay'. It seems this made the ladies day because she had the biggest smile on her face. I made her order, and I wrote down the amount it would be. Once she gave me the money, I held my finger up and told her to wait. I came round from the till, picked up the tray and signed for her to follow me. I took her to a seat by the window. She smiled and thanked me. I managed to sign 'my favourite seat' or at least what I thought was 'my favourite seat' and walked away. As I was going back to the till, I noticed the elderly lady still had the biggest smile on her face. I know it should have made me happy, but all I felt was sorrow. I realised that I was probably one of the only cashiers who knew basic sign language. She was used to having to write everything down to be able to communicate. She must feel so lonely and yet that one gesture I did made her day.

Life is cruel and unfair. If I believed in God, I'd think he was a hypocrite. At least Satan is openly evil; God pretends to be all-loving while making bad things happen to good people.

Today was one of those hazy days, I woke up feeling empty, I went to work feeling empty, and I still felt empty when I came home. I shouldn't complain, it's better than when I feel like I have the whole world on my shoulders.

Sometimes I wonder what it would be like if I were an ordinary woman. I get envious of the women who wake up every morning ready for the day, eat breakfast, get ready for their good job, and look after their kids. They do all of the ordinary things a woman would do, and they enjoy it. They don't ever wonder if they're good enough, they don't stay awake at night thinking about all the bad things that might happen to them or go to bed hoping not to wake up the next day. They live and enjoy life. I wonder if I could ever have that life, one where I would date, get married, have children. But it is not a dream that seems attainable to me. I must remember my plan, and unless that all happens in the next two months, then I will never live that dream. The dream of a 'normal' life. Like Sinatra sings "That's life." I am taking control of mine and choosing my own fate.

I have yet to find the right time to talk to anyone about my feelings. My mother has been talking about her work colleagues, my mate is away with her boyfriend, and I don't speak to my dad or brother about feelings, I think they might be inept to feelings.

With Love,

Maddie x

95 DAYS LEFT

Dear Diary,

I wish I could forget today. I want to be able to sweep it under the rug, to lock it away into an external memory stick and forget it forever but that's not how it happens.

I decided to take Dr Goodall's advice, to talk to someone about my feelings and emotions. Nothing bad can happen from talking to someone about how I'm doing, can it?

I'll paint the picture.

I asked my mate Beck's to hang out. I haven't seen her for a while, so I thought it would be good to catch up. Maybe get some gossip about her boyfriend drama. We met up at Bennett's Castle, our favourite area to hang and smoke.

Beck's is the opposite of me personality-wise, she's loud, shows her emotions too much and is incredibly funny, but when it comes to looks, we look similar to the point where people think we're siblings. Becks is shorter than me by one inch but with a similar build to mine. She has dark, brown hair that comes down to her waist that she often puts into a high ponytail. She has this wicked sense of humour, a dark one, she's the type of person that laughs at videos of children falling over. She can make me laugh, and luckily when I'm around her, I don't have to talk much, which is fine by me. I like to listen.

We have been mates for as long as I can remember. We can go weeks without talking but then when we do it's like nothing has changed. We often meet up for a smoke and chat session, she "quit" smoking five months ago when she got together with her boyfriend, but whenever we meet up, she'll join in and go halves with me. I don't have an opinion of her boyfriend; I don't know him, all I know is his name Matt, and he's built like a rugby player. Apparently, he makes her happy, and as a friend, which is all I want, I want her to be happy. I don't want her to be like me.

When I asked Beck's to Bennet's Castle, she initially asked if Matt could come, I tried to be kind, so I told her that I wanted it to be us two, mainly because I decided I would talk to her about my feelings. I knew it might not end well because in the many years we've been mates we've hardly ever spoken about feelings. Even when Bampy died, I didn't confide in her because it's something we've never done. I sometimes wish I had a friend I could share all of my darkest thoughts with, but I had to deal with what I had.

I got there early, like always, and she arrived about 15 minutes later, which gave me enough time to roll a joint and light it. We walk over to our favourite bench; it is positioned perfectly for you to see the entire village below. It was beautiful.

Within no time at all, she began talking about Matt. "We went out for food the other day, and Matt got so drunk that we had to leave before the desserts came out. Luckily, the waitress put them in a goody bag for later...." On and on, she went talking about her life and how useless Matt was. It can get annoying when she is more interested in her problems than anyone else's, but I just took it all in, because the clock is ticking, and 96 days will come around quickly.

"You seem quiet today, what's wrong mate?" She asked. I remembered what Dr Goodall said about being honest. I guess now was as good a time as ever. "Honestly? Or are you asking to be polite?" It came out rude, our friendship wasn't talking about feelings, so I didn't want her to feel pressured. "You're my mate, and I do actually give a shit about you. Obviously, you don't think that, though." Becks had raised her voice, which was the first time in ages that she had gotten pissed off at me. I decided now was the time to drop my guard and let it all out.

"I've been seeing a therapist for a little over a year now." I confessed. Beck's face remained angry. I didn't understand why, I hadn't actually told her the worst of it yet or the fact that it's been going on for five years. "Why didn't you tell me you started counselling? Or that you were feeling shit?" She demanded.

I was ashamed. I didn't talk to her because I felt like I couldn't, but I wasn't going to turn around and say that was I? "I felt like I couldn't talk to you about stuff like that" Oh wait, yeah, I did actually say that and regretted it instantly. "You serious? You can't talk to me?" She was mad, and with how it came out of my mouth I understood why. But this was why I often kept things secret from people, in fear of this kind of reaction.

"It's hard. We just don't do that. That's not our friendship." "Not our friendship? I tell you about everything in my life. I tell you about Matt and me, I tell you about my work and how shit it is, and you can't even tell me you've had a therapist for OVER A YEAR." She scoffed. Okay this was being blown way out of proportion, I mean I understand why she's upset, but I didn't expect her to shout and scream about it.

"I thought we were mates; you can't even tell me you're seeing a shrink? Maybe we ain't as close as I thought." She stands up from the bench and goes to walk away, but I stop her. "I'm sorry, okay? I get depressed and anxious. Talking about stuff like that makes me uncomfortable, and I know you well enough to know you feel the same. So, I never did." She seemed to loosen up a bit. "I don't care if I'm in the worst mood possible. If you want to talk to me, you should." She said, calmer now.

I felt like I had just been told off by my parents, like when they tell you they weren't angry but disappointed. That's when I realised that Beck's wasn't mad at me because I never told her, she was disappointed because she felt like I couldn't trust her. "Beck's I really am sorry for not telling you sooner. My thoughts often eat away at me. They tell me I'm worthless, that I have no friends, that it would be better if I weren't here, and sometimes I agree with them. There are days I can't get out of bed, and I have to ring work up saying I'm sick when in reality the only thing I'm sick of is living." There. Everything I wanted to say was out in the open. Now I just had to let the chips fall where they may.

"I wished you'd told me. I would have been there. I feel like I don't know you at all Maddie. You were my best mate for so long and yeah, I noticed a change in you, I'm not blind. I just thought it was me, but this whole time it's because of something that's going on inside your head, and you never told me."

I stood there. Head bowed down in shame, admitting defeat. I agreed because at that moment that's all I could do. At that point, Becks tapped me on the shoulder and told me that she hoped I got better soon and walked away. That was the most heart-breaking thing about the whole thing. It wasn't the argument that wasn't an argument. It wasn't the fact she was disappointed. It was the fact that in the whole moment after I had spilled my guts out to her, showed her warts and all, she told me to get better and then left.

She didn't understand, I don't think she ever truly will. I can't just get better; I don't have the flu.

I picked my bag up, went back to my car, drove home and then I cut myself. I didn't know what else to do. I felt horrible. I felt terrible. I felt like a waste of space. I'm not a great person, most of the time I'm not even a good one, so I did the one thing that I always did when times get tough, I put myself in pain. I didn't want to argue with my only friend, I wanted to feel relief, but the only time I felt relief was at home with the razor blade across my thighs.

I wish my birthday would hurry up so my miserable life could be over with.

With Love,

Maddie x

93 DAYS LEFT

Dear Diary,

It's been three days since my last entry, and that's for one reason. I haven't done anything. I have spent the previous three days wallowing in my own self-pity. I still haven't properly spoken to Beck's, I send her messages, and she responds but vaguely, not like she used to when we would talk over text for hours. Maybe she's just busy with Matt.

Who am I kidding?

I pissed her off, she's upset with me, and honestly? She has every right to be because I am someone who thinks the world revolves around me and that other people should share my misery. After all of this time, I always wondered if my thoughts were speaking the truth and they are. I'm selfish, and horrible, and I may as well die because nobody likes me.

Since speaking to Becks, I feel like I'm going off the rails. In the last three days, I have had a joint before and after work, and I've drank until I fall asleep. Anytime I feel hopeless, I self-harm. I wonder what Bampy would think of me if he could see me now. I know he wouldn't be happy. He would be angry and sad. Probably at the same time. He would sit me down and ask me what's going on and he would listen. He would then tell me to pick myself up, brush off the dirt, and continue walking. He would say that 'no matter how hard the wind is stopping you, you keep going because soon enough, the wind will stop, and the sun will shine.' I like to think that we could talk about life's important questions without getting too mushy.

We were a lot alike, and now all I can think about is how miserable I am without him. How sad I am that my only friend has a boyfriend, and how selfish I am for not wanting her to be happy because I want her all by myself. Then I realise that that's the reason I don't have more friends.

I can't share them because I'm so scared, I'll lose them.

My mind has been going a thousand miles an hour ever since I got back from talking to Becks and I can't seem to shut it down this time. I've tried my usual stuff. I've tried hurting myself in all the possible ways I can think of, but none of it is working this time. It takes it away for an hour, and then it comes back just as bad.

Yesterday after being unable to stop the terrible thoughts that had invaded my mind for the past two days, I rang the number Dr Goodall had given me to call if something like this ever happened. It was a number for a suicide hotline. I couldn't call it at first. I had the number in my phone, but I couldn't press the call button. After 15 minutes, I finally did it. The phone rang twice, and then a lady picked up.

"Hello, you're through to safe space, I'm Pam, how may I help today?" I couldn't answer for a moment. It felt like my vocal cords had restricted, and I was unable to speak.

"Hello, is anyone there?"

I managed to let out a quiet yes. "What's your name?" Pam asked. She was calm, only asking once and not pushing me. She knew what she was doing. "I'm Maddie." I said in almost a whisper. "Hi Maddie, I'm Pam. Are you able to let me know what's happening?"

"I've been getting bad thoughts recently. Normally I can shut them off or distract myself, but in the last couple of days, it's been impossible." I confess. There was silence for a second, the only known noise was the tapping of a keyboard at Pam's side of the phone. "What kind of thoughts?" She asked, her voice not changing an octave. She was used to this kind of conversation. I didn't want to tell her everything. I didn't want to scare her.

"Bad ones." Was all I said. I think Pam understood this answer as a sign I wasn't comfortable talking about it because she moved on quickly. "Okay, what do you normally do when these thoughts happen." That was an easier question for me to answer because I didn't care that my coping mechanisms were questionable. "I drink, I smoke and sometimes if those don't work, I self-harm."

Another moment of silence while Pam wrote some notes and then she spoke "Sometimes when you've done something for so long your body and mind become immune to it. It's like if you had a cold, you might have one cold for the year and then your body's immune system knows how to fight it off, so you don't get it for another year. Your mind is like that but with your coping mechanisms instead."

Well, that is disappointing to hear. My coping mechanisms didn't work because I had become immune to them. Which means I'm going to have to find other ways of coping, or harm myself in a way that's even worse than what I already do. "Do you speak to anyone, Maddie?" Pam asked. "I have a therapist. I'm due to see him in a couple of days." Pam let a little sigh out, not one of frustration, but one that came out before something important was mentioned.

"Okay, here's what I would like you to do. When you see your therapist tell him what you've told me. He may be able to help you on a more personal level. In the meantime, I need to assess how at-risk you are now. Have you already tried hurting yourself? Because I can get an ambulance to come to you now?" "No." I answered sheepishly. "Do you intend to harm yourself tonight?" She pushed on. "No. I am feeling much better now." I lied, knowing that I would not commit suicide tonight. I have a plan to follow.

"If you'd like, we can talk for a bit longer. I'm glad you called here Maddie."

That last part for some reason got to me. Why would someone be glad that I was depressed to the point that I wanted everything to end? Deep down, I know that's not what she meant, but the cruel part of my brain convinced me otherwise. "I don't need to talk anymore. Thank you anyway." With that, I hung up.

It didn't work. I went to bed that night with more on my mind than I knew what to do with. I laid there, feeling useless. I don't remember falling asleep that night, but I must have because I woke up today to my mum and brother screaming at each other. Sometimes they do that. They're both very similar people, so they clash a lot. I got dressed, brushed my teeth, and went downstairs to see what was going on. They were arguing over what I assumed was some dirty dishes. I walked out in the garage where I found my dad fixing the washing machine.

"Alright?" He asked. Dad wasn't like most dad's. He was always joking around, to the point that everything was a joke. We didn't spend a lot of time talking about serious stuff, and even when we did, he had a smart or funny remark about it. "How long have they been going off at each other?" I asked. "Oh, they're arguing. I thought it was the washing machine. All sounds the same to me." He laughed, rolling his eyes.

I laughed. His sarcasm was like none other. Dad doesn't do emotions. Unless he's had a few to drink and then his soppy side comes out. "David put dirty dishes in a clean wash, and your mum went mental." He explained after a moment. "Makes sense." I chuckled.

I always stay out the way when David and mum argue because it's easier. I don't have the energy for petty disagreements. I always walk away because it's easier. My brother, however, puts up a fight, and mum loves a good argument. I think mum and dad may have argued recently because he's taken to calling her "Your mother." Rather than her actual name.

When I heard the front door slam, I gave my dad a nod and headed back in. Mum was furiously putting the dishes away, and I helped. A good way of calming my mother down is to help her. She didn't talk, and neither did I. The last thing I needed was to hear an in-depth account of what just happened, despite clearly walking out to avoid hearing what was happening.

"Hey mum, no one knows how long they have left on this Earth, so no matter if you're annoyed at him just don't be nasty." Mum turned around, she looked angry. "Well maybe if he weren't so selfish, I wouldn't have to get like that. You're not a mother, you have no idea what I deal with." "Okay, nice talk, mum." I smiled and with that, I headed back upstairs.

I'm seeing Dr Goodall tomorrow. I don't know if I will mention the hotline. I don't want him to have to talk to my parents about it, from what it sounded like earlier that's the last thing they'll want to deal with. They don't need my burden on top of that.

With Love,
Maddie x

92 DAYS LEFT

Dear Diary,

I spoke to Dr Goodall today.

"How have you been this week?" He asked. "Not good." I answered, honestly. He put his pen down and crossed his arms, signalling to me that he was listening. "What's been happening this week?" "I told my friend about the sessions; it didn't go so well and ever since I've... I felt worse." He pushed a tissue box towards me, but there were no tears in sight. Despite being so down, I didn't cry.

"Sometimes, things get harder before they get easier. She might have been upset that you didn't tell her but if she's truly your friend she will come around." Dr Goodall explained. "That's the thing I'm scared of. Sometimes the worst thing you can find out about your friends is that they were never your friends to begin with. Not truly anyway. A lot of people are only friends with people for a reason. When that reason goes, so does the friendship." As I spoke the wheels started turning in my head, like for once I questioned Beck's intentions. I wondered whether or not she was actually a friend. Should I have to question whether someone wanted to be my friend or not.

I think Dr Goodall understood what I meant, which made my fear seem valid. "There's a quote by Lucius Seneca that goes, one of the most beautiful qualities of true friendship is to understand and be understood." Dr Goodall was always on hand with a cheesy quote. "That should be put on a card." I joked and Dr Goodall smiled. "Perhaps, but I think it applies to you and your friend. You've told her, she's gotten upset, you understand why she's upset. Now you have to wait, wait until she understands."

"But what if she doesn't understand?" I asked. "Then she isn't a true friend." Dr Goodall made some excellent points, but I don't know what I would do without a friend. For me having one fake friend is better than having no friends.

I remember my time in Primary school, when I would walk around the playground looking for someone to play with, but nobody would want to play with me. I would go up to kids and ask to play tag, and they would walk away or ignore me. I never understood why, but as a child, I was so alone. You're supposed to have loads of friends when you're in primary school because everyone wants to play together.

I spent from age 6 to age 10 on my own, the only time I would connect with other kids is when teachers would force them to interact with me, and even then, they would give me the worst thing to do. Like in tag I would be the one tagging people, and because I was terrible at running, I would never catch anyone else. I always got picked last for sport and was the first to go out when playing dodgeball. I never understood why at such a young age, the kids were jerks. I was just like them, wasn't I? I mean I was chubbier than them and I liked reading but for some reason that I still don't know, nobody wanted to be my friend.

I remember the first time Becks came up to me and asked me if I wanted to play with her. She had a cat's cradle, I told her I didn't know how to do it and she said she would teach me. That was it. That simple interaction made me a friend. She came up to me and asked to play, and it changed my life. She did teach me cat's cradle, and we both got really good at playing it. I remember it so well because when the other girls saw us doing it, they wanted to learn. Beck's made me feel special because she refused to teach anyone else how to play. The other girls looked on in jealousy and for once I felt as if I had the upper hand. She was my one friend back then and she's still my one friend to this day.

Maybe that's why I hold on to the friendship more than she does, maybe I'm waiting for 10-year-old Becks to come back to me. Maybe I'm trying to prove that her single act of kindness back then wasn't for nothing. The last thing I want is to ruin a 13-year friendship especially when she was the one that took the time to be my friend.

By the time I zoned back into reality, I had realised that Dr Goodall was staring at me.

"What were you thinking about?" He asked. I smiled, "the happiest day of my life." and it was. I don't remember a day afterwards that was just as happy or joyful. "What day was it?" "It was the day Becks asked me to play cat's cradle…" and I told him the story.

"Maddie, I think that's the first time in these lessons that I've seen you smile. Becks is obviously a big part of your life." He beamed. I had never seen him smile so genuinely. I nodded. While I agreed with him, I was still hurt over Beck's reaction.

****

Once I left Dr Goodall's office, I picked up my phone and tried ringing Beck's; it went straight to the answer machine. I left her a message.

Hey Becks, I just wanted to say that I'm sorry. Can you call me back? I would love to talk to you.

I finished the call, put my phone away and headed to work. I've been doing a lot of overtime lately. For two reasons, one I can buy more weed, and two, it means I'm not at home as much. I don't want my family to see my pain and to worry. That's the last thing I would want from this. I NEVER want my family to feel this. I want them to live like there's no next week (I know the expression is live like there's no tomorrow but in reality, if tomorrow was your last day, you would spend it with your family saying goodbye, whereas if you knew there was a week left of your life you would have enough time to do something before leaving).

When I got into work, I was greeted by Sophie and a new guy that looked familiar, but I couldn't figure out from where. I guessed he was new because he wore a beaming smile on his face; one that will fade after a few weeks of customer service- freshly ironed clothes -that lacked the coffee smell- and a refreshed look. He had dark brown hair, styled in a quiff, blue eyes and was pretty skinny.

"Hi, I'm Tom." He grinned. "I'm Maddie" I smiled half-heartedly. Sophie clapped her hands together "Right Maddie, I've shown Tom some of the basics, but I need you to show him the rest. I have a meeting in 30 minutes, so I need to prep for it." I stuck my thumb up "no problem Soph, you sort your meeting out. I've got it." Sophie gave a huge grin, patted me on the shoulder and walked away.

"So, what's Sophie already taught you?" I asked. Tom looked at me with his bright blue eyes and smiled "Umm she's taught me the till and what sizes are which, but that's about it. I only got in half an hour ago." I nodded "Okay, well a customer is coming in, I'll deal with this one and show you how it's done." One of the regular clients came in; she was a businesswoman who wanted a double espresso to go. I put in the price and went to the coffee machine making sure Tom was behind me; I told him what to do. "So, with certain people, they like quick service, some want slower, you have to read the room. This lady wants a double espresso."

He nodded, I showed Tom how to fill the machine, and make the espresso. When I was done, the lady walked away. "She didn't say thank you." Tom said, confused. "Yeah, most of the time anyone wearing a suit who comes in here won't thank you. They think they're above you. They're stuffy, rude, and also mainly order espressos or americanos." Tom laughed; I didn't realise what I said was funny. It was a fact not a joke. "How long have you been here?" He asked. "About three years. Sophie wants me to go for supervisor, but I don't know if I want to." I sighed. I knew that I couldn't commit to being a supervisor when in less than 95 days I wasn't going to be alive anymore.

I served a few more customers until I gave Tom a chance at it. I made sure the customers weren't in a rush because he needed to get it right. A few elderly people came in, and while I made small talk, Tom made the drinks. When it got to trickier drinks like cappuccinos and lattes, I would make him serve the customers and I made the drinks. This went on for 2 hours until Sophie came back out from the office looking flustered.

"You alright?" I asked. "Yeah, our sales aren't doing too well, so they just wanted to know why. Just a random question. Do you ever give extra shots to customers free of charge?"

I did. I always gave nice customers extra shots, and I always gave them free of charge. I wonder if Sophie knew it was me. I didn't realise that an extra shot for customers would cause so much loss in earnings. I was just trying to be kind.

I remember when I first started and Sophie made sure to tell me that I couldn't give extra shots because it was money going down the drain and I could get in trouble, but I didn't think it would actually be such a big deal. I thought she just had to say it because corporate made her.

"No, I don't think so. Not that I remember." What an idiot, why didn't I just say no? I think Sophie bought it because she smiled. "Okay cool, how are you getting on Tom?" She asked, turning to Tom, he smiled, "It's a lot to take in, but Maddie has been helping out in case I get overwhelmed." Sophie smiled at him "good" and then mouthed "thank you" to me.

It was strange, I usually work on my own for most days, there are a few days Sophie will come in or someone will help out for an hour before I finish, but no one has done a whole shift with me since Alice. It was nice to have someone to talk to again. Hopefully, there will be enough money in the budget to allow both Tom and I to work together now and again.

Tom finished his shift before me, and when I spoke to Sophie, she said that he would work two full shifts with me, the crossover shifts. We will both be working 30-hour weeks. She also mentioned that I might not be able to do as much overtime as I have been because they employed Tom which I didn't mind. It might be nice to work with someone again.

With Love,

Maddie x

90 DAYS LEFT

Dear Diary,

Since Toms started working with me, I can't stop thinking about Alice. We worked together yesterday, and I showed him how to make more drinks, including our summer frosted drinks. Every time I made a drink, I would get flashbacks of Alice showing me how to make them. Tom must have thought something was wrong with me because he kept asking if I was okay.

Alice was an old employee. She had bright pink hair, but her roots would always show even after she had freshly box dyed it. She wore an eyebrow piercing and would often come to work wearing band t-shirts, plaid leather skirts and Doc Martens that had been graffitied with marker pens. She had this punk chick exterior that made customers feel uncomfortable when ordering with her, so I would have to take orders most of the time.

She was a character. She was friendly and fun but now and then would have this switch where she would be aggressive. When she was in one of her moods, she would often make me do most of the work, threatening me when I would resist. When she was nice, she would buy me donuts and make me drinks. I always loved working with Alice when she was friendly, but I worried for the day that she would come in aggravated. You could always tell by the way she opened the door which mood she was in. I was fortunate to not have to deal with her bad moods too often but when they did happen, I felt scared for my life.

She was an old schoolmate of Sophies. Sophie gave Alice the job as a way of reconciliation. Alice told me that Sophie grassed on Alice for bullying a kid. Sophie found the kid in the toilets crying her eyes out and said Alice had done it. Alice had sworn she didn't and that the kid was making it up. Anyway, Sophie told the principal and Alice got expelled. Apparently, Sophie found out a week later it was another classmate who was doing it, Alice had been wrongfully accused. This caused friction between the two, but Sophie apologised and apparently, they sorted it out.

Alice never quite got over what Sophie did but was willing to be civil during work times. I remember certain things Alice would say, she would always make me uncomfortable, and I made sure never to get too close to her. She was strange. The things she said should have been a red flag for me, but instead, I ignored it. She always passed it off as a joke.

Tom didn't remind me of Alice one bit. He was a complete nerd who loved watching shows like Doctor Who and Sherlock. I did too, but I wasn't going to mention that. He would go on about the shows and how he loved them. He also wasn't a raving psychopath who would go off on you if you expressed an opinion that wasn't the same as his. He was much, much more normal than Alice. I didn't feel threatened by him when he was around. I didn't feel like I would do all the work and he would take the praise for it. He seemed normal. I liked normal.

Tom picked up the skills very quickly. By the end of yesterday, he knew how to make the basic hot and cold drinks without needing to be told or reminded. I have learned that he is incredibly intelligent and has many questions and theories on how the universe works. He is a very philosophical person.

"Do you ever look up at the stars and realise that the solar system is so much bigger than you imagined. Like you spend so much time walking around doing the same things, living in the same area that you forget there's probably another world out there with someone like you in it. I mean in the grand scheme of things nothing we do matters, but that means at the same time all the things we worry about don't matter either. Do you ever wonder if there's a version of you in another world that has an easier life than you do here?"

I laughed, the questions he has remind me of the way I think when I'm stoned. Only, he looked and acted nothing like a stoner. He asked questions about my life. I wasn't usually the type to offer up that sort of information, but the way he looked at me expectantly made me want to answer.

"How many siblings do you have?"

"1 you?" I answered.

"2 sisters. Do you have any pets?"

"I used to. You?" I answered with as little information as possible. I'm not one for small talk or long talk really. Normally people don't give me the time of day, so I've come accustomed to short answers only. Tom didn't seem to mind and continued answering and asking questions "I don't anymore, I used to have a lot of hamsters, but they all died after a couple of years. What did you have before?"

"I had a dog called Rory." I felt like every time I answered, he had another question ready to ask. "I like that name; did he pass from old age?" I don't know why he was so interested. I felt like I was at a Q&A for a magazine.

"No, he was run over." I answered. My dog hadn't been run over but I was seriously out of energy answering and asking all these questions. I just wanted him to stop talking for 10 minutes.

Of course, he didn't, he talked about everything he could possibly think of, and when I thought he had finished; he took a breath and then talked even more. Tom gave me Golden Retriever vibes. One that's always jumping up and down and wanting constant attention. Luckily, Sophie came to relieve me from my shift. I retrieved my bag from my locker and got ready to leave. As I walked away, Tom shouted after me.

"Have a good day Maddie, don't miss me too much."

I laughed and waved goodbye. Tom was what I would call a good egg. I certainly get a gay vibe from him, not that I would say anything unless he felt he could tell me. I would not want him to feel uncomfortable with me, especially as we have only just met. It would be nice if he and I could get along for the time I have left, well that's as long as he calms down on asking questions. I don't mind him talking as long as I don't have to participate, I'm happy to nod along and continue working.

While I was walking home, I put on my favourite playlist. The songs are all sombre ones, with their sad lyrics and melancholy tunes. I like to pretend that I am in my own film, and these songs are the score. I listen to these songs every day. These songs had soul. They made me feel something; the most recent time I cried was while listening to them. I mean, I was also high as hell. However, they spoke to something deep inside of me. These songs got me. I don't know how to explain it, but everyone has that one song that gets them every time they listen to it. They resonate with you. I don't know; maybe my funeral song is in that playlist?

When I got home, my mum and dad were sitting in the living room, talking to each other. I stuck my head in, said hello, and started walking to my room. "Maddie, can you come down for a minute?" Mum asked. I stopped in my tracks; I was overthinking like mad. What could they possibly want to talk about? "Bampy's birthday is coming up and we're going to go to his grave and clean it up, are you able to come?" Mum continued.

I used to go to Bampy's grave all the time, but I haven't gone to see it in over a month. Somehow it became harder and harder the longer he was there. We used to go once a week on a Sunday, put some flowers down and clean up the grave. As the years went on, my grandma stopped going because it was too hard for her, then my mum stopped going because she was always working. I was the only one that would go; I would sit beside his grave and talk to him. I remember one time when I was in college. Just before I finished the course, I went there.

"Hi Bampy, I have my final exams this week. I would love some of your words of wisdom right now. Something like 'you'll be fine as long as you think you can do it; you will do it' and 'hey even if the results aren't what you want as long as you try your hardest that's all that matters." I sighed. "I wish you were here to tell me the things I need to hear. It was always better coming from you."

When I finished college and left with semi-decent grades, I went to his grave to show him my certificates. I remember because there were kids outside that day, and they made stupid remarks. I was trying to talk to him, but all I could hear was the sound of the kids laughing after one of them called me a 'grave kisser.' When I left, I grabbed one of the kids by the collar and told him to piss off.

It's funny how memories work, you open one memory, and they all start coming out.

"Maddie?"

I looked at my mum, who was still waiting for my answer. "Oh yeah, I'll be there." It would be good to visit one last time. I walked upstairs, put my bag down and laid on my bed.

I opened my phone and found a missed call from Becks, we hadn't spoken since that day on the bench, and I was surprised, in a good way, that she would call me. I called her back straight away.

"Hey, Maddie." She answered after two rings. "Hi Becks. How are you doing?" I asked sheepishly. "I'm okay, thanks. How are you?" I was relieved to speak to her. I had thought that our friendship was over, and that had upset me more than I thought it would. Obviously, our friendship meant more to her than I realised.

"I'm fine, look I'm sorry okay. I can't apologise anymore, but your friendship means more to me than anything else." I know it won't make everything better, but I had to try, I can't ruin the one good friendship I have.

"Maddie it's fine, I can't imagine what you're going through. I've never felt like that so I can't understand why you didn't tell me." Becks sighed. I smiled, not a happy smile, but a relieved smile. It was so good to hear from her.

"I know we don't have conversations like this, but it would be nice to talk more."

"It would be nice if we could. What are you doing tomorrow? We can meet up at the usual spot." She asked.

My smile grew even more now, and I realised Dr Goodall was right, I was only ever happy when I was with Becks.

"I'd love to. Usual spot and the usual time?"

Becks agreed, and with that, we hung up. I laid on my bed, smiling. I couldn't stop. That one conversation with Beck's put me in a good mood for the rest of the evening, and for once, I went to bed happy. I forgot how good it felt to be happy. Thing's turned bad with me and Beck's, but we have fixed it. Maybe Dr Goodall knows what he's talking about.

I look forward to seeing Beck's tomorrow. and hopefully putting all of this behind us.

With Love,

Maddie x

85 DAYS LEFT

Dear Diary,

A lot has happened in the last five days, and I guess the easiest way of explaining it would be to start four days ago when I went out with Becks. It was an average day up until I met her. I went to our usual spot and waited for her to come. I rolled a spliff, knowing she would want some. I sat on my own for about ten minutes before I saw her pull into the carpark and walk over to me. "Hey." I said.

"Hey" she replied. I went to hand over the spliff, but she put her hand up and shook her head. I frowned but put it back up to my mouth and finished it off.

"I'm not going to smoke it anymore." She explained.

"Fair enough." I nodded, I never forced Becks to smoke, it's not like she ever paid for the weed anyway she always just took mine.

"So, what's been up?" I wanted to keep the conversation as normal as possible. I didn't want it to be awkward between us, although it was clear that it still was. I feel like we've only just met, the Becks I saw in front of me wasn't acting like the Beck' I thought I knew.

"I've just been working, and spending a lot of time with Matt. We argued a couple of days ago... about you. But it's fine we sorted it out."

"Why did you argue over me?" I asked, confused. They had no reason to disagree over me, I had never really spent time with her boyfriend. Becks started kicking the dirt on the floor; she wouldn't look me in the eyes.

"He said you weren't good for me anymore. He was worried I would catch what you have, but I told him that's not how that depression works."

Right. I shut my eyes, put my head down and finished the spliff.

"No, it's not how it works, but all I want is for you to be happy Becks, so if that meant for you to move on from me, I would never stop you." Perhaps losing me to suicide would be easier if we were no longer talking.

"I'd never move on from you. You came first no matter what, I just think some people don't understand that things like depression can't be spread like the common cold." She scoffed.

"How did you know I was depressed and not just mental?" I chuckled.

"Because I know you. I noticed you becoming quieter; I noticed you wearing long sleeves throughout summer. I saw you change, but I didn't say anything because I thought you would tell me and when you didn't, I assumed I was connecting dots that didn't need to be connected." Beck's explained. It was good to know that although she didn't make a fuss about it, she knew something was different with me, but I couldn't understand why she wouldn't just ask me.

"Becks, I'm sorry. I'm not good with words. Talking isn't my forte; I would never want anyone to feel the way I do."

Becks came to sit beside me and took my hand. "Mate, you know I'm here for you. Please don't do anything stupid." She raised her baby finger in the air. "Pinkie swears?"

"Pinkie swears." I repeated and wrapped my baby finger around hers. I wasn't going to tell her about my plan. "Anyway, how have you been?" She asked. "I've been alright, some days I struggle more than others, but at the moment I have my coping mechanisms." I explained. "Are they good coping mechanisms, though?" She asked, eyeing the space where I had stubbed out the spliff. I smiled at her. I think she must have done some research because she sounded like Dr Goodall for a moment.

"No... No, they're not." I answered, honestly. Becks put her hand on my shoulder. She didn't say anything, but her face was crossed with sympathy. "Sometimes I feel like the world is caving in on me and I have no idea how to stop it and sometimes I don't want to stop it, I just want the world to consume me." I continued.

In that moment with the heaviness of the whole world on my shoulders, my closest friend knowing my darkest secret and the exhaustion from telling her, I broke down. I cried and cried. Becks pulled me close to her, and I just sobbed. Becks tried her best to cheer me up, but it was useless, the floodgates were open. I think after a while, it began to scare her a little. "Maddie, listen to me. It will be ok." She said, I don't know whether I was too exhausted or too high, but I told Becks my darkest, deepest secret.

"Becks, I want to die."

I wept into my hands. There it was. It was out in the open now, and I could not take it back. She didn't move or pull a face. She simply sat beside me, her arm around my shoulder and listened as I poured my heart out. She said she would be here for me.

I don't know how long I cried for, or when I finished, but when I did Becks drove me home. I was so exhausted that I fell asleep in the car. "Maddie we're here," she shook me gently. I arose from the short sleep that I had and thanked her for dropping me home, as I got out of the car, she wound down the window.

"Maddie, tell your therapist. I don't want to lose you. It might be selfish, but I don't want you to die." I managed a half-hearted smile, waved, and walked into my house. Luckily, my mum was still at work, so I went straight upstairs to my room. I changed into my comfy clothes, and I got into bed. I was so tired I just wanted to sleep all day long. Of course, that didn't happen because when my mum got home, she came into my room and told me to get up. "You shouldn't be in bed; it's only 5 o'clock, you're supposed to be young. Stop lying around and do something useful." I groaned and got out of bed. I made tea for my family—Katsu curry. Then hurried away to have a shower.

As I was in the shower, I caught a glimpse of myself in the mirror. I quickly looked away. I hated seeing myself naked. All of the scars and fat that covered my body was another reason for hating myself. It made me feel like less of a person. Like I was worthless because to me, my body was so abnormal.

Once out of the shower, I got into my pyjamas and went to bed. I didn't sleep well that night. I kept thinking about what Becks had said, about how she didn't want me to die. How I pinkie promised her I wouldn't do anything stupid. I never understood that phrase 'don't do anything stupid' because stupid is a relative term; different people have different levels of stupid. What I think is stupid, someone else doesn't. I didn't completely understand what she meant by that. Did she mean me harming myself or me ending my own life? I didn't feel like it was appropriate to ask because she'd probably say both. All I dreamt about was our conversation. Her words went around and around in my head, refusing me a moment of rest.

When I woke up the next day, I was feeling a bit better. I felt like I had accomplished something yesterday. It was the first time in a while that I could cry properly. It was the first time in years I have cried in front of someone.

I had a bit of a spring in my step. It was my day off, so I could do what I wanted with the day. I decided to try out something I haven't done in a long time, drawing. At first, I had no inspiration and found myself staring at the blank paper, pencil poised and ready to go. That was until I remembered what Dr Williams told me about drawing my feelings. Usually, that would mean drawing a dark colour or a black mass, but today I drew fireworks. To me, they illustrated the way I felt inside today. I had achieved something, and that made me feel like celebrating.

I didn't stop there, I kept drawing, and when I finished one picture, I went onto another. By the time I had completed three drawings, it was already 2oclock. I had spent all morning wholly distracted, and it felt good.

But the more I looked at the drawings, the less I liked them. Typical. That's the one thing I hate about drawing and any other form of art, no matter how long it takes for me to do them, I will always find a flaw in my piece. I decided to stop drawing when I started finding too many flaws in the drawings and started disliking them.

When I went downstairs, I found mum at the table doing some

paperwork. She looked incredibly busy, so I went ahead and made two coffees, one white with two sweeteners and one white with no sweeteners or sugars. I handed mum the sweetened coffee and sat down on the sofa that was adjacent to the table. Mum smiled and went back to her paperwork. I drank my drink and looked up at my wonderful mum, who I appreciate more than anything.

My mum is strict, she likes things to be a certain way, but she's also someone who will do absolutely anything for anyone. She loves helping people, and that's what I love about her, her kindness is like no other. I think she realised I was staring at her because she turned to me and said, jokingly, "You can take a photo if you like." I laughed and sipped the last of my coffee. "I have loads of you, mum. I don't need another" As I put the mug in the washing machine, I peered into the living room and then added "I was just admiring your work." and walked back upstairs into my bedroom. I led back onto my bed and checked my phone.

0 messages. 0 texts.

I went onto my messages to make sure that the ones I had sent earlier had actually been delivered, and of course, they had. I know everyone is busy and has their own lives, but sometimes it's hard when no one replies instantly. I always put people first, like if Becks needed me, I would drop everything to make sure that I was there, but it doesn't happen the other way round. I think everyone else is doing it the right way. They focus on themselves, and when they're free, they see their friends. My priorities have always been wrong, but I think that's because I've never had that many friends. When Becks and I stopped talking for a year, I remember I had no one for that entire year.

Becks and I fell out because she promised to give me a lift to my old job. My car was in for an MOT that day and work was a 40-minute walk away. I asked Becks for a lift a week prior to the day as well as checking up a day before making sure it was still okay. Everything was all good, on the day I was waiting for her, I texted her but no replies. It wasn't un-normal for her to not message me, I thought she was driving to come get me. It was about 20 minutes before I was due at work, and I rang her to see where she was. She answered the phone sounding groggy, it turns out she was still in bed and my phone call had woken her up. I was fuming, I was so angry. I told her that she was selfish, and I had checked with her multiple times and that she let me down. She then blamed me for not ringing her saying that I know what she's like and I should have rung. I ended up being half an hour late because I had to walk to work. My boss told me off and gave me a formal warning. Becks and I stopped talking after that.

When Becks and I stopped talking I had no-one. I would go to work, come home from work and that was it. I had nothing else. I had no one else. Yet no matter how much I wanted to rekindle our friendship, I didn't. I thought after everything I had done for her; she could come to me. It took a year, but she did. She messaged me out of the blue one day, and I agreed to meet up. We both realised during that time how important our friendship is. However, during our time apart, she met Matt, and I suddenly was not needed as much.

Sometimes I get down because I have no one to talk to, and I feel jealous of those people whose phones are beeping non-stop. I wonder if you can tell from the family what a child will be like when they are born. My mum is really outgoing. She's a party animal and talks all the time whereas dad is more reserved and doesn't talk much, but he knows what he's on about when he does. I know David got mum's traits which must be why he's got so many friends. So, I guess I have to be like my dad. It's not a bad thing but when I'm depressed all I want is to go out with people and have more friends. I can't just go into a club and make new friends. I know the types of girls that go into clubs, and they aren't my cup of tea. I wonder if anyone has ever done that before? There has to be. How do adults make non-work friends? I know I'm 22, but I don't feel like an adult, I feel like I need to be taught more adult things and then I can go out into the world feeling like a grown-up. I wonder at what point in your life you become fully mature. Like my mum is an adult she has it all together, she knows exactly what she's doing. She's able to work, clean the house and make tea, and when we were younger, she also looked after us. It's insane how people are just able to become adults so simply, whereas I do some housework, go to work, and feel dead.

****

Waking up the next day, I thought I would feel better, but I felt worse off. My migraines were getting harder to bear, and the shakes from my anxiety had kicked themselves up a notch. The thoughts were still just as bad, but the physical signs of depression were becoming more apparent. It took me twice as long to get out of bed. I could have stayed there forever. When I finally got up, I noticed how quiet the house was.

Most mornings I'll wake up to mum and dad chatting or sound from the TV, but it was utterly silent. I enjoyed the peace and tranquillity... until I looked at my phone.

8:44 am

SHIT!!

I need to be at work in 15 minutes! I jumped out of bed and got my clothes on quickly. I grabbed my makeup bag, purse, phone, and keys and ran out the door.

8:55 am

It only takes me 10 minutes to get to work when I walk, but today was not a walking day. I was running, and I was running fast. I had chucked all my stuff into the nearest plastic bag that I could find before leaving the house, and it had started to stretch at the handles. I turned down an alley, it was sketchy, but I was late, and surely too early for creeps to be lurking.

As I came out of the lane, the bag broke and all of my things fell on the floor. Great. I picked up my keys and phone and put them in my pocket, then I grabbed my purse and just as I went to pick up my makeup bag a hand reached down and picked it up first. I looked up and saw Tom smiling down at me.

"Thank you" I gasped, still trying to catch my breath. "My pleasure." Tom smiled. We walked the last stretch of the coffee shop together. "I'm guessing you slept in too?" Tom asked. I laughed and nodded. I was still out of breath from running. I was so unfit, the last time I did this much physical exercise I was in high school. Since then, I've put on two stone.

We got into work 3 minutes late, Sophie is really lovely, but her one pet peeve is lateness.

"Tom you're 3 minutes late, you haven't even completed your trial yet, and you're late." Sophie commented as she came round into the coffee shop, looking at her watch. Tom quickly ran into the back.

"Oh, hey Maddie, you want a drink?" She asked when she spotted me.

"Uh yeah, sure." I answered, confused. "Medium latte with skimmed milk?"

I nodded. This is weird. Why wasn't Sophie pissed at me too? I mean, I've never been late before.

I walked out the back and noticed Tom was struggling to tie his apron at the back, I gestured for him to turn around and quickly tied it for him. He smiled and thanked me. "That's weird. Why didn't she tell me off for being late as well?" I mumbled to Tom who shrugged in reply. I put my apron on and walked out the front.

"What?" I asked nervously as Sophie began laughing at me.

"You know you're not working today, right?" She giggled.

WHAT!! "Are you serious?"

Sophie put her hand up to her mouth to try and hold in the laughter, but it didn't help. "Yeah, you're in tomorrow, not today." You have to be joking. Not only did I get out of bed, but I also RAN HERE.

"Don't suppose you need some help? I'm here now." I laughed, holding back my annoyance.

Sophie shook her head. "Sorry, we've got everyone we need."

"Okay well looks like I'm going home then." I sighed.

"You can have my shift if you like?" Tom said half-jokingly.

"Nice try." Sophie glared at him. I went out the back, took my apron off, grabbed a to-go bag to put my stuff in and headed out.

"£3.50, there you go Soph, cheers for the drink." "Don't worry about it, have one on the house but don't tell management." She laughed.

"You are management" I laughed and then headed out.

When I got home, I sat down on the sofa. Having a free house was nice. I enjoyed the peace and quiet. I looked around, my living room was as neat as always, every photo was neatly in place, the cushions in the chair were straight, and the blinds were perfectly clean. It was like a show home. I stood up and went over to the photos; there was an array, one was of Bampy and I at the aquarium, one was David and I, then there was mum and dad together, David and my grandma, and right in the middle of the photos was Rory, our dog. In front of the photo of Rory was a dark mahogany box with his ashes inside.

Rory was a staffy. He was seven years old when he passed away, which is pretty young for a dog. He was the best friend I could have asked for, except Bampy. After Bampy died Mum and dad knew David and I were struggling, so they bought Rory. He was the cutest wrecking ball to ever exist. He had grey fur with white paws and the dopiest, most loveable face I have ever seen on a dog. As he got older, his mouth started turning white as well. Rory had skin cancer, we noticed a small bump on his leg one day, took him to the vets to check it out and when they did a scan, they found not one but four lumps.

I remember that day so vividly; we were told that they could grow back even if they were removed. We took the chance. He had them removed, and then four months later, two more were found. We tried many different medicines, but we realised that the best thing for Rory was to give him peace. We stopped his medication, and for the last two weeks of his life, he did all the things that made him happy. We took him to the beach, gave him ice cream, burgers, and chips. He went swimming, to the park, and slept in our beds. For the last two weeks, he was treated like royalty. On the last day before we took him to the vets, we went to McDonalds, got him a kids meal (his favourite), and took him for a walk. We walked so far that day because, in reality, we knew once we finished walking, it was time to say goodbye.

At the vets, they asked us if we wanted to go in. I said yes, but everyone else said no. I went in and led down with him; I didn't want him to be alone. I remember speaking to him. "Rory, you have been a marvellous dog, you came into our family when we were broken and bruised, and you have brightened our lives. You are the best thing that ever happened to us. Seven years is short, but it was the best seven years I could have asked for."

As I spoke, Rory licked my hand and rubbed his nose on me. Then he just fell asleep. It was so simple. So peaceful. One moment he was here and the next he was gone. I laid on the floor for 15 minutes before I got up. I remember the vet giving me Rory's collar and tag. I still have them to this day. Rory loved all of us, but we had a special connection. I miss walking into the house and seeing him come bounding up to me, yapping with happiness. Or when he used to lay on my feet at the end of my bed. He would sleep beside me before mum told him to get down. He was a good dog.

I spent the rest of the day in bed. Mum was at work, so there was no one to tell me what to do. Although I could have done without rushing to work this morning, I am glad of the time alone.

****

I spent most of yesterday at work. I had a long shift as we needed to change around the coffee machine for a new one. Tom wasn't in, so Sophie and I got to work dismantling the old one and fitting the new one. Luckily, we knew what we were doing because we had done it before. We were so busy that we forgot the time. By the time I finished and got home, it was 7:00 pm. Three hours after I originally should have finished. I was exhausted. Mum made a cottage pie, which I politely declined. I wasn't interested in food today. I have been feeling very sick recently (another side effect of a depressive episode). I hadn't eaten properly in days, but the strange thing was that I wasn't even hungry.

****

Today, I saw Dr Goodall. It was one of those days. I wanted to miss therapy all together, but it's quite hard when you've paid for the next six sessions, and you're money savvy. I walked into the office and noticed that Dr Goodall's office had had a makeover just like our coffee shop. It was now navy blue and white with photos hanging around the room. It looked more comforting. More homely.

"How are you today, Maddie?" Dr Goodall asked. He got straight into the questions today, leaving no room for chit chat.

"I'm okay." I said with a fake smile.

"How has this week been?" He asked.

"Not too bad. I'm just tired." He nodded, writing my every word down.

"Did you speak to your friend?"

"Her name's Becks." I corrected him.

"Okay, have you spoken to Becks?" He smiled.

"Yeah." I nodded.

"And things went well?" He asked.

"Yeah." I nodded again.

"So, tell me what's getting to you? Because last week Becks was the only thing you wanted to fix and you've done that, which is great. But you seem different from last week; you look deflated." He sighed.

"Yeah, I am. I thought I would be happy, but I'm too tired, to think about it. Nothing I do is making a difference. I've been doing counselling for over four years, and it's not helped otherwise I wouldn't still be needing it. I was always told counselling was a short-term solution. 4 years doesn't seem to be short term." I admitted how I was truly feeling.

Dr Goodall put his pen down and crossed his hands in front of himself. "Counselling isn't a miracle. Not for everyone at least. Some people have six sessions and boom they're better, but for others, it's just good for them to talk, so they don't go over the edge. It's something they may always need." He explained. I nodded in reply. I had heard this before. "Listen, if you ever have any problems and you want to talk to someone, you can call me. I don't want you suffering alone." He slid a piece of card over the table. I picked it up and examined it. It was his number. I smiled and thanked him.

Before I left, I turned to him and said, "you know how we put animals down when they're in pain, don't you think it would be better if we could do that with humans?" Before he could answer, I walked out. Tom asked me the same thing last week, and I had to admit that it had stayed with me since.

I realised how the only people I really talk to are my therapist and work colleagues, even after I have reconciled with Becks, I still feel like we're not as close as we once were. I also think that when I am with Becks, she does a lot of the talking and I tend to agree. I can be with Becks, my family, Tom or Sophie and I can still feel alone, I can be with people laughing and joking around, then all of a sudden, I feel empty. It's like I'm a battery, but I'm an old, warn out one where I have 100% battery for an hour or two, and then my battery needs recharging.

I have been thinking of writing a note, a proper one, not this one. An actual suicide notes, for my parents to read, so they can have closure.

With Love,

Maddie x

80 DAYS LEFT

Dear Diary,

Nothing of major importance has happened over the last five days. Work has been a lot more interesting with Tom there, even if we only work together two days a week. Whatever Tom does in the future he will be great at it; he has this enthusiasm that I have never been able to have or understand. He's one of those who do great at their job, and you want them to do well, they try to help other people, and have this happiness that shines through. I'm not jealous of Tom, but I am slightly envious. The more time I spend with him, the more I've realised that he is a kind man, with an old soul. I half expect him one day to shake his fist and say something like 'in my day we would have respected the elders.'

He's definitely very strange. Just two days ago, in the middle of work, he looked at me and asked, dead seriously, "do you think zombies could be a thing?"

"I don't think so; you'd have to find a virus so powerful that it eats and rewrites your brain cells into becoming a zombie. I don't think there's one powerful enough." I laughed.

Tom nodded his head and then added: "I mean that's true; however, there was a guy in Florida who took a ton of drugs and ended up eating people and having superhuman strength."

I laughed, I remembered seeing that online "Yes, but drugs are different, he took the drugs and for a certain amount of time his brain receptors weren't coordinating, so he basically turned into our ancestors, the ape. Apparently, we only actually use about 30% of our strength. If we used more, we would damage ourselves and others, just like apes." I explained. Tom stared at me, so I continued. "We evolved, but when he took the drugs, he kinda stepped back thousands of years, and the brain receptors failed allowing him to become ape-like strength-wise." I gasped for breath. Tom seemed surprised by my information. He looked at me as if I had grown four extra legs.

"So, if drugs can do that why couldn't the possibility of zombies exist?" He asked.

"Okay, maybe one day they might, but there are so many factors the virus would have to take into consideration. First, it would have to affect the brain, so the brain receptors were killed off, then it would have to find a way of keeping the rest of the body, like the cells alive but dormant so the body itself could stay intact like we see in films. The virus would have to work out a way to kill one part of the body while keeping the rest alive."

"You're smart. I thought I was the only nerd here." He laughed, surprised at my knowledge.

"I, Tom, am not a nerd." I laughed, with mocked shock.

By the time we finished talking about zombies and the apocalypse, it was almost the end of Tom's shift.

"Umm, Maddie, I don't suppose you wanna hang out some time?" He asked as he was leaving.

I smiled and nodded. "Sure, just let me know when you're free."

"Great" he replied, slipped me his phone number, and then walked away.

Sophie came peering out from the back of the shop and smiled. "Oh my god! He's just asked you out."

"What? No, he just wants to hang out." I laughed sheepishly..

"If he wanted just to hang out, he would have asked while working together, not just before he left the shop." She giggled.

I looked at her bewildered. Sophie doesn't know what she's on about; Tom wouldn't like me, there's no way. And I'm still pretty sure he's gay.

"You should text him." Sophie said.

"I will when I finish work." I agreed.

Sophie was smiling the entire time until I left. She wouldn't stop talking about what a 'cute couple' we would make.

Did Tom like me?

No, I'm 99% sure he does not like women at all.

What if he does?

He doesn't. He wouldn't like someone like you, someone so messed up.

Why would he like me?

Why does anyone like you? You are so depressing.

Oh, God, I'm spiralling. Thanks, voice

****

When I got home that day, I couldn't stop thinking about Tom, and how he had given me his number. I checked my pocket and found the piece of paper. I put the number into my phone and saved it as Tom (Work). I debated whether to message him or not. I don't want to sound needy, but on the other hand, he did give me his number for a reason. I tap on his number and send a text 'Hey it's Maddie' Do I put a kiss or not? No, I won't. Just friends.

I headed downstairs, my phone tightly in my hand. I noticed mum is still working and neither dad nor David is home, so I decided to cook food. I've been trying to make more food recently for my family. I want them to think of it as a nice gesture. I wondered how my family would cope when I'm gone. How they would deal with getting rid of my personal belongings. I know it will be hard for them to go into my room and clear my stuff. Maybe I should start clearing things out myself, things I know won't be sentimental to them. I decided to write a list down of things I need to do before I die.

A list of things to do before I die;

- Go through my room and throw away anything I don't need or use.

- Sell items that can give my family some money.

- Make amends with Becks.

- Try to make amends with Beck's boyfriend.

- Spend the day with my grandma.

- Spend the day with my nan.

- Get leaving presents for the family.

- Tell everyone I love them one last time.

It's one thing to think about dying but planning it is another. I thought I would feel sad or empty, but it's the best I've felt for a while. That's how I know that this is the right thing to do. I feel free when I write about it like nothing else matters and all of my problems and worries go away.

What if I fail?

Knowing you, you will, you do at everything.

I need to come up with a plan in case it goes wrong. What can I do?

Always needing to be dramatic, that's your problem, you actually think people will read this when you're gone. No one will because no one cares.

I know. God, the voice is annoying.

I'm not going away until you do.

I know.

****

I checked my phone and Tom had messaged back

T: Hey, Maddie, what's up?

M: My ceiling haha, what about you?

I replied instantly regretting hitting send as soon as my thumb had touched the button. I am terrible at messaging people. Sophie's voice in my head has convinced me that there's the slightest chance he may like me, and I have become a blithering schoolgirl, messaging a boy for the first time.

T: That's a good one haha. I can't reply with that now, unfortunately. I'm just chilling listening to Portishead.

Okay so he didn't get weirded out. He went with it, that's good.

M: Portishead is a good band, what's your favourite song?

They were actually one of my favourites.

T: Wandering Star, one of those I can drive at night to and listen to. You?

M: Glory Box . I know it's the popular one, but that's because it's so good.'

T: Yeah, or because it was the most pop song on their Dummy album.

M: Hey, don't knock it.

I replied, feeling my cheeks turn red.

We must have been texting for hours because when I looked up, it was 11 pm, and I had work in the morning. I texted him to say that I was going to bed and then put my phone on charge and made sure my alarm was on. Once I'd led down, I had to make sure my alarm was on again, and once more for luck. I don't know why I do that. Just my anxiety, I guess.

When I woke up this morning, I was in the best mood I had been in ages. I had slept peacefully without the stress of nightmares or disturbing dreams.

I headed to work earlier than usual because I was doing an open with Sophie, as I turned the corner Sophie was waiting for me inside the shop with a massive grin on her face.

"So did you message him?"

"Morning to you too, Sophie" I laughed.

"Yes, Good Morning." She sighed. "But go on, did you text each other?" I nodded, and she shrieked in excitement

"We're just mates." I chuckled. She looked at me for a suspicious amount of time .

"What are you looking at me like that for?" I asked when she continued to stare.

"It's THE look, you know?" She said.

"Nope, what's THE look for?" I asked.

She sighed and walked into the shop. "Okay, you can't honestly tell me you don't know THE look?"

I shook my head, and she sighed again. "Maddie THE look is basically me saying you're wrong, he likes you and you should go for it."

"Woah hang on a minute. What makes you think I'm interested?" I held my hands up.

"Because in the entire time that you've worked here, he is the first person ever to get you to laugh properly. I've seen you two together. You work great together. You have this connection. Also, I listened to you guys spend an hour talking about the possibility of zombie invasions and I think that was the most I've ever heard you speak in such a small amount of time."

I stared at Sophie. I never realised that that's what I was like. I never got close to anyone because I never needed to. Work was always work and having work colleagues as friends wasn't something I did or having friends at all for that matter.

Maybe Sophie is right?

Of course, she isn't, she's being nice because she is a nice person, unlike you.

But what if Tom does like me?

Are you serious? Why would Tom like someone like you? Look at you. You're ugly, pathetic, and a waste of space, the sooner your birthday comes, the better.

Thanks again, Voice. You always know how to brighten my day.

I went to the back of the shop to open up and was surprised to see Tom standing outside, a huge smile on his face.

"Hey Tom, didn't know you were working today?" I asked.

"Sophie asked me to come in for two hours. She has a meeting, so she asked me to cover."

"Fair enough." I picked up some stock to take out to the front, and as I turned around, Tom was still standing there

"You alright, Tom? You should probably get changed for work."

Tom smiled and looked at me. I was becoming quite uncomfortable. I didn't know what to do so I started walking to the counter.

"Umm Maddie, I noticed there's a new film coming out, it's a zombie film. I thought it would be cool… If maybe…we went… like together?"

He said, twiddling his thumbs.

OMG, Sophie was right! No way! Wait, maybe he means as friends, I used to have loads of guy mates. It could be that. I shouldn't get ahead of myself.

"Yeah sure." I smiled.

He grinned, walked into the back, got changed and came back out. The first half-hour of opening is always quiet. We stood around for a while, and it felt a bit more awkward than it usually does. So, I decided to be brave and started up a conversation.

"If you could be any villain in Doctor Who, who would you be?" I asked.

"Told you were a nerd." He teased me.

"Whatever, what's your answer?" I laughed.

He scratched his head and thought for a second. "I think I would choose a Cyberman, I mean the ones from the later years, the ones that can upgrade all the time, they'd be invincible. How about you?"

"I mean seeing as it's any villain, it would definitely be the master. I mean it's the closest to being the doctor, but you're criminally insane, and in the later years you befriend all of the other enemies of the doctor, so you're invincible in another way."

"That is a good choice, can I change mine to that?" He said, looking impressed.

"Of course, cause I always come up with the best answers to these games." I chuckled.

When I looked around, Sophie had a beaming smile on her face and was sticking her thumbs up.

"Shouldn't you be in a meeting?" I walked over to her, my arms folded.

She smiled, and that's when I knew I had been set up.

"You don't have a meeting, do you?" She smiled and shook her head "Nope"

I looked at her the way my parents would look at me when they're disappointed.

"I just wanted to see if anything would happen, and it did! He asked you on a date!" She said, excited.

"He wants to see a zombie film with me."

She looked at me with a big grin on her face. "He texted you all night and has come in on his day off for two hours with you and has asked you to see a film? You think that's just friends?"

I realise now that chances are Sophie is right; however, I can't get my hopes up, whenever I get my hopes up, they suddenly get shattered. If I remain calm and think the worst, then, whatever happens, can only be better than I imagined.

"Sophie, I've had a lot of guy mates, we see films, hang out, and then they get a girlfriend and move on. Let's not get more dramatic than we need to, yeah?"

"Maddie, what's the worst that will happen if it is a real date?"

"Nothing but that's not the point. There's no point getting in over our heads for something that might not even be a thing. Anyway, I still think he's gay."

We both chuckled, and I headed back to the front of the shop where Tom had finished serving a customer.

"I wonder if customers know we're people and not robots?" He said.

"Bad customer I'm taking it?"

"One of the suits."

"Ah, the worst."

When I turned around, the older lady from before was walking in—the one who was happy that I knew sign language. I signed good morning, and with the biggest grin, she handed me the same piece of paper as last time, with my total at the bottom. She handed me the money, and as I gave her the change, I signed for her to sit down, she thanked me and walked over to my favourite seat, which I'm guessing is now her favourite seat.

"One small cappuccino with a caramel shortbread for that lady." I said to Tom, who started making the drink while I got the tray together with the shortbread. Once he finished the drink, I picked up the tray and headed over to the lady. I put it down on the table, and she thanked me. I smiled and walked away.

"I didn't know you knew sign language." Tom said.

"A little bit, I tried to learn the basics for that lady. She's the only customer we've ever had that's deaf, and then I think about how lonely that must be that she can't talk to people around her like we can. So, I learned basic sign language. You should have seen her face. She was so happy. It's so sad."

"How's it sad? You've made her happy."

"Because she can't do what we're doing. She can't just sit down and start chatting to people. She's an elderly lady who always comes in on her own, so chances are she hasn't got anyone nearby, add that into being deaf. She must be so lonely."

"Maybe she is, maybe she isn't. We don't know her story, but what we do know is how you made her feel. She came in to buy a drink, and you communicated with her. She's probably so happy with that. You've brightened her day. I think you're amazing"

I thought about that for a while. Tom had a way of seeing things that I could never understand. He was someone who would see a drink and say it's half full, whereas I'd see a drink and see the person drinking it and observe their emotions and feelings. I don't see the whole picture. I see the image and the world beyond it, I always have.

I think that's my problem sometimes, while everyone else worries about the trivial stuff I worry about everything. I observe everything, take everything in, and then my brain works at 1000mph to figure out what's good and what's bad. I remember it got so bad once that I would have to run home when I got off the bus because I used to think that people were following me home. People weren't following me home. They were going to their own houses, but I became so paranoid that someone was following me that I would run home. I remember one time when I didn't leave the house for three weeks because I was convinced someone was planning on killing me, I didn't tell my family because I thought they were in on it as well. Anytime I left the house, I would jump straight into my car and drive to where I needed to go, I would take open roads so nobody could jump out and make sure the car rides weren't longer than 20 minutes. Luckily, that only lasted three weeks, and just as quickly as it started, it ended. I don't know how it ended, I simply woke up one-day and didn't feel scared anymore.

When Tom had finished work, he said he would text me with a date for the cinema. Sophie came onto the shop floor and decided to help with making drinks. At this time, the shop started to become quite busy, and both Sophie and I were rushed off our feet, making drinks for everyone. Most people were ordering take out drinks, so it wasn't too busy in the shop, but the queue for the drinks went out the door, so we both rushed to get drinks out as quickly as possible. Once the mad rush finished, I went onto my break and checked my phone. One missed call from Mum. 1 text from Tom. Why would mum be trying to ring me? I tried ringing her back, but there was no answer. I opened Tom's message.

T: That Zombie film is showing tomorrow at 9 pm if you're free?'

M: Yeah, sure. 9 pm sounds good.

When I got home after work, mum was already home sitting on the sofa watching TV.

"You alright mum?" I asked. "You rang earlier, but I was at work so I couldn't answer," I added.

"Oh, hi, love." She looked up. "Sorry, I forgot you were at work today. I was talking to my manager, and she wants a drawing done for her sister's birthday. I said you could do it as you're a very talented artist."

Woah. I can't believe my mum would suggest it to me. I thought she never noticed my art.

"She'll pay for it to be done, I said I'd talk to you first." She explained.

I looked at mum with the brightest smile on my face "Of course I will. Umm, if you can send her my email, then she can email me with the ideas."

"Great. I told you, didn't I? Things get better." She smiled.

Maybe mum was right. Perhaps it does get better.

****

I'm nervous about going out with Tom today to see the film. I'm wondering what I can wear, it's only the cinema so I don't need to wear a dress (not that I would want to anyway), I don't want to wear a blouse because it would look like I was interviewing for a job rather than going on a date. I've chosen to go smart; simple, black, skinny jeans and a flowery off the shoulder top with white boat shoes. I'm still nervous about seeing him outside work. What if he's completely different? What if it's all a setup? What if he doesn't show? My inner monologue never fails to bring me down.

I'm not sure if I want to go now. I'm so nervous, and mum is making it 100x times worse than Sophie did. She's getting excited and choosing jazzy outfits for me to try on, even though it's just the cinema.

I'll let you know what happens.

With Love,

Maddie x

79 DAYS LEFT

Dear Diary,

I went on the date with Tom last night. Before I write about that, I'll write about yesterday.

My mum reminded me that it was the day we were all going to Bampy's grave. I had completely forgotten about it. Normally we would walk there as it's only 5 minutes from our house, but we took the car because of all of the things we were taking to clear his grave up. It was a weird journey; nobody joked around, not even Dad. When we got there (which only took two minutes in the car), we got everything out of the boot and headed over to Bampy's grave.

Bampy's grave was middle left, three from the end. We were all surprised that his plot was much tidier than we thought it would be. The grass had begun to grow over the top slightly, but the grave itself wasn't dirty. Mum started on cleaning the gravestone, and David and I started clearing around the grave. It didn't take long before it looked as fresh as possible. Once we had finished, we set up a new vase of flowers and put some new candles around the side. David, Mum, and Dad all started walking away, but I stayed. I turned to Mum "I'll meet you at home." Mum nodded, smiled, and walked back to the car.

I waited for them to drive away before talking to Bampy. "Bampy, I know I haven't come to see you in a long time, and I'm sorry about that." I waited for some reason expecting Bampy to reply and then continued "I think I have my first ever date today, Bamps. I mean he asked me out to the cinema, but I don't know if that's as friends or more." I waited for a few seconds looking around, making sure no one was listening to me. "You know Bampy; this is probably the happiest I've been since you passed away. Things seem to be looking different than I thought." I sat at his grave for a couple more minutes, touched the top of the tombstone and then headed home.

****

When I got home, mum was waiting for me with a fresh cup of tea.

"Are you okay?" she asked.

"Yeah, I just wanted to spend some time with him, I haven't visited in ages." I replied. Mum smiled and put her hand on my shoulder.

"I know I should see him more, but I find it harder now than before."

Before I knew it, mum was bringing me into a hug. Our family doesn't hug often, so it meant a lot when it did happen, although I didn't know where to put my hands, so they fell motionless beside me.

I remember when we found out Bampy was ill, nobody said anything. We all just sat in silence. It was Dad who eventually broke it, he patted Bampy on the shoulder, handed him a Bacardi and coke and started talking to him about football. It was nice to see my dad start a conversation for once. He knew the rest of us were at a loss for words. Eventually, we gained the courage to join the conversation. We didn't talk about the fact he was ill, we carried on like normal. It was the way we dealt with things.

I remember the day he passed away, right up until the end we believed he would fight it, that he would win. I guess we were all in denial. I remember the day so vividly. David and I were getting ready for school when mum came home from the hospital. She called our names, and we both came downstairs. Before she could even finish "Bampy's gone" she started crying. I had never seen mum cry before. At that moment mum hugged David and me. I remember fighting with myself not to cry. Like I've said, we didn't cry in front of each other. Mum said she would call the school and tell them we weren't coming in, so we both went upstairs, got changed and stayed in our rooms. We've never spoken about it to this day. I know how much it hurts each of us, but we don't express that out loud. It's more of a silent agreement that, well, this is shit.

****

As I was getting ready for the non-date date, I remember thinking about Bampy. I wondered if he would have been proud of me. Of course, the voice then assured me he wouldn't.

It's funny anytime I'm around Tom, the voice is quieter than usual. I wonder if I am happier than when I started the diary, but the voice assures me that even if I am, I still need to stick to the plan because I don't deserve to live. The voice then tells me that I am a waste of breath and ending it, all would be better for everyone. I do love the voice sometimes.

Once I had finished getting ready, it was 8:00 pm. I was going to drive to the cinema and meet Tom there. I decided to leave early in case of traffic and waiting in my house a second longer would have made me even more anxious. As I left the house, Mum said "Have a good night" I smiled and headed out. Once in the car, I remembered that I had a joint left in here from my last endeavour.

As I was driving to the cinema, I listened to my usual chilled playlist. I was anything other than chilled. I started to feel panicked, and the thought of meeting up with him made my stomach churn. I felt sick. I got to the cinema 40 minutes earlier than expected, which allowed me to light up and relax my nerves.

As I was halfway through my joint, there was a knock on the window. I jumped a mile, and as I looked around, I saw Tom. Shit. Okay, he is probably put off by you smoking, stay calm just undo the window and say hi.

"Alright? You're early." I said, my voice betraying me with a slight shake.

"Yeah, I think we both had the same idea." He said as he put his hand up to reveal a joint. I opened the door, and he got in the car.

"I didn't know you smoked." He said, taking a big inhale of the smoke and exhaling slowly.

"I can say the same for you." I replied.

"Helps me chill out." He said, shrugging his shoulders.

"Oh shit, Tom, I just realised. We're watching a zombie film, and we're going to be high."

"Yeah, what's your point?" He laughed.

I looked at him as seriously as possible, took the last drag and said: "If I trip, I'm out of there." He started laughing, and so did I.

When we finished our smoke, we headed into the cinema. I was blazed, so walking into the cinema felt like I had just been hit with a heatwave. I don't get paranoid when I'm smoking, well not all the time, but I felt like everyone was staring when I walked in. Tom and I walked up to one of the self-service machines and got the tickets. The zombie film was called "Zombies in the night." It sounded terrible, but I was high, and I was with Tom, so I didn't mind. Tom wouldn't let me pay for my ticket, so I said I would pay for the drinks. As I got to the drinks section, I picked out the ultimate cinema drink: a slushy, and Tom picked the same. We chose our flavours and went to the desk to pay. It was now 8:40 pm, we still had twenty minutes before the film started. We made small talk, talking about work and the weather. Typical small talk for any Brit's.

From what I learned; Tom was a keen writer. He loved to write stories, especially science fiction books. He came to the coffee shop for the same reason I did, which was to earn money while still doing what we loved on the side. I didn't tell him that I had given up on that dream because in 80 days I would be dead.

We had seats close to the exit. We thought this might be a good idea if I have a trip or the film was just terrible. As we sat down, I noticed a group of girls that I knew from school. They were in the year above me. I remember them because they bullied me endlessly but not the obvious bullying, it was the kind of bullying where they'd try to be friends and then just take the piss out of me the whole time. Another reason I don't have many friends, I don't trust their intentions. Tom had noticed my change in behaviour

"Who are they?" he asked

"Old school friends." I shrugged it off.

"Oh we should go say hi." He smiled.

"No, they were the type of friends who would take the mickey out of me or tell me they didn't want to be my friend one day and did the next."

Tom stopped smiling and looked forward, "Assholes" he said simply, and yes, yes, they were.

The film started, and honestly, it wasn't too bad. We were both laughing the entire time, because of how funny the zombies looked. At one point someone told us to be quiet because we were laughing so much. It was an unintentional comedy film, the plot was basic, and the acting was mediocre, but it was nice to spend some time with Tom outside of work. There was one part in the film where the two main characters are having a loving moment, and right before they kiss a zombie comes out of nowhere and kills the guy. Tom and I had our mouths wide open because usually, films end happily, but this took us completely by surprise. We looked at each other and burst out into laughter, while the rest of the cinema was tearing up. Once the film finished, we sat around for a bit and waited for everyone to leave; we were still cracking up from the ending to the film. A few people walked past and gave us the evil eyes and stared at us, some tutted and complained under their breath. As we stood up, the group of girls at the back of the cinema started walking down.

"Come on, let's go before they do." I said to Tom, grabbing his arm and dragging him out.

"Woah okay, calm down." He said but followed me anyway.

As we were walking out, the girls at the back were behind us, they talked to each other and laughed. Their laughter reminded me of all the times they would laugh at me. Although weed has minimal effect on me, I became quite paranoid. I started checking my shoes to see if there was anything on them. I made sure my shirt was pulled all the way down and that my bum didn't feel wet in case I sat on anything. I didn't want to give them any reason to laugh at me.

Tom noticed my behaviour change.

"Are you alright? Is it those girls again?" He asked. I nodded, picking up the pace. My breathing was becoming erratic. He kept up with my pace and followed me outside. Once outside, I automatically felt a lot better. The fresh air helped me to calm down. We walked to my car in silence. I felt safer once we were beside my car.

"Maddie, are you okay?" Tom asked again.

"Yeah, I just needed to get out of there." I said.

"I get that."

"Do you want a lift home?" I asked. Tom smiled, said "Sure."

"What did they do to you? Like in school?" Tom asked as we were driving home.

"They befriended me, I had no friends at that time, and I thought it was great. I was 15 and they were 16, and they wanted to hang out with me. I was so happy. I didn't really have a group of friends. I had Becks, but that was it. When we first started hanging out, it was great. We would laugh and joke around. I thought I found friends for life. Then, after a couple of weeks, the jokes started. A few jokes turned into constant jokes about me or the way I looked. They called it banter, and I accepted it thinking it was. On one occasion, they locked me in the toilet stall and wouldn't let me out. I started having a panic attack and screamed for them to let me out. But they carried on laughing. They stopped eventually and said they were only joking. Things like that kept happening until they left school. Then they never spoke to me again. They blocked me on everything. I was their punching bag." I had never told anyone about it before, apart from Becks.

"Shit" Tom replied, shocked.

"Yeah, shit." I answered back.

****

Tom gave me directions to his house, which was only 15 minutes from mine. He lived closer to the coffee shop than me but in the opposite direction. His house was small, with an overgrown front garden. I noticed that there were no lights on. I guessed his parents were already asleep. "Well, this is me." Tom announced. He had the biggest grin on his face. "I'll see you at work." I said, returning the smile.

But Tom didn't get out of the car straight away. I felt so awkward. I didn't know what to do next. Why wouldn't he get out of the car? After a couple of minutes of awkward silence, Tom let out a little sigh and said: "see you at work."

With that, he got out of the car and headed into his house, looking back at me one more time before going inside. I drove home, wondering why he was hesitant to get out of the car. When I got home, I texted him letting him know I was home and that I had a good night. When he didn't reply, I put my phone on charge and went to bed.

When I woke up today, I didn't feel any worse or better than I usually do. I enjoyed going to the cinema with Tom, but I feel like I messed up at the end. I didn't want him to think I was weird, even though I knew I was. I checked my phone, and there was no reply from Tom, I checked the text to make sure it had gone through, and it had. Strange. I decided not to text him again as I didn't want to seem too needy.

Today was a dull day, except for checking my phone every 10 minutes to see if Tom had replied. I messaged Becks about Tom, and she got just as excited as Sophie did. She wanted to know when I was free next to meet up, so I agreed to meet her tomorrow after work. Which was something to look forward to.

I know things seem to be better at the moment, but I have to remember this diary's purpose. The plan stays the same, no matter what happens between Tom and me. I have to. I'm committed. The plan was there before Tom was.

With love,

Maddie x

78 DAYS LEFT

Dear Diary,

I saw Dr Goodall today. I told him about Tom and I going to the cinema, about going to Bampy's grave and about Sophie wanting me as a supervisor.

"So, it seems that things have been looking up." He said. "Yeah" I replied with a lack of excitement. "So, what's the problem?" He asked. I paused for a second "I don't deserve to have a good life." "Why don't you deserve to have a good life, Maddie?" Dr Goodall asked, looking at me intently.

"I don't know, I don't think I'm a good person." "Why do you think that?" He asked.

"Sometimes the voice tells me I'm a bad person, that nobody wants to be my friend, they only want to use me and when they've got what they want they leave. The voice tells me I'm worthless, that I'm not a good person and deserve to feel this way. The reason I have no real friends is because I don't deserve it." I let out.

I don't know what's changed about me, but I've noticed that I've started talking more in sessions. Maybe it's because I'm happier in my personal life. Maybe it's because deep down I like Dr Goodall, or maybe, just maybe Tom has given me a reason to want to keep living.

"What voice?" Dr Goodall asked. "My internal thoughts, it's not a literal voice but it's not like me either. My old therapist called it the void, all the bad thoughts. I just never understood why I thought the way I did. Like I don't want to think like this, but I do, so surely there is a part of me that does think this. There's a part of me that believes I'm horrible, and terrible, and the worst person in the world, and I know it sounds stupid as I'm saying it but…" I swallowed "… if one part of me is thinking it then surely, it's true. I just think, what is the point of all of this?"

Dr Goodall left a minute of silence, all while still looking straight at me. "Does this voice ever tell you to harm yourself?" I didn't know what to say. I could easily answer, but what if he ruins my plan. What if he asks the other question?

"Sometimes, but the thoughts are nothing more than thoughts. They get me down, but I don't act on them." I replied. I'm not technically lying, I haven't self-harmed for like two weeks. I prefer medicinal self-harm more nowadays.

"So, you're coping better than you used to? That's great." He smiled at me, and I smiled back, it's not exactly what I thought he would say after I had just poured my heart out to him. "I guess I have made peace with the voice, well on most days anyway." I say simply, knowing all the while that the voice and I know something the Doc doesn't, our peace will come in 78 days.

"What you said last session just before you left, Maddie... where is it..." He looked through his book. "...You said. You know how we put animals down when they're in pain, don't you think it would be better if we could do that with humans." I looked at him, trying to figure out where he was going with it.

"In some countries it is legal, if you're a criminal, most likely murderer, you're put to death. If you're very ill or disabled or in considerable suffering, you can legally be put down. It's called euthanasia. It's legal in places like Switzerland, but before they do it, they ask many questions to make sure that that's the right choice. Some people, who have struggled with illness for a long time, find it easier than carrying on. However, I'm assuming that's not the way you meant it. So, I have to disagree. I don't think people should be in control of their own death date" Dr Goodall sighed. "Is there a particular reason you asked? Do you think about it?"

I didn't know what to say, I mean yes, I did think about it, I spent most of my day thinking about death and the day I'm going to die but I didn't want to tell him that. "Oh, it was just one of my silly thoughts that I had, and I had to share it with someone." I half smiled at Dr Goodall "What do you think about it?" He asked me. "I think people should be able to do with their lives as they please, I don't think people should be punished if they feel so urgently that they want to die. I mean as long as they're not hurting someone else, why does it matter? It's not like we live in a very pleasant world anyway, some might say living in this world is more painful than not."

Dr Goodall looked down at the table for a moment or two "Maddie, I have to ask this because I'm worried about you. Have you been having any suicidal thoughts recently?" I pick the skin between my nails and answer with a quick "no," I don't think Dr Goodall fully believed me, so he then asked "Maddie, it's okay, you can be honest if you do."

My breathing became shaky, I didn't know what to do. "No, I don't... I mean...Sometimes, but I don't do it... I know it's not good so I draw, or I write." Dr Goodall wrote in his book and then looked up at me. I was terrified, I felt like I had bugs crawling in my body, my heart was beating five times faster than it should have and I honestly for a moment thought I was having a heart attack. "Thank you for being honest, it's good that you have found ways to deal with the thoughts. Are you still taking your medication?" He asked me but all I could do was nod a yes.

"I would recommend talking to your Doctor about increasing your medication. I think it would be beneficial and it might help reduce the negative thoughts. I do think you're opening up a lot more though Maddie, you should be really proud of yourself. The first couple of months of sessions you barely spoke to me but now you're able to verbalise your thoughts. Maddie, you should be proud of yourself."

I smiled, I didn't know what else to do, I just wanted to get out of there. Luckily, it was time for us to finish, so I said goodbye to Dr Goodall and headed out of the office. Dr Goodall had no idea. I wasn't doing better; I was just lying at this point to get through the sessions. Despite wanting to go ahead with the plan I somehow felt annoyed that Dr Goodall didn't realise how bad I actually was. I know he's not a mind-reader but if I was a therapist, I wouldn't let me out of my own sight. It's not his fault, he's doing his best, but telling me I should be proud of myself was stupid. Why should I be proud of myself that I told him I had suicidal thoughts? That's not something to be proud of. Something to be proud of is when I sell my paintings or secure a place in one of the top Universities, but I've done neither of those things so I shouldn't be proud.

As I headed to work, I started dreading it. I wondered if I would see Tom at work today. He still hasn't messaged me, so I was wondering if the date went badly or not. I didn't overthink it because I knew I would have spiralled otherwise. I don't know whether this diary has helped to keep the bad thoughts at bay, but in writing them down, I'm letting them out. Perhaps that's all they need, a way out of my mind.

When I got into work, Sophie was on her own. She looked utterly flushed with bright red cheeks, and her hair was messier than usual. "Maddie, you're late." She said, I looked at her waiting for her to laugh, but she didn't. She looked stressed and was frowning at me. "No, I don't start until 12 today. I told you a while ago." I headed out the back, got changed and headed straight out the front to help her clear up what seemed to have been an already busy morning.

"I asked you three weeks ago when I was doing the schedules if you could come in earlier today because of the new drinks we were making." She said exasperated. I don't remember her asking me that she knows I wouldn't be able to. Why didn't she ask Tom? "I don't remember agreeing to that, I'm sorry. I must have thought you meant a different day." I started cleaning the shop and putting my cakes in the trays.

"It's fine, I'm sorry, I know you have counselling on Thursdays. It's just been hectic, and Tom's off sick so there's one less person to ask to come in." Sophie sighed, annoyed at herself for getting annoyed at me. "Sophie I am sorry; I've just had a lot going on so I must have forgotten."

Sophie smiled at me, her face was flushed, and sweaty, stray bits of hair were clung onto her face. She suddenly stopped what she was doing and hugged me "It's fine Maddie don't worry. I'm proud of you by the way. I wanted to say that" She pulled away and smiled at me. "Thank you." I smiled back, but I was embarrassed. I didn't need people to be proud of me, I needed them to prove that my negative thoughts were right. I needed Sophie to hate me so that I could stick to my plan.

I finished off the displays. Sophie continued to serve the customers, and when the shop became quiet, we had time to chat. Sophie tried to talk about Tom again, but I interrupted her, not wanting to think about Tom. "How's you and your boyfriend by the way?" "We broke up." She said with a sad smile. "He wanted to travel, and I wanted to settle down." "Oh, I'm sorry to hear that," I replied. I tried to sound sincere, but it came out more stern than sincere.

"It's fine. I was happy to travel with him, but I realised he wanted to travel with someone else. Specifically, his chick on the side." Oh no. Sophie is the nicest girl going. How could her boyfriend cheat on her? It's times like this that make the voices louder. They tell me that I'm worth less than her and if she got cheated on then I deserved worse.

"Sophie I'm sorry mate, you deserve so much better than someone like that." Sophie smiled at me "Thank you... Do you ever think that you don't deserve better though?" She asked and the way she asked it was like a child being told Santa didn't exist. The sadness radiated her entire body language, and I could tell how deflated she was. I went over to the coffee machine and made one of my favourite drinks, an iced latte with salted caramel. I got some money out of my pocket and put it in the till and handed her the cup. "This is my favourite drink; I always find it cheers me up a bit when I need a boost." Sophie took the cup with a smile. I took over the counter, but as the shop was still so quiet, Sophie wanted me to start putting up new posters around the shop.

As I was putting some posters up around the coffee shop, I got a tap on the shoulder. When I looked around, it was the deaf lady. I signed him and walked over to the counter. As I was putting the shortbread on a plate, the lady pointed towards the poster I had just put up. I signed 'you want?' and she nodded. I smiled and started making the mint hot chocolate, adding whipped cream on top. The lady gave me the money and took it over to what was becoming her usual spot. As I went back to the till, I noticed the lady had left a note. It said:

To the young lady who serves me,

Thank you for taking the time to learn sign language. It has made me so happy that I can have a tiny bit of communication. You make my day every time I come here.

From Doris.

I put the note in my pocket. I wanted to take it home. It made me feel like I had done something good, and I wanted to remember her name. Maybe I could learn more sign language so that we can communicate more. The rest of the shift went by slowly. It felt like every 15 minutes was an hour, and every hour was a day.

When I got home, I went straight upstairs and glued the note into my diary. I don't particularly appreciate boasting about stuff like that. It's basic human decency. It shows that my parents brought me up correctly that they showed me that giving people respect and kindness are the most important things.

I've been thinking about how everyone will react when they find out. I know it's a morbid thing to think about, but people act differently to that type of news. I think my mum will cry, I think dad will work to stay busy and not think about it, and I think my brother will pretend nothing happened. I think Becks would stop going to Bennetts Castle altogether and Sophie might be sad, but eventually, she can just hire someone else. Then I think about Tom, about how he might react but then I remember that we don't know each other that well. I'll be nothing more than some girl he kind of liked. I know that my family will be sad, but it's better than living on and being a waste of space and disappointment to them in the long run. I think they'll understand when they read this that it's all for the greater good.

With love,

Maddie x

75 DAYS LEFT

Dear Diary,

I always wondered what it was like to plan for the future knowing that you'll actually have one. When I was a teen, I never thought I'd make it to 18. So, when I turned 18, I had no idea what I was doing. I had no plans for my life. I had no ambition. I barely scraped through school because I assumed it wouldn't matter. By the time education was finished I assumed I would be dead.

Now I'm 22. No career in line, an art diploma I spent three years on with nothing to show for it and struggling to find anything exciting. I think that's the problem. I've never enjoyed anything. I don't find anything fun. I don't get any enjoyment out of life.

I always thought I would have a career by now. Something that I loved doing. The one thing my mum always made sure was that my brother and I would never have a job, that we'd have a career. I spent my life working towards something that wasn't feasible because I enjoyed it, and now I don't have it.

I have nothing. What's the point in being alive when you aren't even living? I don't have anything to live for. So, I may as well not.

And I'm exhausted, and sad, and angry and worst of all; I'm so fucking lonely. I have no one, and even when I try to talk, nobody gets the hint. I truly believe it would be best for myself and everyone if I took the problem out of the equation. The problem being me.

I feel different, like I'm on the wrong planet or something. I struggle doing anything, getting up for work is more difficult than it used to be. Getting changed out of my clothes, having a shower, all these things that should be so simple, I'm struggling to do.

When I should be sleeping, I'm wide awake, and when I should be awake, I'm falling asleep. I know mum and dad have noticed, they've noticed me staying in my room for longer, going for a spliff more than once a day. They've noticed, but they haven't said anything, so neither do I. I shouldn't have to be the one to mention it, they're my parents they should come up to me.

****

The last three days have been a blur. The void is coming back, and it's heavier than it's ever been before. I spent all of last night trying to stop the voices from taking over me. I haven't seen Tom since the night of the date, and he hasn't replied to my messages. The voices let me know that it was all my fault and that I scared him away because I am a freak.

FREAK.

That word has been circulating my brain for the last three days. I am a freak, and everyone knows it, that's why I don't have friends. That's why Becks cancelled meeting me four days ago. She said it's because Matt needed to see his dad and she had to take him, but I know it's because I'm a freak.

Whenever I'm at work, I want to be at home, and whenever I'm at home, I want to be anywhere but there. The voices are getting stronger, and the void is spinning like a whirlpool.

I know that there's a scientific explanation. I lack chemicals in my brain, which means that my brain tells me I'm depressed. I then think about the type of people who suffer from depression, the ones who were abused, the ones who were heavily into drugs, who didn't have a good home life and then I think of me. I don't fall into any of those categories, I should be considered happy, but I'm not.

I think that's the worst part about having a mental illness, is that if you don't have a specific cause or reason for it, you think you shouldn't have one at all. I know that's not the case, I know that Dr Goodall would say "Celebrities who have everything suffer from depression, it's not the person, it's the brain." but I can't help but think of celebrities having their own battles. They battle with paparazzi and the constant fame and trying always to be a role model. They can't walk out of the door in pyjamas to go to the corner shop and get some milk. They have to dress up to walk 5 minutes. They have their own little battle.

I don't. I have nothing that I've struggled with, and yet I still feel the same way, and it's killing me. Sometimes I wish I could find a reason, but there isn't one. Bampy passing away isn't a reason to suffer from depression because everyone dies. That's the whole point of being a living organism, is that one day you'll die. That's the worst thing to happen in my life, and that happens to everyone, so there's no reason I should feel depressed because of it, right?

The last three days I've been working. I've been staying on because Tom's been calling in sick. I didn't want to ask why he's off, but Sophie mentioned that he might not be in until next week, so I assumed he's ill with the flu. We don't have that many staff members, and I usually work on my own, so for one person to be out, it means we all have to muck in. I tried asking Sophie how she was, especially after telling me that she and her boyfriend broke up. I've been asking more, but she would say she was fine and would then walk off. She seemed to be getting distant, which was the worst thing for me when the voice was already teasing.

She doesn't like you anymore.

You forgot to show up, and now she wants you gone.

Maybe you should go and disappear.

She wouldn't miss you.

Nobody would.

I don't see why you don't hurry up the process and kill yourself now.

Why are you waiting until your birthday? They won't miss you anyway.

The voice started becoming more prominent after seeing Dr Goodall, but the last two days were the worst. It felt like there were seven different people in my head all talking at the same time. All saying negative things to make me anxious or depressed. All wanting to be heard simultaneously. I tried to write down the thoughts to get them out of my brain, but it wasn't working.

I started panicking. I couldn't breathe. I was crying, and Sophie wanted to know what was wrong.

My vision was getting smaller, and it felt like the room was closing in on me. I managed to walk to the bathroom and sat on the floor with my head in my hands, sobbing.

After about 5 to 10 minutes, I heard a tap on the door. It was Sophie. "Hey Maddie, how are you doing?" I got myself up, blew my nose with some tissue and opened the door. "Do you wanna go home? I can manage myself, is it normally quiet at this time?" She asked. "No, I'll be fine, thanks" I smiled and went to walk away, but Sophie stopped me in my tracks. "What's going on?" She asked.

"Nothing. I'm fine." I replied, trying to walk out of her way, but she kept moving in front of me. "Maddie!" She shouted, which took me back. I've never heard her shout before, and it definitely stopped me on the spot. "You had a panic attack. I know what they look like, so don't even try to tell me you weren't. You've not been yourself recently. I know you're quiet, but this is different."

I kept quiet with my head down. The worst thing about a panic attack is how embarrassed you feel afterwards when the rational part of your brain creeps in. "Just tell me what's going on." I sighed and looked up at Sophie. "I don't know, things were great and then all of a sudden the last two days haven't been."

Sophie pulled me into a big bear hug, and when she eventually let go, she said: "We have good days, and we have bad days, embrace the good days and share the bad days." This was precisely why I liked Sophie. She understood. With one last hug and a deep breath, I walked back out to the front of the store.

When I got out there, I was shocked to see Tom standing waiting in the shop. Great. I looked at him and awkwardly smiled. "Hey." Tom smiled, his hair wasn't in a quiff like usual, but was instead stuck to one side of his face, covering one of his eyes. Sophie came out and told Tom to go out the back.

"We're going to have a meeting, are you okay for 10 minutes?" I nodded, and Tom followed Sophie to the back. I awkwardly stared at Tom, wondering if he was going to say anything else, but he stayed quiet. It looked like all of the life had been drained out of him. I tried not to overthink because I didn't want to panic again. When Tom came back, he hugged Sophie goodbye and walked over to me.

"I'm sorry for not texting you back, I've had some family shit to sort out, and my phone broke. Here's my new number." He handed me a piece of paper with his new number on it. I smiled, and he smiled back, but his did not seem genuine. It wasn't the usual happy smile he gives me when he's being chirpy and cheeky. Today was like looking in a mirror. It's the same smile I show every day. It's the sort of smile that's reaching from either side of their face, but the eyes always show genuine emotion. Tom looked empty. He looked like I do when everything is falling apart.

When I got home, I texted Tom *'hey it's Maddie.'* A couple of minutes later he texted back

T: Hey, sorry about earlier.

M: It's fine you alright?

T: Yeah, my life has been a bit hectic recently. Thanks for covering my shift earlier.'

I looked at my phone and smiled. I felt happier knowing that it wasn't something I had done. I put my phone down and went into the bathroom, as I got undressed to get into the shower I looked down at the faded scars on my legs.

I remember the days where I would self-harm every day. It used to be part of the routine. I would get out of the shower after a long day at school, I would get changed into my pyjamas, and just before I got into bed, I would pick up a razor blade and bandages (to make sure my family didn't find out) and then I would self-harm. It started with one cut and then to 6 or 7. Every night it was the same thing. Then one day I just stopped, I think because I started smoking, I stopped harming myself. I quit one addiction and replaced it with another one instead.

As I laid in bed, I sat there and thought about Tom and why he had such sadness in his eyes. I knew it was family-related, but I didn't want to ask further and feel like I was intruding in his personal life. We don't know each other that well. I then thought about how people see me, do they see me the way I saw Tom today? Becks said she noticed a change in me, but I don't understand why she wouldn't simply ask. Did she not care enough to ask?

With love,

Maddie x

73 DAYS LEFT

Dear Diary,

In the last two days, two massive things have happened.

The first one is that Becks and Matt broke up. I know I shouldn't be happy about it, but there was a sense of relief when she told me. Not for me but for her. I'm not a fan of Matt, from what she's told me he can be quite controlling and likes to make sure that his needs are put first. She was obviously upset about it. Apparently, they were at his house when a massive argument arose because he wanted to see his family instead of seeing hers. He was rude about her family, and she told him to grow up. In the end, he broke up with her saying it wasn't going to work if she didn't like his family and didn't get along with them. I think he was looking for an easy way out. He found a way of creating a simple argument by being a dick, so she would leave and hate him. I'm not in the relationship so I shouldn't have an opinion but from what she tells me, it's a good thing they broke up.

Becks apologised for cancelling a couple of days ago and said we should go out soon, on a proper night out. I agreed as long as it wasn't at one of the grotty clubs in town. Then she carried on talking about her fight with Matt for the best part of an hour. She said that it was for the best, but I can't help but think she didn't mean it at all. I know Becks, she wasn't someone who got close to people, but when she did, she clung on. She would do anything for that person to make them feel special. I wondered whether Matt had cheated on her; it was the only thing that made sense as to why he was heartless. Just before she hung up, Becks asked how I had been since we last saw each other. I said I was fine and just working more to get money. She seemed pleased that I was doing better. She also said that if I needed to talk to someone, then I could always talk to her. It was a sweet gesture but seeing as she's just broken up with her boyfriend, I think I'll need to be there for her more now.

The other big thing happened today.

I was heading to work when I got a text from Tom saying that he would be at work today. I was quite excited because I hadn't seen him since the cinema, which seemed like months ago now. I walked a little faster when I saw the text wanting to get into work sooner.

When I got there, I saw Sophie pottering around because it was quiet. I walked in and when she saw me, she had this beaming smile on her face and started jumping around. "Maddie, I have exciting news!" She exclaimed before I even had a chance to get into the shop properly. "What is it?" I asked, less excited than her.

"So corporate rang the office today, to let us know that we've been given £15,000 to update our store!" If this is the news Sophie gets excited about; it's easy to see why she's the manager. "What does that mean?" "It means we can get new counters with built-in pastry windows; we can get new tables and chairs that all match, and we can decorate it." Sophie was jumping with glee. I tried to look as happy as her. "Wait. Why? Weren't they struggling with money?"

"The sales have really hit off in the last couple of weeks, especially in our store. I was told that one of the executives has come into our store a couple of times and really liked our attitude. So, we've been given money to make the store look better."

Oh wow, that's pretty cool.

I'm nowhere near as excited as Sophie, but I understand why she is. She has put in blood, sweat and tears to make this coffee shop not only a great place to work but somewhere customers enjoy coming. She works tirelessly to make sure that everything is perfect. I'm pretty sure she works all six days that the store is open as well. She wants to make sure that she knows everyone on a personal level.

Sophie then went on to tell me that the store would be closed for five days while the changes were being made but that we would all get paid in full for our contracted hours and we would all be able to help out if we wanted to. Sophie then turned around and asked me.

"Hey, you're great at drawing, can you draw something for the coffee shop? I'll pay you." Oh wow, someone else that wants a drawing. I guess the three years at college weren't a total waste. "Yeah of course."

"Great, I'll think of some ideas and let you know." Sophie smiled. She left to go into the back room, and as I looked around, Tom was coming into the shop. I smiled, and he smiled back.

A customer came into the shop, so he went straight out the back, and I got on with making the drinks for the customers. The shop started picking up speed as Tom came out of the back and behind the till "Hey, if I do drinks do you mind serving?" I asked. I knew it would be faster and efficient if it was done this way.

Tom smiled, "sure, and hey... it's nice to see you."

I smiled back, my cheeks going bright red, and Tom turned around to serve. I really missed Tom while he was away, even just his presence made me happier.

The shop was busy for 3 hours, and we were non-stop serving customers and making drinks, at one point, the queue went around the shop and out the door. We opened up the fire exit by the tables to allow for customers to get out easier. When the queue eventually died down, we started clearing up.

I was wondering who would be the first to break the silence. Normally it was Tom, but he was still incredibly quiet. So, I decided to take a page out of his book.

"Who would win a fight between a shark or a lion?"

Tom continued to clean the counter but started giggling. "It's a bit unfair. It all depends on the place where they're fighting. If the lion was in the sea, then the shark but vice versa if the shark was on land, then the lion." I stopped what I was doing to look at him.

Seeing him properly for the first time in ages I realised how attractive he was. His hair fit his face perfectly, his smile was contagious, and his eyes were like the ocean on a calm day. He seemed happier in himself too. I realised quite quickly that I was staring at him and smiling, so I quickly continued the conversation.

"See that's logical, but what if both lion and shark could live on both sea and land, which one would win then?" He stopped what he was doing and looked up at the ceiling as if thinking intently. "I think... hmmm... that's a difficult one. A shark. They have so many teeth that they could easily rip a lion in two within seconds." I held my finger up which stopped him. "But a shark doesn't have legs, so it has to shuffle over to the lion if it's on land like a seal does, that gives the lion enough time to pounce and attack."

He started laughing, which made me start laughing. "Ahh the difficult questions, we're getting to the real gritty stuff now." He chuckled. "Can I ask you a question?" He suddenly stopped laughing and now looked more serious. He looked at me directly in the eyes "Do you think people should be happy?"

"That's a sudden change of mood. What do you mean?" I replied puzzled. "Well life is a strange thing, it's a mystery. Nobody knows what the right thing to do is, everyone has their own opinion on what's right and what's wrong. Is it okay in a world that is corrupt and terrible for people to be happy?"

I looked at him and his beauty shone. Now not from his face but his heart and it was beautiful. He was wonderful.

Oh God, nope.

Nope, I cannot be catching feelings for him. I'm still 50% convinced he's gay, or maybe I'm hoping he is so if he thinks I'm disgusting it's not because of me being ugly and being mental but because I'm a woman and that's not his thing.

"I think despite what's going on in the world, how bad something is, you should always be able to find something good out of it. Happiness isn't as easy as people think; it's a construct based on our ideas of happiness. A homeless man can be the happiest man on earth despite having nothing because he's realised what life is all about. Then you have millionaires who aren't happy. We create this idea of happiness that we want, but if we're always looking for it, we might not see the happiness that's in front of us. Does that make sense, or am I rambling on?"

Tom looked at me seriously. "Maddie, are you happy?"

Out of all the questions he's ever asked me, this is the hardest to answer, because it's not based on theoretical evaluation, or statistical knowledge. It's real, and it's one I don't even know the answer to, so I didn't. I continued cleaning and remained silent. Tom stood looking at me for a minute or two and then continued cleaning as well.

I couldn't lie to Tom, I didn't want to, but I didn't want him to think I was a freak. I didn't want him to see that side of me. I didn't want him to know what was happening. So, I stupidly stayed quiet. It was another 10 minutes until I plucked up the courage to say something.

"Umm...I'm leaving in 10 minutes, is there anything you need before I go?" I asked, trying to make conversation, wanting to seem normal.

"Na, I think I'll be alright. Thanks though, and thanks for covering, it means a lot. You're a good mate." He thought I was his mate, not a workmate but a normal mate. This made me happy. "And Tom." He turned around and looked at me as I headed towards the back. "It's good to have you back. I missed you." He went bright red, and I walked out the back before he could see that I had too.

I went into the office and shut the door. "Sophie, I could draw a photo of all the employees that work here, but without faces, so it has that personal element, but won't be too irrelevant in case anyone leaves." Sophie looked up and smiled at me "Oh wow, that would be great, how much do you want for it?" I paused for a second "I don't want money, but could you give me September 24th off full pay?" Sophie checked the calendar. "You're already off that date." Okay, so I had forgotten that I had taken that off. "What about the day before?" Sophie checked the date and agreed I could have it off paid in full.

Our work gives us 20 days holiday if we work 30 hours a week. I have already taken or requested all of my holidays, so I thought if I could have the day off beforehand, I'd have a final farewell.

Once Sophie had put it in, I got dressed, signed out and walked home.

As I left the shop, I waved goodbye to Tom, who was still red from what I had said. When I got home, I started on the drawing for the coffee shop. We had six employees altogether, including Sophie and myself. I knew what they all looked like so I went about starting the basic drawing, the background would be the shop and in front would be all of the employees. The drawing would be more cartoony/animated to make it a bit more artistic. I wanted the photo to be simple but allow the employees to know they're part of the company. As I was drawing, I heard a knock on my door, and mum walked in.

"Hey Mum" I said, continuing to draw the artwork. "Hey Maddie, that lady has gotten back to me about the artwork, and she's given me a few photos for you to work with. She said she's happy to pay, and she's emailed you all of this as well." "Cheers mum, I'm just doing one for work. They want it to go into the shop and then I'll start on hers." "It's good to see you doing what you love again." Mum smiled and left the room.

I wasn't enjoying what I was doing, but I thought I wanted to leave a little present for Sophie, that she could keep up and that the other artwork would be extra money for the family.

I completed the outline of the art and stopped to have something to eat. I looked at my phone and saw that Tom had messaged me a couple of times

T: Hey, I was wondering if you wanted to hang out tomorrow.

T: I still think a shark would win by the way.

T: It's nice to be hanging out with you again at work.

I laughed to myself, not only did he send three texts in a row, but he also sent them within 5 minutes of each other which meant he sent it, waited, sent another, waited then sent the last one. I don't know why, but this made me smile. I felt a warm feeling in my stomach, one I did not recognise. I messaged him back

M: Sure, after work sounds good? Also, a lion has many advantages over a shark.

I tapped send and headed downstairs.

I'm looking forward to spending more time with Tom. I know I have to remember the reason I started this diary, but that doesn't mean I can't have a good time with the time I have left, does it?

With love,

Maddie x

71 DAYS LEFT

Dear Diary,

I finished the art for Sophie yesterday. It only took two days. Thankfully, it gave me something to focus on. It turned out better than I expected it to. It was a simple outline of the staff and shop with a light tie-dye background. When I gave it to Sophie, she raved about how amazing it was and gave me a massive hug. She also made me my favourite drink at no charge. It made me feel good when she told me how good the drawing was. I felt like I had achieved something.

When Tom came in, Sophie showed him my painting straight away, he smiled and said I should be proud because of how good it was. He tried to guess which one was him, which I found hilarious. Every time he got it wrong, I corrected him and laughed even more. Eventually, he found himself.

"Is that you?" He pointed to the one next to him, and I nodded, which made him smile. "You put us next to each other." I didn't realise until he mentioned it that I had. I drew everyone as I remembered us, and he happened to be after me. "How long did it take you to do?" Tom asked. "Only two days, which is fast, but it was easy."

He looked at me surprised. "That only took two days! I'm terrible at drawing. I could never do something as good as that." "Yeah, but you're intelligent, you can't be both intelligent and good at art that's not fair." He let out a laugh and then he suddenly looked sad. "Yeah, but that's not fair, I should have special treatment and be allowed to be good at both." and looked at me with puppy dog eyes which made me laugh uncontrollably.

Tom and I talked like nothing happened that night at the cinema, and like he hadn't asked me one of the most difficult questions a couple days ago. I liked that, and I liked that he didn't ask anything else. I didn't like the idea of talking about it around him or with him. Even though we were close, we weren't close enough for me to talk to him about stuff like that.

"Do you ever think we will evolve to be able to breathe underwater?" He asked. "Are you high?" I asked. He laughed. "No, but seriously" I thought about it for a second. "No, unless, we were to start mating with sharks," He laughed. "Okay, that's a good point."

He continued by asking me an array of questions. "Do you think we will evolve again? Like having an extra thumb for social media.," "Do you think there would ever be an app that showed you, your soulmate?" And "If you were in a movie and the only way you could get out was if someone let you out, how would you let them know you needed help." Finally, "If you had to make one animal extinct, which one would it be?"

He always tried asking pointless questions, but he would always call them tricky because one answer for him was different from mine, even though it was simply due to how the brain worked. I told him it was simple psychology, but he went on a rant about how everyone is different, just because you might agree with someone on one thing doesn't mean you will agree on something else. No two people are exactly the same, even twins think differently and have different likes and dislikes. I knew what he meant, but I went on to tell him that that's because our personalities, likes, dislikes etc. stem from our family, so we have a bit of them in us.

This went on back and forth until two people came in, one was a business lady, and the other was Doris. The business lady surprised me with how polite she was. "Hi, can I get a small latte to sit in, please?"

I smiled at her and made the drink. "That will be £4.00 please." She handed me the money and thanked me. She took her drink and sat down in the corner. Then took out her iPad and started typing. Doris came up next, and I smiled at her, and she pointed at the poster in the mirror and signed 'same again,' I made her drink and got her, her usual caramel shortbread treats. When I put it all on the tray, I brought it to the same seat that she always sits in. Once she sat down, I signed 'thank you,' and she did it back. I went back to the counter and started cleaning up, Tom was out the back getting the delivery, so I focused on the front and made it look tidy.

Fifteen minutes later, the business lady came up and handed me the drink back. I thanked her and hoped she had a good day. I took the cup and took it out the back ready to be cleaned. When I came back, the lady was still standing there, but Doris had joined her.

"Is everything okay?" I asked. "I'm Sandy Phillips. I'm an executive for this coffee shop and the other chains." I nodded, and she continued, "This is my mother, Doris."

What! The lovely lady I've been serving for weeks is the mother of our shop's executive. "My mother has told me how kind you have been and how you have been able to talk to her using sign language. She feels so much happier coming here than anywhere else." She explained, while signing so that Doris too understood what she was talking about.

My mouth was open, and my eyes were big. I was shocked, I couldn't believe what was happening. "When mum told me what you did, I spoke to the top guys, and they allowed me to give Sophie the cheque. We want more people like you." She continued.

What was happening?

"I was one of the reasons that the shop got £15,000?" I asked Sandy with complete disbelief.

She looked at me and smiled "Yes, that's exactly right. When my mum told me what you do, and how kind you are, we knew we wanted to treat the shop to a well-deserved redo." I didn't know what to do. I was buzzing. I couldn't believe that I was a reason for something good happening.

Sandy asked me to get Sophie, which I did. When Sophie was told about what happened, she couldn't stop smiling and told Sandy about how good of a person I was. She kept saying how proud she was of me, and it made me feel good. Something about being told I had made such an impact made me feel worthy.

Like I had a reason to live for once.

****

Today I went to see Dr Goodall. I told him about the artwork and what had happened at work. "I'm happy that you seem to be doing better." I smiled because it was true. I did feel better than when I started writing this diary.

I know there have been moments where I've dipped but they're blips, small moments of madness in an ordinary tale.

"I guess so, yeah. I do seem better." I wasn't even taking the medication, and things in my life had started to seem better. I wondered why all of a sudden, I felt better, and I could only think of Tom and how since he started at the shop, I have felt better, I've felt normal. Even when I had a panic attack at the cinema, he was there to calm me down. He was something that was good in my life, even if nothing came out of it, I had made a really good mate.

Dr Goodall also suggested that I start writing poems seeing as I love writing as well. He said it's a good way of staying busy because I have to think of the wording and the format. I might try it out. It might help.

When he asked me if there was anything that wasn't so good in the week, I told him I didn't. My blip was just that, a blip. Tom is back at work and we're having a great time together. The void has been incredibly quiet recently, and I'm hoping it stays that way. I'd hate to think that it would come back when everything in my life seems to be turning out good.

I feel something I haven't felt for a long time... Hope.

With love,

Maddie x

66 DAYS LEFT

Dear Diary,

I haven't written in so long and it's simply because I've been busy trying to enjoy the little things. I've noticed when Tom laughs a single dimple shows on his cheek. I have also noticed that he laughs a lot. He finds a lot of things that I say are funny even if I don't think they are.

I've never really had a friend like Tom. He's different compared to Becks. Tom asks questions, even if they are really dumb ones. I could have conversations with him for hours about random things, whereas with Becks, we only ever talk about her now ex-boyfriend and work. We never laugh like Tom, and I do.

Tom is an incredible guy, but I find myself holding back. I don't want to get too close because I don't want him to find out how screwed up I am. I think I like Tom, like him more than a friend but I'm scared that he doesn't feel the same way. I mean why would he feel the same way about me? He's like ten times more attractive than I am.

Tom and I were working a shift together a couple of days ago when he suddenly changed the subject.

"Have you always worked on your own?"

"No, I used to work with a girl called Alice." I replied.

"Did she quit?"

"No, she's actually in prison." Tom looked at me, confused. I knew a spiral of questions was coming.

"Why?" He asked.

"Well, Alice was an old friend of Sophie's, Sophie gave her the job because Alice needed one and there was a position going here. Alice had... problems. She was angry. Mainly she was angry at Sophie for something she did like seven years ago. The first year she worked here, she was absolutely fine, she had an attitude and sometimes got angry, but she was pretty normal when we were together. Anyway, a couple of months back Alice came in, in a terrible mood, she told me that Sophie was writing her up about being late too many times and being rude to customers, and you know Sophie she's pretty easy going..." As I spoke, Tom seemed focused on watching my lips move. It made me feel shy, I wondered if my lips were dry and cracked like they usually were.

"...on this day it happened to be me, Sophie, and Alice in the shop, it was just after lunch, so there were no customers. Alice came straight into the shop and went straight out the back and into the office where Sophie was. Suddenly, there was screaming coming from the office. I ignored it at first because I knew it was Alice. She would shout a lot. I think it was her only volume..." Tom chuckled. At this point, I was checking to make sure that Sophie wasn't anywhere to be seen, because I know it's still raw to her.

"... After a couple of minutes of shouting all of a sudden, I heard Sophie screaming, she wasn't arguing back, she was shouting, she was telling Alice to stop. I ran straight to the office. It was locked, I couldn't get in. When I knocked on the door, Alice told me to call the police, so I did. About 10 minutes later, the police showed up, but those 10 minutes were the longest 10 minutes of my life. I just stood there listening to Sophie screaming. I felt useless, trapped on the other side of the door. When the police showed up, they were able to kick the door down and found Alice on top of Sophie. She had been hitting her for like 20 minutes straight. Sophie was a mess. There was blood everywhere." Tom looked astonished.

I continued "Alice went to prison, not for long though. It wasn't proper justice, she got off easy. But Sophie, she's still living with that every day. She was in the hospital for two weeks. I don't understand how Soph can still be so kind and caring after what happened. But that's Soph for you, she's a good person." Just as I finished explaining, Sophie came around the corner, she looked sad, and that's when I realised, she had heard the whole story.

"Sophie, I'm sorry, Tom asked, I didn't know you were listening." Sophie gave me a sympathetic smile "It's fine Maddie, you often have to talk about your experience to overcome it." She looked over to Tom "It's true, I spent three days in the hospital. I had lost vision in my left eye where she had hit it so many times. I had broken ribs, a broken finger, and she even broke a tooth. She ended up with a reduced sentence of three years because she pleaded guilty. But, after only eight months, she could get out on good behaviour."

Tom looked at both of us one at a time, shocked. He couldn't believe the story he had just heard. "Luckily, I have a restraining order against her so she can't be anywhere in the vicinity, otherwise she goes back to jail."

We all stayed quiet, mainly because Tom didn't know what to say for once. It seemed like 20 minutes until a customer came in. That's when Sophie went back to her office. I finished cleaning the shop. I knew Sophie found it hard to talk about, so when Tom had finished serving the customer, I bought her a cherry Bakewell tart (which is her favourite cake) and took it to her office. Her office door no longer has a lock because of that situation. It left Sophie too shaken to have it repaired.

As I knocked, I heard sniffing noises, I opened the office to see Sophie sat with her head in her hands, sobbing. I walked in slowly, put the Bakewell tart down and told her "You are the bravest person I know; you have dealt with so many bad things, and you still have a smile on your face. All you want to do is make people happy, and if I were even half the person you were, I would be damn proud of myself."

Sophie looked up at me and smiled, this time I went over and hugged her, I knew she needed it. I quietly said "Nobody is strong all the time, everyone has bad days, it's like a battlefield. There are some days you think you're winning, and you get excited thinking the war is over. Then there are days when you start losing, and you think it's all over. It's all about enjoying the good days and overcoming the bad ones."

Sophie let go of me and stared at me slightly confused. "I've heard that phrase before. My old therapist told me that once."

How strange. Perhaps, it was a common phrase?

"What was his name... Dr... It began with a W?" I looked at her more intently, she wasn't talking about THE Dr Williams, the one I had. "Dr Williams?" I questioned. She clicked her fingers "YES! He was the nicest therapist I've had, but he moved a while back. Wait. You know him?" She stared at me, and I could see her tears were drying up and no new ones were coming. She had the making of a smile on her face. "Yeah, I had him before my current one." That's probably the most I've ever told a work colleague or anyone about my counsellors. It felt nice to talk to her about it. I couldn't believe that she, not only went to counselling but also, had the same one as me. It made me feel closer to her, knowing that she had had a similar experience to me.

When I went out to the front of the shop, Tom had finished serving customers and was working on making the drinks. I got the trays ready for the customers staying in and got the to-go customers' cardboard holders. The rest of the day was busy, I spent most of the day either serving or making the drinks, and when Tom left Sophie came out to help for the busy moments. By the time I finished, I was exhausted, I was ready to go straight to bed, and that's what I did. I didn't even eat my dinner because I was too tired, all I wanted was to sleep for the rest of the night.

****

I woke up the next morning feeling pretty refreshed and felt ready to take on the day. I got dressed, ate breakfast (which is something I haven't done in a long time), drank a coffee and headed to work. Work was busy today. Which meant I didn't get much time to talk with Tom. I was glad when I finished, because it meant I could go home and get ready to go out with Beck's tonight. On my way out I popped in to say goodbye to Sophie. She had framed my picture and placed it proudly on her desk. I felt better about myself today than I have in a long time.

I told Becks I would go out with her tonight to a bar, and as I rang Becks to ask her when she wanted me to come over, mum came into my room. She smiled, stuck her thumbs up and mouthed "You look nice."

This made me smile again.

"Hey," Becks answered.

"Hey, what time do you want me to come over?"

"About 7:00 pm?" I agreed and hung up. Beck's seemed a lot more excited than I thought she would be. I was happy to be going out with her tonight. In the last 48 hours, this is the happiest I've been in around ten years.

When I got to Beck's I knocked on the door, and it was Matt that answered. I didn't expect to see him. "You coming in or what? Beck's upstairs." He groaned and left the door. I walked in and shut the door behind me, I went upstairs and into Beck's room. She looked up at me and smiled. "What's he doing here?" I whispered. "He's coming out with us; sorry I didn't say because I knew you wouldn't come."

I stared at her blankly "ARE YOU SERIOUS. Of all the things he's said to you." Becks stood up and grabbed my arms. "Maddie, calm down, he's apologised, he said he wouldn't do it again." I rolled my eyes "Seriously. You're intelligent Beck's surely you know that's a lie. He's a jackass."

Becks let go of my arms and sighed. "I love him okay. I know he's not the nicest and I know that you two don't get along, but I love him." "You love him? You hardly know him" I chuckled. "Maddie, you haven't had a boyfriend, so excuse me if I don't take your word for everything." Becks replied sarcastically. She sat back down and continued to do her makeup. "Maddie, you don't have to come out if you don't want to, I don't want to make you uncomfortable, but I want you to come out more than anything. Anyway, Matt won't be with us all night. He's meeting up with his friends." I sat on her bed and watched her do her makeup while trying to choose some good music to put on and got us some pre-drinks sorted.

After an hour, she was finally ready. We ordered a taxi, and while waiting, we drank a couple of vodka and cokes. The journey there was the most awkward journey I've had to deal with. I knew Matt knew, I didn't like him, and it was clear he didn't like me either. I didn't try to talk to him, and he didn't talk at all. He was too busy on his phone texting his mates. I bet his mates are just like him, complete jerks. When we got out of the taxi, we headed into a bar called Cookies. It's a bar that sells sweet cocktails. Also, if you know the bar staff you can get weed brownies there, the brownies are expensive, but you only need one bite to feel the high. Matt's only good thing was that he knew everyone and managed to hook me up with a brownie. I think he did it because he wanted to seem nice in front of Becks. Either that or the brownies were actually poisoned, and he wanted to kill me. I'm unsure of which one it was.

At around 8:00 pm, Matt met up with his mates, who all seemed pretentious and not my cup of tea. Becks and I went outside for a smoke. In the distance, I noticed someone who looked familiar. They started coming closer, and I realised it was Tom! I didn't want to seem creepy, so I pretended I didn't notice him. Tom must have noticed me because he shouted my name and started walking towards me. I turned around, acting like I hadn't seen him at all.

"Oh hey, Tom, what are you doing here?"

"I'm meeting a mate inside."

"Okay nice. Well, I might see you in there." I smiled, and he walked on in.

"Who's that?" Becks asked while nudging me on the shoulder.

"Tom, he's a workmate." I replied, and I realised I hadn't told her anything about Tom. I didn't tell her how he could make me smile by asking a stupid question. How he made sure I was always alright and never asked anything too personal. I especially didn't tell her how I felt like I was closer with him in the month that I'd known him compared to the 12 years I'd known her. I didn't tell her anything.

When we got back inside, we tried finding Matt luckily to no avail. We walked onto the dancefloor and started dancing. I was aware that Tom was somewhere in the bar, so I was hypervigilant, I was hoping to bump into him again. While we were dancing, I caught sight of Matt, who was talking to a girl. I tapped Becks on the shoulder and said, "Matt's over there." knowing she would see him talking to a girl and would go up to him and confront him, but she didn't do that. She shrugged and carried on dancing with me. I didn't understand what was happening between those two, how Becks had become so calm about situations that used to make her explode and why she invited him out if she didn't want to dance with him. Were they going out or not?

Suddenly, I see Matt kissing the girl he was talking to. I knew he was a sleaze bag. I didn't think he was that much of a sleaze bag. I tapped Becks on the shoulder and pointed towards Matt, she looked at him, and I could tell she became angry, but she didn't do anything. This made me even more confused. Becks was always up for a good argument, she loved it, but she didn't, she didn't move from the dancefloor.

"Becks, what's up with you two?" Becks sighed "We're together but also in an open relationship."

"What!" I shouted in shock. "He said he wants to get back with me, but he feels it would be good to try something new, so suggested an open relationship." I stopped dancing. "Are you okay with this?" I asked her, I knew people did stuff like that and I didn't care about it because I don't know those people, they aren't my friends. I know Becks and I know she would care about something like this.

"I told him we could try it for a month. If I didn't like it, then it would stop, and he agreed." I scoffed and continued to look at her in disbelief. I can't believe that she would be up for something like that. It didn't make sense. I think Matt's manipulating her somehow but unless she tells me I can't do anything but be supportive.

As the night was getting on, the bar became quieter. With people either heading to clubs or going home. We stayed until last orders, spending most of the night in a booth talking about life. The only time we get real with each other is when we're intoxicated. We talked about how different we were now and how life seems to worsen as we get older. We talked about how hard it is to be an adult with adult responsibilities. We talked about so much stuff, and it felt like I was talking to Tom for that moment.

Speaking of Tom, I never saw him after that encounter. He probably left with his mates to go to a different bar or club. He never texted me, but it wasn't like I was expecting him to message me. I knew that I had some feelings for Tom, but I could understand why he wouldn't have feelings for me. He was probably wanting to come out and enjoy his night but couldn't be there while I was, so went somewhere else.

Matt texted Becks and told her to go home by herself because he was going to his. She said he was hooking up with someone else because that's the only reason he would go home. She said she wasn't bothered, but I could tell she was. I just didn't want to intrude on a relationship I know nothing about. We both headed home and went to bed. We always let each other know when we got home safe, and that's exactly what we did.

When I got in bed, I thought about the night and how despite the beginning being rocky, the end wasn't too bad. I missed going out with Becks. We always had fun going out. This is the first time since she's been with Matt that she's come out and that's only because they're in an open relationship so he can shag whoever he wants. I know for a fact that Becks wouldn't do anything with anyone else because she's not that type of person, and I think Matt knows that as well. He's getting the best of both worlds. He can sleep around with whoever he wants and have someone he can come home to.

****

Yesterday I spent most of my day lying in bed, I was bored out of my mind, scrolling through Facebook and Instagram. I got up out of bed at 2pm, thinking I should probably spend some time actually doing something, so I decided I would write a poem.

I thought about what I wanted to write, whether I wanted to write it creatively, so there's a hidden meaning, or if I wanted to write it as obviously as possible. Then I thought about what I wanted to write it about, whether it was going to be a silly poem or a deep, meaningful one. I decided I wanted to write something serious. I wanted to try to explain my emotions in a written way or mainly how I feel about dealing with depression. I wanted to write about how I feel my depression interacts with my brain and how I should simply be happy, but I'm not.

In reality, I don't think I will ever be truly happy. That's why I'm still writing even though everything seems to be going well at the moment. I know this 'happiness' is only temporary, and the next time the void comes, it will take over my body completely. If you asked me deep down whether I actually wanted to leave this world and never see my family again, I would say no.

No, I don't want to go up to Bennetts Castle and kill myself, but I know there's no other way. There is no other way to make myself feel better. There's no other way to put my family out of the misery that I put them through. I think that writing has really helped in a way I didn't think it would. By putting my emotions into creative writing, I was allowing them to find freedom in my words. So, here it is…My first ever poem

What is Happiness?

What is happiness but a thought process,

Something that makes people constantly obsess.

The perfect family, the perfect life,

The perfect husband, the perfect wife.

People don't realise that it's not real,

Being happy all the time isn't part of the deal.

When we come into the world, we're born crying,

And then we grow up, and our body starts dying.

What is happiness except for one big, fat lie,

When in reality we're simply born just to die.

If happiness is used to fill in that time,

Then I myself lack some of that enzyme.

The mind within lacks some delight,

But the body outside is ready to fight.

Two parts of the body fighting each other,

both wanting to win against the other.

The pain becomes too much too bear,

I never signed up for this sordid affair.

What is happiness without many sad tears,

And trying to find it throughout the years.

Happiness is different for everyone on Earth,

As long as we remember each person's worth.

There will be some people who don't have a smile,

So, show those people their life is worthwhile.

After I finished writing, I put my pen down and just looked at it for a while. I read it aloud once, and then I read it aloud again. I liked it, it wasn't great, I wasn't even sure if it made sense, but I liked it. It was different from anything I've done before, and I actually enjoyed writing it.

I used to enjoy writing. I liked writing small fictional stories about detectives and solving cases. I stopped writing when I started drawing because I found I was better at physical art. I did miss doing it. It was a way for me to express myself verbally. I might try again soon.

I picked up my phone and saw that Tom had messaged me. I opened the message

T: Hey what are you doing later?

M: Nothing, I'm literally so bored right now that I will do anything.

Almost instantly he replied

T: You'd do anything like skydive? Well, I'm not that exciting, unfortunately. I was thinking of a drive to the lookout?

I enjoyed spending time with Tom and spending time with him outside of work was even better.

M: Why not? What's the worst that could happen? Yeah, sounds good.

Again, he replied almost instantly.

T: You know death is a big one, and okay 7oclock sounds good?

I laughed. Tom was the opposite of me. He was scared of death while I was welcoming it.

M: We all have to go at one point, at least it would be doing something fun. 7 o'clock is good.

With that, I put my phone away and went downstairs. Mum was in the front room watching TV. My mum wasn't one of those Facebook mums. She didn't use much social media; she always tried to stay connected in the real world. She would always say 'social media is a trap; people portray the best lives on social media.' She was right. Social media didn't help. My mum would get into loads of trends - she loved making stuff. She would make cards at birthdays and Christmas. She made cakes, and she made Christmas reefs. Anything you could think of mum would make it. At the moment she is making hats for my grandma and nan for Christmas. I won't lie, she's pretty good at it. I told her she should sell them, but she's happy to do it for fun. She would also tell me 'I would stop enjoying something if I was paid to do it. I like the choice of doing it and not being forced.' It made sense to me, I guess I was like that with drawing sometimes.

My mum was incredibly chatty. She could talk for hours. If she saw someone while we were out shopping, she would leave me to do all the actual shopping, and by the time I finished she would still be nattering away. I wish I could do that, but I'm not like mum, I'm not chatty, I'm a listener. My mum had this hard as nails exterior, but inside, she had the biggest heart. I remember when Becks got kicked out of her house, and my mum let her stay with us rent free for the week. My mum was always doing things like that. She would volunteer for so much, which is why we don't really see each other anymore. It's weird how you can live in the same house but hardly see each other. My mum has this random rage as well where small things would bother her more than big ones, most of the time it was to do with housework. When I was younger, it would be scary, but it's become quite funny as I've gotten older. I wouldn't say that in front of her face.

As I walked into the kitchen to get a drink, mum got up and stood by the kitchen door. "You alright mum?" I asked. She looked at me with sad eyes but a small smile "Yes, love. I haven't really seen you properly in a while, come sit and have a chat." I walked behind her into the living room and sat down on the sofa.

"So, how's work been?" she asked.

"Yeah, it's been alright, it's been quite busy." There was something up with her. She seemed distant.

"How have you been?" She asked.

"I've been alright." I said. I smiled and the smile she gave back to me was tinged with sadness.

"Good. Good." She said quietly.

"You alright?" I asked back.

"Yeah, I'm just tired, that's all, work has been busy as usual." I didn't really know what to say, so it just twiddled my fingers together

"So did work like your painting?" She asked a few moments later.

"Yeah, they loved it. The manager has put it in a frame and has put it in her office. When they redecorate the shop, she said she's going to put it out front on display." Mum's face lit up. She suddenly looked very happy.

"Oh, wow that is wonderful news, Maddie. You would have made Bampy proud, you know." I half-heartedly smiled. I knew why mum was upset now. She was thinking about her dad.

I always thought about mum when Bampy passed away. She became more reserved when it first happened. She stayed in the living room a lot watching tv and not really talking to anyone. I knew she was depressed, so I tried to help. I would make the tea and do the housework, but it didn't help much because all she wanted was for her dad to come back, and we couldn't make that happen. There was nothing we could do to help mum except being there when she needed us. A few times she would go off the rail where she would drink a lot and then cry, but she was mourning. After a couple of weeks, mum started to come back out of her shell, she started laughing again and was able to go back to work. Sometimes she still gets down, but that's the part of mourning nobody tells you, it's always there. There isn't a day where all of a sudden you forget about it and move on, you always remember, and there are days when it will come back, and you miss a loved one as much as the day you found out they passed, but as time goes on, those days happen less often.

When I knew mum was sad about Bampy, in a way, it gave me a bit of relief. I loved that she wanted to talk to me because she was sad. I sat with mum for a while. "The new guy that started work has asked me to go out again tonight." Mum's eyes shone. She always enjoyed it when I went out because I hardly ever did. "Oh, that's a brilliant sweetheart. Where are you going? What time are you going? Are you having dinner out? Will you be home before I go to bed?" Mum asked questions one after another with no break in between.

I told my mum the truth about 80% of the time unless it would get me into trouble or worry her. Yes, I wanted to smoke, and no my mum didn't officially know, I'm sure she had guessed but I hadn't told her the truth, and that's because she would be so disappointed in me. I hate the feeling of disappointing people. "So, we're going for a drive, leaving at 7, no I'll have dinner here, and I have no idea." Is exactly how I answered the questions. I had gotten pretty good at being able to guess what Mum was going to ask me because when it came to boys (whether they were friends or not), it was always the same questions.

I remember when mum tried purchasing me a rape alarm because 'I'd hit the age where men are interested.' I was 13 and I remember thinking what guy would be interested in me? Mum made dad buy me one. Dad was surprisingly fine with it. He said he just wanted to know I was safe. The alarm would go in my bag, and I thought I was the only one in my school who had one until someone else went off in their bag one day. Everyone started laughing because we all knew it was a rape alarm, the teacher went up to the girl who's bag it was, and while the girl was trying to turn it off, the teacher took it off her hands and turned it off for her. He then turned to the class and said "Class, as you all know this is a rape alarm. It's something that's supposed to keep women safe when they travel home alone. Let me show you how to use it," and he did. He told us what each button did and if someone is trying to take it off you there's a particular piece of rope to pull on that will make it automatically start. I remember this because the teacher said women, not anyone. I thought it was strange because I knew that men could be victims as well, but the teacher assumed it would just be women. I remembered how every time I would walk home at night that I would put my keys in between my knuckles so if someone tried anything it would hurt.

Tom texted me saying he was ready early if I wanted to head out, so I got in my car and drove to Tom's house. Tom was waiting outside when I got there and didn't even allow me to put the handbrake on before jumping into my car. I always wondered about Tom and his life because we didn't speak about stuff like that, he didn't ask me questions about my family, and I didn't ask him questions about his. We knew the basic information and that was enough for us. It was this unspoken rule that we knew not to bring up.

As I drove to the lookout, which was 20 minutes away from where he lived, he spoke about Doctor Who and how much he enjoyed it. I just listened to the way Tom spoke about the things he was interested in, I listened to how his voice would get louder the more passionate he was and how he would go red when he would talk too fast. I noticed the wrinkles on his forehead that arose when he scrunched his face up because he talked about something that confused him. The way he would laugh when he realised that he was talking too much and wanted me to talk and how it got quieter when I told him I enjoyed hearing him rant about things like that.

When we got to the lookout, he got a spliff out of his pocket and got out of the car. After a couple of minutes of walking, we found ourselves at the highest point of the lookout, we could see the entire town below us, and for that second, I felt invincible.

He sparked up and started taking drags of it and handing it over to me. I took some tokes and handed it back. When we smoked, we sat in silence, it was nice to be outside and just enjoying the view. It was quiet. There weren't any noisy kids or cars zooming past. We were at the right height to be away from the loud and bustling scenes of the town.

I turned to see Tom staring at me. "What?" I asked while laughing nervously. His eyes found mine, and he smiled. "I think you're amazing Maddie." He told me with a beaming smile. "I think you're amazing as well Tom." I replied. Then nervously looked ahead at the view again. I could tell Tom was still staring. "Take a photo, why don't you Tom?" I exclaimed.

He awkwardly laughed, ran his fingers through his hair and then looked away. I didn't know what was happening. It felt like Tom was keeping something from me. He was quieter than usual. He was more awkward than usual. It's the first time I've seen this version of Tom.

I stood on a rock that was next to the railings and looked over the edge. A couple of moments later, Tom joined me. He was tall enough to be the same height as me while I was still on the rock. "Isn't it beautiful." I said. "It sure is, that's why it's my favourite spot." I closed my eyes and took it all in with my other senses.

Hearing - I could hear the faint sounds of cars driving in the town below, the wind made a whistling noise and now and then you could hear an owl hooting.

Smell - It was fresh, it smelt like a cold winter morning with a slight added extra of hot dogs and burgers from the restaurants below.

Taste - Except for the after taste of weed and a dry mouth, the smell of hot dogs and burgers had salivated my mouth, allowing me to experience those things without actually eating them.

Touch - The cold railings shook with the wind, and the rock that I stood on was rough and would move side to side when I moved my footing. I was warm with my coat on, but the wind would interrupt now and then by swooping inside of the coat, making me shiver.

This is an exercise that Dr Williams taught me. He told me that a good way to stay grounded was to think of the five senses and to concentrate on those things describing what we were feeling with each one of those senses. It was an excellent way for me to prevent panic attacks when I used to suffer badly with them, but now I use them to appreciate things, to take everything in, in what could be the last time I have a chance too.

When I opened my eyes, Tom was also doing the same thing. I looked over, and he was smiling. This made me smile too, and I enjoyed the peace because I knew it wouldn't last forever. Sure enough, Tom was about to ruin it.

"How does something that was fun become an addiction? Like how does someone who enjoys drinking become an alcoholic, and what's the difference between an alcoholic and someone who drinks a glass of wine with dinner every night?" Tom had this way of speaking that intrigued me, he would always ask these pointless questions or at least what he called pointless questions, but when you think about them in further detail, they have meaning. I think it's his way of talking about things that makes him feel too uncomfortable to come right out and say.

"I guess the difference is dependency, if someone is living simply to drink that's different than someone who wants one glass of wine a night. It's the amount and the reason." I replied. I hope this helped him, although I could not tell. The sun had set quickly, and now it was dark out.

"Tom, are you in pain?" I asked him. "Sometimes, but that's life. No one should be happy 24/7 because that would make them normal and normal is very ordinary and boring."

I then tried to repeat the question "Okay, are you in pain now?" I turned my body and gazed into his eyes. "No, right now, I'm so fucking happy." He answered, his eyes glistening, I smiled and laughed at him.

After a couple of hours of talking, we decided to head back. Tom was stern that he needed to be home before his mum got home at 11. We got back into the car, and I drove him home. As we got closer to his house, Tom became quieter, and his smile began to fade.

"Thanks for the great night, Maddie"

"I like hanging out with you, Tom."

Tom unbuckled his seat, but he didn't get out straight away, he sat and smiled at me for a second. He was goofy, but I liked it. He waved goodbye and went into his house.

On the drive home I couldn't stop smiling, we had a really nice time out, and he opened up about stuff that I never knew. He spoke about his mum and dad and how his dad left when his twin sisters were born. He spoke about how his dad doesn't bother and how that left him feeling a little empty but then said it was okay because he had a family that mattered. Tom did a lot of talking, and some of it might have seemed like he was rambling on about nothing, but if you took what he said and took it less literally, things started making sense. A lot of the time what he says seems cryptic.

Maybe Tom was like me, maybe he was more like me than we both knew. I hoped he wasn't because I wouldn't want Tom to feel the way I did.

I hope that we can spend more time together because I really enjoy his company, every time I spend time with Tom my heart skips a beat. He seems to just get me in a way nobody else does.

With love,

Maddie x

64 DAYS LEFT

Dear Diary,

I saw Dr Goodall today and told him about Tom and how I am starting to feel about him. I told him how he would ask strange questions and how I was unsure if they had hidden meanings. I told him how I wanted to get Tom to talk to me more about his life and how I wanted Tom to know that he could trust me.

Dr Goodall told me that people take time and used me as an example. He reminded me how long it took me to open up to Becks, and that I should be patient and maybe tell him more about myself. That way Tom knows he can talk about himself too. Dr Goodall said it was good that I made a friend but that I needed to make sure I was also happy on my own and not just with him because I can't become dependable on other people for my happiness.

When I told Dr Goodall that I didn't know if I would ever be dependable on my own happiness, Dr Goodall explained that it is good to rely on yourself for happiness and not just others. Because the moment you lose touch with those people it means all of your happiness goes with them.

I didn't like Dr Goodall's session today. He made me feel terrible. I didn't say anything, though. Dr Goodall doesn't get it, it's not the people, but it's the memories. It's knowing that I spent a great day with Tom, and he made me feel good. It's knowing that Sophie loved my painting and has it next to her computer. It's all these things, and happiness isn't just an object, but it's people as well.

I went to work in a bad mood, and as soon as I arrived, Sophie could tell I wasn't happy. She made me a drink and took me into the office. "I'm guessing it wasn't a good session today." She asked. "No, he told me I shouldn't find happiness in people but in something else like my art or whatever." I complained.

Sophie sat down next to me "I kind of agree with him. I thought I found happiness with my ex and look what he did to me. I thought I found it by giving Alice a job and look how that turned out. Happiness isn't just people because people can leave your life." I dropped my head and stared at my coffee. I didn't want to hear it, because my only happiness lately has come from others and not myself.

"Having friends is great, it's a great booster but don't rely on them, you have to find the happiness within you." I chuckled because that's exactly how Dr Goodall said it. I knew both Sophie and Dr Goodall had a point. I knew how my mood changed depending on if Becks was talking to me or not. I knew that they were right but having Tom became a great distraction from the void. I rarely thought of the void, I only thought of Tom.

****

Tom was serving Doris, when she saw me, she smiled and waved. I made Doris' new favourite drink, and I took it over to where she was already seated. She thanked me with a smile. As I walked over to Tom, he stuck his tongue out so I put my middle finger up to him, we both laughed. When I got back to the counter, a group of older people came into the shop with two younger women who must have been care assistants. They came in and ordered seven tea's and seven brownies. They went to find a seat while we prepared their order.

Doris looked at the group that had just come in and then looked back out the window. One of the old ladies noticed this. "Hey, you over there." She shouted to Doris. One of the care assistants told the lady not to be rude and to let Doris enjoy her drink alone. "Excuse me, lady?!" The same lady shouted. Of course, Doris was oblivious to the women's rudeness.

"She's deaf." I told the elderly women when I took over the tea.

"Well, she needs a sign then, just cause she's deaf doesn't mean she has to be rude." The elderly lady continued.

"Unless she's looking at you, she won't be able to tell you're calling her." As I bought the last cup of tea and set it on the table, the elderly lady turned to me and said: "You should lose some weight lady, your stomach is going on the table." The care assistant told her off and apologised to me. "Don't apologise for her. She knew what she was saying, but if she's rude again, I'm going to ask you all to leave." I replied and walked out the back of the shop. I felt my breathing becoming erratic, my throat felt like it was closing in, and my eyes began to water.

It hurt. I'm not going to lie that it hurt like someone had just stuck a knife in my back. The thing this lady didn't know was that I had been losing weight. Last time I checked, I had lost 15 pounds. She may as well have pointed at me and said "Oi Fatty!" My body is the one thing that I'm ashamed of and to be told by a stranger that I need to lose weight hit me back a couple of steps. I was feeling better, but now I feel like I did two weeks ago.

I wish that words didn't hurt me so much, but words like that made a mark on my body. Much worse than the wounds I inflicted on myself. My mind tells me these things all the time. I'm fat. I'm ugly. I try to convince myself it's just my brain's way of upsetting me, but when someone actually says it, it proves that it's true. If she's saying I'm fat, then everything else my brain is saying is correct as well.

She's right. Look at you.

You're pathetic.

Can't even stick up for yourself properly.

You walk away and cry like a little baby.

God.

You are so pathetic.

Absolutely useless.

I steadied my breathing, trying to stop the void from taking over again, and walk back into the shop. I cleared a few tables and loaded the dirty plates and dishes into the dishwasher. I felt a soft hand pat me on the shoulder, when I turned around, and saw Tom.

"Are you okay? Look. Don't listen to the evil, old bat. Thinks because she's old she can tell everyone what she thinks, she's got another thing coming. Don't worry. She'll die way before us, so we can have the last laugh."

Tom was trying to make me feel better, but the last comment was what got me "she'll die before us.' I thought about it over and over, and the one thing Tom doesn't know is that she won't die before me. I'm sticking to this plan. I have to.

With Love,

Maddie x

62 DAYS LEFT

Dear Diary,

Usually, when someone upsets me, I would go home and eat my feelings and problems away, but I didn't. After being called fat, I've been walking the long way home. I've even started going on walks after work in bids to lose more weight. I don't know why this comment out of all comments has affected me, I guess anytime kids used to be cruel my mum would tell me it's because they're either jealous or have their own problems dealing with, but this lady was simply nasty. She stated the obvious as if I would turn around and be like 'Woah, thank you; I thought I was a size 8 and in perfect shape.'

The comment niggled at me and went round and round in my mind. Everything I tried wasn't working, even talking to Tom at work didn't help. It was like I was a cartoon character with a cloud over my head. The only short time I felt better is when I would exercise because I knew I was doing something to help myself.

She's right, you know.

You are fat, and if you're fat then you're ugly.

No matter what you do you'll always be fat and ugly.

That's who you are.

If you exercise, you'll lose weight and then you won't be ugly.

Tom might actually want you if you lose weight.

He might actually like you back.

Obviously, he doesn't like you right now because you're fat.

No guy would ever like you when you're fat.

I remember when I was younger, I didn't look like the rest of the kids. I was always fatter and taller, while most girls were skinny and short. I was the opposite. I looked more like the boys than I did the girls. In Primary school, I was always the one to stand out from the crowd because I was taller than most people. I wondered why I had to have both genes from my family and why I couldn't be skinny. I remember the feeling of being the odd one out in school, the one that would walk from group to group never fitting in and eating lunch by myself because no one wanted to eat with me.

I remember in secondary school there was this one really nice teacher. I felt like she was more of a friend than a teacher because we both enjoyed the same things. My class had to plan our English-speaking assignment, and I wanted to do mine on Doctor Who, but I was embarrassed that people would laugh at me.

When Miss Westlake asked what I was doing mine on, I said I was unsure. She sneakily saw that I had written a paragraph on Doctor Who in my textbook, but she could also see I was too nervous to talk about it in front of everyone else. She got down to my level and told me she enjoyed watching it too. She told me that her favourite Doctor was David Tennant and I had to agree. As soon as she said that it made me feel a lot more comfortable to write about it and speak about it. She was a great teacher, anytime I didn't have anyone to eat with, I would knock on her door, and she would allow me to eat my lunch with her.

Often, I was early for school so I would go into her classroom before it started and sit and read. I always bought a book into school as a reason to eat by myself. It kept me company. She was a good teacher, and she was a nice one. She understood me without me telling her anything personal.

I'm sure Miss Westlake actually wanted peace and quiet, she didn't want me there talking to her, distracting her, generally annoying her, but she never said anything. She never told me to go away (unless I had lessons), she never told me she wasn't interested when Becks and I would fall out. She was always kind, she came up with solutions, she told me to make amends with Becks. She always asked how I was, and she always knew when I wasn't doing good. She could tell when I was depressed or anxious, she never forced me to say anything but the way she asked questions made me feel safe. I never outwardly told her how I was having terrible thoughts, how every night I went home and self-harmed. I never told her any of it, but I knew if there was a day where I wanted to tell someone, then I would go to her.

I'm sure Miss Westlake doesn't remember me, she's had hundreds if not thousands of students that she's taught and I'm sure that there have been many that are so much better than I am, but I remember her.

I remember her lessons, I remember the first time she properly spoke to me, and how she made me feel comfortable about something that I had been picked on for liking my entire life. Miss Westlake was a kind and caring person, and even if she doesn't remember me, I will always remember her.

Just like how Sophie reminds me of my old teacher. I see the kindness in Sophie, and she always knows if something is bothering me. I always wonder how Sophie does it, how she's so happy and kind to everyone and doesn't show any negative emotion. She has this outlook on life that is just so positive. If I ever had or wanted kids, I would want them to turn out like Sophie. I would want them to see the positive in everything around them. I would want my kids to be happy, that's all I'd want from them even if it meant having a job at a shop or being a binman whatever they wanted to do as long as they would be happy, that's all that matters in life.

When I went to work yesterday, Tom was already there, which was weird because I normally start before him. I'm known as a 'senior' member of staff (it's an easier name for someone who's been there for two years or more). Which meant I always had to be there a little earlier than normal staff members. When I came into the shop, Tom was standing behind the counter looking all chipper.

"Good morning, Maddie, it is a fine day today." He shouted as soon as I came into the shop. "It's raining outside, and it's before 9 am why is it a fine day?" I mumbled as I walked behind the counter and to the lockers.

"Well, Maddie, dear..."

I laughed at that, that's something my nan would call me after I made her a cup of tea.

"...today may be rainy, and it may be early, but it's a new day, and I'm positive that it will be a marvellous day." I rolled my eyes. He wasn't convincing me, and it was obvious.

"Okay, I'm excited because one of my writing pieces has been picked up by a publisher" He started jumping up and down. "Oh, My God! Well done! I'm so proud of you, Tom!" I hugged him. Sophie came out to hear what the commotion was all about. Tom told her the good news, and he was beaming like a Cheshire cat the entire time. "Oh wow, that is amazing, Tom!" Sophie said and hugged him as well.

I was so happy for Tom; he deserved every bit of good news that he could get. He looked so fresh and full of life; he was practically bouncing off the walls in excitement. I was happy for Tom, he really did deserve it, he was one of the good ones. I was so glad that he was able to experience the happiness and joy that he deserved. I knew Tom hid behind this happy/hyper facade and that deep down, there was something going on, I could spot that sort of thing a mile away. I just didn't want to burst his bubble or make him feel uncomfortable. Right now, he seems genuinely happy, and I'm glad of that.

During our shift, Tom tells me all about his book. It's a Sci Fi story about a man who travels back in time to save as many Jews as he can from the evil concentration camps. I asked if it had a happy ending, but Tom explained that although the man does save many Jews, he himself gets trapped in Auschwitz and is never seen again.

I told him to let me buy a copy when it came out, he said it would be a long time until it was published as he had to make some changes, as well as sort the contract and cover out. I was still over the moon for him.

"You wanna hang out tonight?" I asked him once the initial excitement had died down. Tom's face lit up "Of course I do, what are you thinking?" I thought for a moment. I didn't really know what we could do. There's not much around our area to keep us entertained.

"How about we go to my favourite place? We've been to yours. I'll take you to mine." Tom smiled and agreed. I told him we would go home, get changed and then meet at the coffee shop because where I wanted to go was a 20-minute walk from there.

I ran home again tonight. I enjoyed it, and it meant I could get home quicker. People stared, which made me feel awkward, but I put my head down and pushed on.

When I got to my road, I stopped to catch my breath. I should buy one of those watches that show your heartbeat because I reckon mine would be off the scale. I thought it was going to pound out of my chest. I walked into my house, and it was dead quiet. Typically, my mum is home by now from work, but it was empty. I shouted hello to see if anyone was in, but they weren't. I went upstairs and got undressed to have a shower. I looked down and saw the faint scars on my legs. Both legs had scars dating back 6 or 7 years that were still showing.

Self-harming isn't something I'm proud of, but it's something I did as a way of relieving any feelings or emotions I couldn't handle. I always thought 'Sometimes hurting yourself is the only way not to hurt the ones around you' That was the thought process I had. I cut myself to hide the truth. To hide the hurt I felt, so I wouldn't have to share it with anyone. I tried so many different methods, and they all hurt, they really fucking hurt. It's not like in movies or shows when someone does it and automatically gets this euphoric feeling. It happens, and the first thought I have is shit I need to stop the bleeding. There was a sense of relief afterwards, but it never lasted. After a while, I slowly stopped doing it and instead changed to alcohol or weed because it helped but wasn't leaving a physical mark on my body.

Once dressed, I heard a knock on my door, it was David. "Come in," I shouted. "You going out?" He asked me. "Yeah" "Okay, I am as well." He replied. He smiled at me and then left the room. That was it, which was actually a pretty long conversation for us. I texted mum to let her know we were both going out. She texted back quickly saying she was at Momma's (her mum) and wouldn't be back until late.

Once I finished getting ready, I messaged Tom to let him know. Luckily, the rain had stopped, but I took a jacket just in case. I picked my bag up and headed out the door shouting Bye to David. I headed to the coffee shop, and when I turned the corner, I saw Tom was already there waiting for me. I walked up to Tom quietly.

"BOO!" I shouted, and Tom jumped a mile, I started laughing hysterically, and he held his hand to his chest. "You scared the living daylights out of me." He said and then joined in with laughing.

Once his heart started beating normally, we headed to Bennetts Castle. The entire walk we were talking about his book and my artwork and how suddenly we've both gotten something we wanted. Tom had been looking for artists to draw the cover for his book and he asked if I could give it a try. "I'll pay you of course." He said. I shook my head.

"I don't know that's a huge deal drawing for a book." I told him, but Tom kept begging me, and eventually, I gave up. "Okay, I'll do a cover, but if it's no good, you find someone else." He smiled at me and thanked me. "Your artwork is amazing, you'll do great."

When we got to Bennetts Castle, I took him to my favourite spot where you could see the village and sat on the usual bench. "What a lovely view!" He said.

"Yeah, it's my favourite. Isn't it weird how our favourite spots are views of built-up areas?" I asked him.

"Yeah, but we're just high enough that we can't hear the noises, so it's quieter. I like to think that it's a good way of seeing the bigger picture, you know?" Tom replied.

I looked at Tom, who was happily enjoying the view. "Sometimes, it's hard to see the bigger picture without removing yourself from it." I mused. Tom looked at me and nodded, "Yeah, exactly like that."

We both looked back at the village below. I knew at some point I wanted to ask Tom about his life, to try to get him to open up a bit, but there was never an appropriate moment. Every time I went to talk to him, Tom would ask me random questions again.

"Do you think Bees will go extinct and wasps will take over honey duty?" "If we gave fish feet, would they swim as well as they do now?" "You know how sharks die if they stop swimming, do humans have an equivalent of that?"

I always laughed at his questions because they were so strange. I have never known another person like him. Just as I thought I wouldn't be able to talk to him about what I really wanted, he turned to me and asked: "Do you think there's a way that you could have everything you wanted and still be unhappy?"

I tried to catch his eye, but he was too busy staring ahead of him. "I think whether people have everything, they can still feel sad, and I think that's okay." Tom nodded but didn't say anything.

"Tom, do you ever get depressed?" I asked him. Tom stayed silent for a while before answering.

"Sometimes, do you?" He muttered.

"Yeah." I chuckled knowingly. "I've been depressed for like ten years." Tom looked over. His eyes filled with sadness, a new look on him.

"Ditto"

He replies. I think that is about as much as he can share for tonight. There's a part of me that is so proud of him for telling me. It took me years to tell Becks, and in just a few short weeks, he felt comfortable to tell me. He rolls a joint and sparks it up. Then smokes in silence.

It wasn't an awkward silence though it was a nice silence. A comfortable silence.

When we finished smoking, we headed back. "Let me know when you get home. I wanna know you got back safe." He said embracing me into a hug, for a moment I didn't know what to do, but I then found myself wrapping my arms around his waist and placing my head next to his. When we let go, we both laughed and awkwardly waved goodbye.

When I got home, I went straight upstairs and laid on my bed. My phone beeped straight away, and Tom asked if I had gotten home safe, I replied I had and thanked him for the good night. I put my phone against my chest and laid there for a second. Tom's hug was warm, it was nice. He was nice.

The only problem is I shouldn't be adding people to the list of people I need to say goodbye to. I don't want him getting the wrong impression, but I also can't deny my feelings for him.

I only have 62 days left, and I'm more confused than I have ever been.

With love,

Maddie x

59 DAYS LEFT

Dear Diary,

Tom and I have been spending a lot more time together. I enjoy his company, and I'm guessing he enjoys mine because he's the one that keeps asking me to go out.

On Saturday, the day after Tom and I went to Bennetts Castle, he messaged me to let me know he was doing overtime so would be at work with me for two hours. I didn't mind that, one it's nice spending time with him, in and out of work, and two it meant that I could do a lot of cleaning, which was my favourite thing to do to make the shift go quicker.

Most Saturdays I'm able to manage serving customers and making drinks, but I think because kids are out of school, it was even busier than usual. There was a long queue, and at one point, I had to bring Sophie out to help make drinks. (She's faster than I am because she lives and breathes coffee). When Tom came in, Sophie and I gave a huge sigh of relief. "You've saved us." I told him as he came round the counter. Tom put his jacket down. "That bad, ay?" he asked.

"It hasn't stopped. I haven't even had a break." I told him. As soon as he was out the front I went on a quick break. We were allowed 30 minutes, but when it's that busy, I always like to eat my food and then go straight out to help.

When the shop finally settles down, Tom suggests we play 100 questions. He says it's a good way to get to know each other. I agree, it helps to pass the time while doing mundane jobs.

"Okay, 100 questions, I'll start." Tom jumps in. "Favourite colour?" He asks.

"Blue." "Favourite artist?" I ask.

"At the moment Muse." He replies. It goes on like this for ages.

"Worst nightmare?"

"Drowning. Ideal holiday?"

"Australia. Favourite food?"

"Curry. One million pounds or going on holiday with your favourite celebrity?"

"One million pounds, my favourite celeb is dead. Favourite season?"

"Autumn. Your favourite season?"

"Autumn or Spring. Favourite drink?"

"Non-alcoholic is diet coke. Alcoholic is Bacardi and coke. Worst habit?"

"Always apologising even if I wasn't in the wrong. Worst fear?"

"Frogs can't explain why but I hate them. Favourite animal?"

"Giraffe. Your favourite animal?"

"Turtles. Your weirdest trait?"

And on and on we went, asking each other the first question that came into our heads. We got to about 50 questions when the shop started getting a bit busier again, and we had to stop. We then spent the last hour of my shift making drinks, sorting out orders and cleaning tables. Sophie came out 10 minutes before I was meant to finish my shift.

"Hey Maddie, do you mind staying on until this queue is down?" She asks. "Of course, I don't mind." I didn't mind because Tom was there and I was happy to stay on, he made it more bearable even when he didn't say anything. Tom had agreed to stay on for another 4 hours, giving Sophie the chance to sort out some problems in the office without leaving me by myself.

I ended up staying for another half an hour until the queue had gone down significantly, and only two people were waiting for their drinks. "Do you wanna hang out tonight?" Tom asked as I was leaving. The shop was shut on Sundays, so neither of us had to get up extra early. "Sure. Same time?" I smiled and he nodded in reply.

"You can pick where we go this time." I said as I left the shop. I ran home again not because I was rushing to get home but because I wanted to lose some weight. I didn't want Tom thinking I was fat and didn't want to spend time with me because of it so I was specifically trying to lose a few pounds a week. I had already lost over a stone, which in just over a month isn't a long time, however I have barely been eating, and when I have its salads.

I remember the first time I started a diet. I was annoyed because I only lost a pound. Dad saw I was upset and explained: "You know even if you lost 1 pound every week for a year you would have still lost 52 pounds, which is over 3 stone." It made me feel better because he did have a point. I was too busy trying to lose loads in a small amount that I didn't think of the big picture (no pun intended). I started making my aim to be to lose a pound a week so that I would be 3 stone and 7 pounds lighter in a year's time. My plans never fully worked, at Christmas time, I would get loads of chocolate and snacks in my presents, which would push me back or lose interest in exercising because I had no reason to be slimmer. Sometimes I was too depressed to get out of bed or put on clothes to exercise, so I didn't.

This time I've been better, I have been able to stick to something, and it's because of Tom. I wouldn't want him hanging around with a heavy load like me. Tom's lucky though. He can eat whatever he wants and doesn't put on weight. It's really annoying. He came to work once with a 12inch sub and then bought some brownies from the shop. He ate all of it during his lunch break. I was gobsmacked to see nothing was left. I couldn't eat like that without putting on 5 pounds. He was lucky.

I got home and headed straight to my room to change. When I opened my drawers, I found the plastic bag. It took me back for a moment because I hadn't seen the bag in so long. I picked it up and looked inside, in that bag was everything I needed to go through with my plan. There were packets and packets of paracetamol, there were razor blades still with the packaging on, and there was one final spliff I had already pre-rolled. It was the first thing I did when I knew I wanted to end my life. I made my final bag, everything I would take up to Bennetts Castle on my last day. I took it out of the drawer and checked to make sure no one was home. I tipped the bag out onto my bed and looked through it all. Did I really want to do this? Life was getting more bearable. Did I want to say goodbye to it all?

I heard the front door slam shut. Someone was home. I quickly put all of the stuff into the bag and put it back into the drawer. "Maddie, it's me," David shouted. He walked upstairs and went straight into his bedroom. I got the bag back out and considered putting it in the bin. I knew if I emptied the bin straight away, my family wouldn't find it and I wouldn't be questioned. I didn't know what to do. I headed downstairs with the bag in my hand. As I got to the bin, Dad came into the house.

"Alright, Maddie?" He asked. I swung around and held the bag behind my back. "Alright, dad? How was work?" He took his shoes off and headed into the living room. I followed him with the bag still behind my back. "Yeah, it was tiring. How was work for you?" He asked. "It was good. I stayed on a bit, so that's good." "Good, Good. What's behind your back?" He asked.

My body started heating up. If he found out about this, he would not be happy. He would tell mum, and then they would take me to the Doctors again. Think. Think. "I went to the shops before I came home. It's for your birthday." "My birthday is in a month." He told me. "You know me, dad, always buying early presents." I smiled at him, and thankfully he didn't question me anymore. I ran upstairs and put the plastic bag back into the drawer, this time making sure it was right at the back so nobody would go snooping.

****

I met up with Tom at 8. He chose to go bowling. I'm no good at bowling, I throw it, and it always ends up in the gutter. He told me I could have the guards up, and I told him I wasn't a five-year-old child, which made him laugh. When we got there, he had already pre-paid for the tickets, so we went straight in and started bowling. As usual, I was terrible. I ended up getting 50.

On the other hand, Tom was amazing, he got strikes and spares and ended up with 101! He doubled my score. I was amazed at how good he was. I wasn't a sore loser because I knew no matter what I would lose, so I congratulated and clapped him when he won. He took in the moment and started bowing and thanking his family. I thought it was hilarious. We didn't talk that much when we were bowling because we were too focused on hitting the pins, so when we finished, we sat down and had a drink.

"Thanks for staying on the other day. It was an absolute nightmare when you left." He told me. "It's fine. I don't mind at all. I like you... hanging out with you." He stumbled on his words then quickly changed the subject, explaining how most of the customers he had after I left were rude and how they were telling him to hurry up. "You have to ignore them, ask Sophie to come out and serve if you get someone like that." I encouraged him. "I always ask Sophie for help when it's busy. She's happy to help all the time." I added.

Tom and I spoke for hours, we laughed, and I cried at one point (of laughter I may add). We talked about tv shows, films, we even finished the 100-question game we didn't have time to earlier. When we eventually finished talking, we realised it was 10:30 pm, this made Tom agitated, he told me we had to leave now because he had a curfew of 11. I downed my drink, and we headed to the car.

Heading home, we continued talking of shows and films and what we thought of Doctor Who episodes and things like that. He didn't seem as agitated as he did in the bowling alley. When we got to his house, we had 5 minutes to spare, Tom unbuckled his seat but remained in the car.

"Maddie, I really like spending time with you."

"I like spending time with you too Tom"

"And I... I've been wanting to say this for a while, but I guess I was scared."

Tom stopped for a moment, we had both contorted our bodies so that we were facing each other in the car, but Tom couldn't keep direct eye contact. "I guess... what I've been wanting to say is..." and before he could finish his sentence, he looked at me, reached his hand out to my cheek and moved his body towards mine. His lips pressed mine and we kissed.

I felt fireworks exploding in my body.

Butterflies in my stomach.

My heart skipped a beat.

He was kissing me.

Me!

Of all people.

Tom was kissing me.

Tom moved back after a couple of seconds, and we both smiled and chuckled to each other. "I've been wanting to do that for so long." Tom whispered and got out of the car, and into his house.

I sat in the car for a couple of minutes thinking about what had just happened. I held my hand against the cheek he had just been touching, it was now red and hot, and smiled. He kissed me. I drove home with the biggest smile on my face. I couldn't believe what just happened. Even when I got home, I was still in shock. I led down and kept thinking about that moment. I checked my phone and Tom had messaged me.

'Thanks for the good night.'

'It was amazing. Thank you.' I replied.

Within seconds he had messaged again.

*T: **Thanks for getting me home so quickly, mum doesn't like it when I'm late.***

I smiled at my phone. I didn't know anything about his mum except that his dad left his mum when he was younger.

M: That's fine. I like spending time with you.

T: So do I :)

Anytime I spend time with Tom, the void is quiet. It doesn't make a noise, maybe Dr Goodall and Sophie are wrong. Maybe, Tom is the one that will make everything better.

****

I woke up the next day as if I had woken up from a heavy night of drinking. My head was pounding, and I felt sick. I hoped I wasn't coming down with something, but before I could even think about anything else, I ran to the toilet to throw up. It's so annoying, I had a great night last night, and now only 10 hours later I'm throwing up in my bog. Amazing. After I finished getting close and personal with my toilet, I dragged myself back to bed.

"You okay, Maddie?" Mum shouted up to me. Mum hated being sick so she wouldn't come up and rub my back. "No, I've just been sick." I groaned down to her. "Well get yourself in bed. I'll make you some toast." I never understood why toast was the go-to meal to have when you were ill, but it was the traditional sickness food.

I headed back into my room and laid back in bed. I felt horrible. I couldn't think why I had all of a sudden felt ill, when yesterday I was absolutely fine. I started going through everything I had eaten. It wouldn't be food poisoning because I ate the same things as everyone else yesterday. It wouldn't be alcohol because I didn't drink and wouldn't be weed because it would have happened that night. It seems like I've picked up a bug. Luckily, I wasn't at work today or tomorrow so I could easily stay in bed all day.

I laid in bed all day only being woken when I needed to be sick or when mum was checking in on me. She checked my temperature and told me I had a fever. "How are you feeling?" She asked me. "I feel like death." I moaned. "Do you want any toast or some orange juice?" Mum asked, but I simply shook my head and went back under my covers.

When I woke up, I was boiling hot. I undid the covers and spread myself on my bed, starfish style. My pyjama shirt was wet, and eventually I built up the strength to go and put on some different clothes. I couldn't be bothered to have a shower, so I put some deodorant on, wiped my face with face wipes, brushed my hair and put it back up.

The whole day was a write-off. Monday was a bit better. I was able to get out of bed and eat some toast. I decided I would have a shower as mum always says a good shower makes everything better and she was definitely right. It made me feel slightly refreshed. I still felt sick, but the shower made me feel less groggy.

I checked my phone for the first time since Saturday night and saw that Tom had messaged me a couple of times.

T: Hey, are you free?

T: How's your Sunday been?

T: Sorry if the kiss was weird or I was out of line.

He messaged me three times in a row, and despite feeling terrible, it made me feel good. I quickly messaged him back.

M: sorry I've had a fever and was sick all day yesterday. I like you, Tom, like, really like you.

Before I sent it, I re-read it over and over, I didn't want to seem desperate, I didn't want to come across as a beg so I deleted the text. Suddenly my phone went off, and it wasn't a text. I looked at my phone and as if by pure telepathy Tom was ringing me.

"Hello?" I answered.

"Hey Maddie, how are you doing?" Tom asked.

"Yeah, I'm doing better, how are you?"

"Good, I'm glad to hear you're feeling better and yeah I'm good, I'm just on my break at work, it's mental in here." Tom sighed.

"Monday's not normally that bad, I wonder why it's so busy?"

"Yeah, kids are off though for summer holidays, so it's been completely mad at the moment." He explained.

"Oh, that old lady came in today," He added.

"Doris?" I asked.

"Yeah, Doris came in. She seemed sad because I didn't know sign language." Tom pointed out. "She's sweet." I told him, there was silence at the end of the phone and for a moment I had assumed he hung up.

"Hey Maddie? I know you're not feeling well, I was wondering if maybe I could come over after work? I'll get you some soup if you like that kind of thing. And maybe one of those tiger baguettes, they're honestly the best bread to have alongside tomato soup. Like top tier bread in general but with soup it's like heaven in your mouth." I chuckled, he was so funny, and I don't think he realised it. I think he was being sweet and sincere but his rant about tiger bread made me feel better.

"Of course, you can Tom. I'll message you, my address."

Tom hung up shortly after as Sophie was shouting that his break was finished, and she needed help on the shopfloor. I fell back asleep basically straight after Tom had hung up.

I awoke at 4pm, to mum talking very loudly downstairs "Oh my god, how nice of you. Yes, she's not feeling very well, but what a lovely gentleman you are." I assumed mum was talking to Tom as her usual voice had changed to her customer service voice.

I quickly got out of bed, threw some dirty clothes under my bed, quickly sorted my hair out, put a bra on, sprayed a load of deodorant under my armpits and gargled some mouthwash before heading downstairs.

Tom was sitting on the sofa, a tin of soup in one hand and half a tiger baguette in the other. He was intently listening to mum talk and had clearly been engaged in conversation prior to me coming downstairs. "Oh, here she is," mum says as she clocks me at the bottom of the stairs. Mum stood up and walked over to me.

"Well, you could have at least changed or told me someone was coming over" she whispered. Mum then turned around with a fake smile and "it was so nice to meet you Tom, I have to pop upstairs now."

Tom exchanged a "nice to meet you too" and then walked over to me, bread, and tin still in his hand.

"There you go, ma'am, one tin of Co-op's finest soup and one-half loaf of tiger baguette from the bakery."

He held them up in the air and slightly bowed like one would for the queen. I laughed and took them out of his hands "Thank you, but question. Why didn't you just get the bread in Co-Op?"

Tom held his finger up as if to stop me from talking anymore. "Well, the bakery bread is made fresh that day, of organic and natural ingredients, plumped and preserved..." Before he could finish his sentence I jokingly added, "Co-op didn't have any tiger bread, did they?" and he quickly nodded "nope, they ran out, so I had to go to the bakery..." I laughed and so did he. "...that is a £4 half loaf of tiger bread, so I hope it's the best goddamn tiger bread you've ever tasted in your life."

I went into the kitchen and Tom followed me. I cut up the tiger bread, lathering butter onto the pieces, poured the soup into a pot, placed it onto the hot stove and got out two bowls. When the soup had cooked, I separated it and gave Tom half of everything. We sat down in front of the TV and watched Scooby Doo. Turns out Tom was as big a Scooby-Doo enthusiast as me. We agreed that the Sarah-Michelle Geller films were elite, so we ended up watching both.

I asked Tom if he would be able to do my morning shift if I did his afternoon. I was pretty tired and wanted extra sleep to make sure I was ready for the morning. He said it would be fine because it meant he was able to take his sisters to school for breakfast and would be able to pick them up straight after he'd finished.

"Hey, I should probably go, mum won't be too happy if I'm home too late on a work and school night."

"Yeah, that's fine." We both got up off the sofa and headed towards the door.

"Thank you by the way." Tom did a random twirl on the spot and took a bow. "What for?" He asked.

"For coming here today, for swapping my shift, for being just really fucking cool."

I looked at Tom, he seemed happy, and I was too. For the first time in ages, I was so happy, it felt amazing.

"I really like you, Maddie. I thought the other night I had ruined it by kissing you."

"You didn't ruin it. I really like you too, I thought maybe you were pulling some kind of prank on me." Tom frowned.

"I would never do that, not to you. I can't stop thinking about you, like, all the time."

I pulled Tom into a massive hug and kissed him on the cheek, he didn't seem happy with that so yet again he grabbed me and just like the night in my car, he kissed me. The fireworks were still there, and so were the butterflies and the drop in my heartbeat. I couldn't believe for a second time that Tom was kissing me.

"I have to go, but I'll see you tomorrow, okay?" He announced and walked out the door, I watched him get to the end of my road and when I couldn't see him anymore, I shut the door and lent against it. I couldn't believe that Tom liked me. He liked me, and I liked him.

I know Dr Goodall doesn't want me to focus all my happiness onto Tom, but he's made everything brighter, he's made me enjoy drawing and painting again, he's made me laugh and shown me a beautiful side of this town. Sure, now, and then at night when I'm lying-in bed I'll have thoughts, and they can be dark, but then I think about Tom and how happy he makes me, and it makes the thoughts a lot quieter.

I've been thinking about this Diary a lot, and the point of it. If I'm happier, why am I still writing to it? Am I still interested in getting to day 0 and completing the Diary?

With love,

Maddie x

52 DAYS LEFT

Dear Diary,

It's been a week since I last wrote, mainly because of the events that followed after the night Tom came to visit.

I woke up the day after Tom came round, and I felt a lot better. The bug I had was gone so I headed to work knowing that I would see Tom. I had a spring in my step. I wanted to get to the shop a bit earlier to have extra time talking to Tom, I wanted to talk to him about the night prior and I was intrigued to see what that meant for us. Were we dating? Did he want to do official dates? Did he want to take it slow? Did he want to take it fast? I had so many questions.

From a distance the shop looked remarkably busy, there were cars everywhere, some were white, and some were black. Usually, Sophie would call if the store was busy because she wanted more help serving, but she hadn't. As I got closer, I realised the store wasn't busy with customers but a lot of police officers, the cars were police cars both marked and unmarked.

As I went to walk into the shop, an officer stopped me. "You can't enter here" He told me. "I work here. What happened?" I asked him, but he wouldn't tell me. I mean I was wearing normal clothes and had no proof of working there, I wouldn't have told me if I was him.

I waited outside, took out my phone and tried calling Sophie, but she didn't pick up. I then tried calling Tom, but he didn't answer either. What was happening?

I waited outside the shop for 40 minutes until Sophie came out, she wasn't wearing her usual work uniform, she was wearing her casual clothes instead. She had been crying, it was obvious from the tear tracks on her face.

"What's happened, Soph?" I asked her as she came out. She threw herself on me and started crying heavier than before. I put my arms around her confused, we stood there for 10 minutes, Sophie was just sobbing.

"Soph, what's happened?" I asked sympathetically when it was clear that most of Sophie's tears had run out. Sophie pulled herself away from me, wiped her face with her sleeves and managed to stutter out:

"Alice."

"What about Alice? She's still in prison, isn't she?" I asked her, but the pit in my stomach was growing. "No, she got out two days ago, apparently for good behaviour." I looked at her shell shocked. "Shouldn't you be told when she's due out and don't you have a restriction on her?" Sophie was distressed. I wasn't any closer to finding out what had happened. Also, I hadn't seen Tom anywhere. If Sophie was out here, Tom should be too. Where was Tom? Did she send him home? Why wasn't he answering my phone calls?

"Yeah, they told me yesterday." I pulled Sophie into another hug. "What happened Soph?" I asked calmly. "So, we were serving customers, I was making drinks, so my back was turned to customers. Tom was serving a lady who wanted a hot chocolate with mint and orange syrup. We both know there's only one person who orders that." Alice.

"I'll be honest, at that moment I didn't think anything of it. I was busy with the previous order that I completely ignored what was said until the receipt came directly to me. I looked at it and actually laughed for a second because I thought how funny it was that there was more than one person who liked this horrible drink. So, I turned around to double check with Tom when I saw her. She was in my shop, with a huge grinning face, and I was stuck. I didn't know what to do." Sophie took a moment to wipe her tears again before continuing.

"Hello, Sophie.' She said, she had this grimace joker look on her face. I ran to the back of the shop and tried to shut the door behind me, but while I was doing that, she jumped over the counter... Oh, GOD!!" Sophie covered her face.

"It's okay, Soph. You're safe." I reassured her.

"Alice was saying how she was going to finish me off and how would I like it if I was in a cage 23 hours a day. She was horrible. Poor Tom, he just stood there. He didn't know what to do. She tried running towards me, but Tom stopped her. He put his arms out and caught her off guard. He put her to the ground and told me to call the police. So, I did." She explained…But there was more. "Oh God Maddie, if I had known." She cried.

"If you had known what?" I asked her. For some reason, panic began to rise in me.

"When Tom grabbed Alice…" Sophie couldn't continue; she just kept crying. I didn't know what was going on, and it made me begin to panic.

"Maddie, Alice had a knife…" She cried out.

OH

SHIT

No

Please No.

"When Tom tried to stop her, she stabbed him." Sophie sobbed.

Not Tom.

Anyone but Tom.

I froze, I didn't know what to say. I was in shock. I leant up against the store window. "Oh my God!? Sophie, Is he alive?" I managed to say.

Sophie seemed to turn grey when I asked. "I didn't realise he was injured until he fell to the ground." Sophie explained.

"Is he okay?" I repeated.

"The ambulance told me the wound was big, that he was lucky even to make it this far. They've taken him to hospital."

I slid down the window and onto the floor. Sophie sat beside me. We sat there for a while saying nothing. I looked at Sophie, who was still crying. I didn't cry. I was really fucking sad, but I didn't cry, and I wished I could because at that moment I wanted to cry. I wanted to drown the city with my tears, but nothing would come out.

It was my fault. It's my fault Tom's in the hospital. I should have been there. It should be me in the hospital. It's all my fault. We sat there in silence until I tried to do what Tom would in this situation.

"I guess that means none of us are getting paid today." I laughed, trying to imitate Tom's happy-go-lucky sarcasm. Sophie half-heartedly smiled. "No, you may as well go home. I have to stay awhile. The police want to talk to me some more."

I stood up and grabbed my bag that at some point, I had thrown onto the floor. "Did they get her?" I asked, and Sophie nodded.

"Yeah, she was taken back into police custody, awaiting another trial. God, I thought we were finished with her." She told me.

"I hope one day, you will be." I said.

I hugged Sophie goodbye and started heading home but took twists and turns. When I got to my house, I didn't know what to do so I just stood outside and looked at my home. The one with the brickwork, the white windows, and a big white door. I looked at the knocker that used to scare me as a child because it looked like the one of Scrooge, and I looked at the garage that was not used as a car garage, but my dad's fixing station and that attached to the garage was a white door that looked like it hadn't been used in a couple of years. I looked at the house, and I walked away.

I walked and walked and walked, not knowing where I was going but also heading to one place in particular. The lookout. It took me an hour to walk there, but I just walked and thought of nothing, and everything, and sometimes both of those things at the same time. When I got to the lookout, there weren't many people there. It was only 1pm, so I guessed most people were at work. I walked to the same part that Tom and I went to. I found the same rock and stood on top of it. I took in the senses, but this time I used sight too. I looked down on the town and saw blue flashing lights. It made me think about Tom. As I was thinking about nothing and everything, I felt a tug on my jeans. I looked around, and it was a little girl, about nine years old. She had dark brown hair and blue eyes. She was wearing a summer dress even though it was quite chilly outside. I looked round to see if I could see her parents, but they were nowhere to be seen.

"What are you doing up there?" She asked.

"Just admiring the view," I told her.

"Are you going to jump off?" She then asked me, I was taken back

"I hadn't planned on it," I told her again.

"Okay, don't jump, my auntie did that and now she's gone forever" she said. I turned back around, and she had disappeared. "What a strange kid" I whispered to myself.

I got down off the rock, rolled a spliff and decided I would head home. I texted Tom 'Hey I heard what happened, I hope you feel better soon.' I put my phone away, lit my spliff and started walking back. I knew I would be home earlier than I would have finished work, and I knew if someone were home, they would question it, and I would have to tell them about Tom.

As I entered my house, I realised how quiet it was. The place was so hollow with no one in it. I sat down on the sofa, which I rarely do now, and I enjoyed the peace and tranquillity because as soon as one person came home, the house would be a lot noisier. I was right, my brother came home an hour later than me. "You're home early." I commented. "Half day" He replied "So are you? You bunking again?" He asked, jokingly.

"No. Someone got stabbed at work today, so we have the day off." I said deadpan. I was exhausted, my mind consumed with worry about Tom and nothing else. I didn't want to talk to David, I just wanted to think about Tom, but David stopped in his tracks and came back into the living room where I was sitting.

"Shit Madds, how are you doing?" He asked me sympathetically. This was the first time in years we'd had a normal conversation. He wasn't a mushy brother. "I'm alright I didn't see it happen, but he is a friend." "Was it Tom?" He then asked, and I nodded.

"Oh god. Maddie, I'm sorry." David seemed to show sympathy, something I didn't think he could possess. I didn't realise that David actually listened to anything I said in the house, or anything related to me in the house. It's sibling code to hate your sibling but to not allow others to hate your sibling. Eventually, the tension in the room got awkward so I walked upstairs into my room "If you want to talk Mads, I'm here" he announced right before I shut my door "Thanks" I answered.

This is your fault.

This is all YOUR fault.

If you just hadn't asked him to change shifts.

None of this would have happened.

This is ALL YOUR FAULT.

I tried to steady my breathing; the void was right. This was my fault. I should never have asked Tom to change my shift. I should never have changed the shift. I should have just gotten up early and had an extra coffee at work. This is all my fault.

****

When I went to see Dr Goodall on Thursday, I told him about Tom and what had happened. He expressed his sympathy to me and asked if I would go see Tom at the hospital. I told him I didn't know whether I would or not because I didn't know if I was allowed. I knew that a lot of patients are only allowed to be visited by families. Dr Goodall told me that as long as the family hasn't specified, I could visit him. This made me feel a bit better. Unfortunately, Dr Goodall didn't want to spend the entire lesson talking about Tom. He wanted to talk about me.

"How are you feeling?"

I didn't know how to answer the question because there was a mixture of emotions happening. No, the void hadn't been interfering with me for a while, but with what had happened with Tom, there were strong emotions and feelings, and I couldn't quite understand all of them. I wanted to know he was okay, that's all I wanted. I just wanted to know what was happening with Tom and if he would be alright. Dr Goodall didn't seem to understand that my emotions were all Tom related and was trying to bring them back to me.

"Do you think you feel this strong because of your own personal battles and it's brought you back to a form of reality?"

What! What was he even talking about?

"No. I know what Alice is like, I was there the first time with Sophie, and now Tom is injured, and I don't know if he's going to survive, and it's all because I asked to switch a shift" I was now angry at Dr Goodall.

"Maddie you couldn't have possibly known Alice was going to come into the store. What happened to Tom is absolutely devastating and we can talk about your emotions around that, however I think it's important to talk about you more than Tom."

I didn't know what to say, I felt like steam was coming out of my ears. My heart was beating, and I was clearly showing agitation because Dr Goodall told me to "calm down" and that was it. I went off on him.

"Here's the thing Doc, I have spent the last 2 months being so fucking happy, because of Tom. Sure, I shouldn't rely on people to be happy, I get it. But for some bizarre reason, Tom is the only person to ever bring me out of the void, Becks could never do it. Sophie never did. My family certainly never did it, but Tom did. The void was quiet when I was with him, and even when it was there, it's like Tom knew. He knew the void was there, so he made me smile, even when I didn't want to.

He asked me a hundred pointless questions about sharks and lions, and the possibility of the multiverse. He asked me stupid, bizarre, strange questions that anyone else might think were mental, but I loved them."

Dr Goodall tried to interrupt "I think you're missing my point..." but before I allowed him to finish his sentence, I continued talking "I haven't finished talking. I sit here every week, talking, and talking, and I'm getting nowhere. I was always told therapy was a temporary thing, a way to find your voice so you can use it with the right people, but I've been here for over a year and the only time I have felt truly better is when Tom came into my life. So don't you dare turn around and say that I can't talk about him in my therapy sessions that I'm paying for. If I wanted to talk about Flamingos and why they're pink, I should be allowed too, which by the way is because of the type of food they eat."

Before the session was meant to finish, I stood up and walked out. Dr Goodall tried talking to me before I left but I paid for my session, wished him well and left. I was done with him, and I wasn't going back. He didn't understand, Tom was everything to me and now he's gone.

I don't know why Dr Goodall had to always make me feel worse. I had decided on my walk to the coffee shop that I wouldn't go back to counselling, not only did he charge me £40 for a session, but most of the time I left feeling worse than when I entered. I think it's good for me to cancel my sessions for a while. I'm feeling a lot better without his advice, so I don't see why I'm spending money. Plus, I wouldn't need him when I'm gone.

I didn't know whether or not work would be open. I hadn't heard from Sophie, so I assumed I would be. When I headed to work the realisation that I would be working on my own hit me, the day would be longer. Tom wasn't there so I would be on my own. I will miss him today. When I got to work, I saw that Sophie was working, I thought she might have found someone to cover. I walked in slowly. The shop had one or two customers, so it was quiet. I went around the back.

"Hey soph" I shouted, trying to seem happy and cheerful so she didn't just burst into tears as soon as she saw me. She was too busy to talk so just smiled and waved. I put my apron on and put my things in my locker. When I went to talk to Sophie, I noticed she looked different.

"How are you doing?" I asked. "I'm doing better, work always helps." She told me. I understood that because I did the same, but it would surely be good to get away for a bit. "But it happened here, doesn't it remind you? Like shouldn't you take some time off?" I asked. Sophie smiled. "Thanks, Maddie." Then she walked away. "Sophie, I'm sorry! I didn't mean it like that." I shouted after her. I wanted it to come out as understanding and kind, like how Tom would say it, but instead it came out sarcastic and cold, like how I, Maddie, would say it.

I turned around to the customers waiting, smiled and took their order. When the store quietened down, I quickly ran out of the back, knocked on the office door and entered. "Sophie I'm sorry, I thought it would help. I didn't mean to be a dick." I stayed by the door because I didn't want to take up too much time. "Maddie, it's fine. I know what you meant. Maybe you're right. You know, in the 5 years I've been the shop owner I've had 2 holiday days off." I smiled sympathetically, it's all I could think of doing. Sophie stopped doing her paperwork for a second.

"Have you visited Tom yet?" She asked me. "No, I don't even know where his room is." Sophie held up her finger, got a piece of paper, wrote something down and then handed it to me. "I'm sure he would like you to visit." "He hasn't replied to my messages, or anything, are you sure he's not mad at me?" I asked Sophie, who moved around in her seat. "Umm, I'm sure the signals, just bad." She tried to smile but the way she did it was suspicious, it seemed like she was hiding something, but I didn't know what.

I went back to the counter and waited for customers to come in. I found myself looking at the floor, despite it being cleaned, I could somehow see what looked like red stains. I became obsessed with it. I kneeled on the floor with damp clothes and started rubbing, all that was coming off was coffee stains, but the thought of it kept troubling me. While it was still quiet, I got a mop and bucket and thoroughly cleaned the floor. I had to make sure there was nothing left. I had to make sure that there wasn't anything left behind for Sophie to find. I had to make sure that when I changed the water, the water was clean. I needed to be sure nothing was done wrong.

"What are you doing, Maddie?" Sophie asked.

"I'm just making sure I get everything." I told her while still mopping the floor.

"Maddie, it's already been done." She said, but I continued mopping.

"It has to be done perfectly." I declared.

"Maddie, the police called cleaners, they did it. Just stop!" Sophie demanded, still, I continued, I had to make sure everything was clean. I don't know why. Something just came over me.

"Yeah, but they could have missed something." I answered back. I was now cleaning faster. Sophie came over and tried to take the mop off me, but I wasn't having it.

"Maddie, give me the mop!" She repeated. "MADDIE" Sophie shouted and took the mop off me.

"It needs to be clean!" I shouted back.

"Why? It's already clean!" She asked.

"Because I don't want you to find anything that could upset you." I told her. Sophie put her head down, and then after I had calmed down, she looked me in the eye.

"Maddie, I'm fine. Look at me, yes, it's upsetting what happened. But I'm fine. Are you though?" I looked down, and my shoulders dropped.

"It's my fault. I asked him to change shifts. It should have been me." Sophie put the mop down and came over to me. She put her hands on my arms and tried to comfort me. "What happened is shit, but it's not your fault." She paused for a moment, looked me in the eyes and then asked: "Have you stopped taking your meds?" I looked at her strangely. I didn't know she knew I was taking meds. "I'm not on meds." I told her. "So that's a yes. Maybe you should call your doctor, Maddie?" She stated, and before I could tell her I was fine, a customer came in to be served.

When I finished work, I realised how different today was from the last couple of months of work. It was quiet, I had no pointless questions, I didn't laugh, and I had the urge to clean for the first time in ages. I used to clean a lot when I was anxious, I used it to cope, but then the thoughts told me that I had to clean otherwise something bad would happen. It wasn't really bad thoughts like 'someone will die if you don't do this,' it was more like 'if you don't do this, this person will be really upset with you.' These thoughts would make me clean until I could see a shine or until the thoughts stopped. I stopped doing it a while ago one day I woke up and the thoughts weren't as obsessive. But today it was bad, I hadn't been like that for eight months. Maybe Sophie was right, maybe I should start taking my meds again.

****

I went to see Tom on my day off. I took the bus to the hospital because parking costs are ridiculously high. When I got to the hospital, I had to try and figure out where his room was. I went to the admin's desk and asked. The lady gave me directions, and I headed to the set of stairs that she told me to take. I then followed the signs to rooms 100-200. Tom was in 146. I kept following the signs until they started to become more specific and had only 20 rooms on each sign. 100-120 left, 121-140 right, 141-160 second left, 161-180 second right, 181-200 straight forward. I took the second left. As I went down the corridor, I looked for the sign with his number. When I found it, I stood close to the window to check that Tom was in there.

I entered the room; I saw Tom on the bed with loads of tubes in. He wasn't awake. I slowly walked in and sat on the chair next to him. I was unsure whether he would wake up when I was visiting him or not, so I sat and waited. I had brought him a card, so I put it on his desk-side facing towards him. On the inside of the card, I put.

'Tom,

I hope you feel better soon,

I can't wait for you to ask me pointless questions, go on adventures, and have meaningful conversations.

With love, Maddie x'

I was sitting by the bedside when a nurse came in.

"Um, is he going to wake up?" I asked the nurse.

"Mr Johnston is in a coma." The nurse told me.

"Wait, what? I thought he was just asleep. Why's he in a coma?" I asked the nurse. Stab wounds don't usually result in comas, not from the movies I've watched anyway. "When Mr Johnston was stabbed, the blade hit a major artery, with so much blood loss, his body began to shut down, and he fell into a coma when he came into the hospital." I sat back in the chair, astonished. Why didn't I know he was in a coma? Did Sophie not know? Or did she know and just didn't tell me? I didn't know what to do. The nurse took his vitals and then walked out of the room. I just sat there in the chair for what felt like 30 minutes. I stood up and walked over to Tom. I looked at him. He looked peaceful. I bent down and kissed his forehead. I then took the card and put it in the drawer next to him. I didn't want anyone else to see what I put. I wanted it for Tom only.

When I left the hospital, I felt tired. I dragged myself to the bus stop and waited for the next bus. I felt deflated. I felt sad. The one and only person I wanted to talk to right now was in a coma. I didn't want to talk to Becks or Sophie or any member of my family. I wanted to talk to Tom.

I wanted to tell him how happy I was when he kissed me, twice. That I feel like I'm walking on the moon whenever I spend time with him. I wanted to tell him everything, but I couldn't. While I was waiting for the bus, I kept thinking about Tom.

It's all my fault

Well, duh, everything's your fault. You suck.

I want him to wake up and talk to me.

He's in a coma. He won't get up just for you. This isn't a love story.

Maybe the thoughts were right.

Tom was the one that kept the thoughts at bay. I never had bad thoughts when I was with him.

That is so sad. You actually think one boy could keep me away from you? I will stay with you forever. That's a promise.

Tom made me happy.

Yeah, for him, and he'd do exactly what everyone else does when they get what they want from you.

They leave you.

They always leave you.

Nobody likes you.

The thoughts all of a sudden came back, I need to find something else to do, I need to take my mind off what's happening. The bus turned up and opened the doors "Are you getting on?" The bus driver asked. I paused for a moment .

"No, sorry. Wrong bus."

The bus driver shut the doors and pulled away. I stood there for a second taking in everything, thinking about everything.

When I zoned back onto planet earth, I headed home. I decided walking/running would be a good idea. It took a lot longer than anticipated to walk home, but I enjoyed the tranquillity of it. I thought not only about Tom but about Becks too. I realised that we hadn't properly seen or talked to each other for a couple of weeks. The last time I saw her was the night we went out, she had messaged me to tell me she had gotten home safely, but apart from that, we hadn't had a full conversation. It must be to do with Matt. Anytime he gets involved with Becks in this way, she always shuts out everyone and then shows up a couple of weeks later apologetic, saying he was treating her like a princess and was too busy to message.

If I wasn't thinking about Becks, I was thinking about my mum. I was thinking about how when David and I were younger we had this trampoline that mum bought us. She told us to be careful on the trampoline every time we were on it, especially if we were on it together. I remember when we were messing around one day, and David fell off. Mum came running out to make sure he was okay. He was okay, but mum's panic expression had us scared. We decided to not go on the trampoline at the same time anymore because we didn't want to scare mum. I remember for Christmas when I wanted certain clothes and despite how mum didn't like what I wanted to wear she still bought it for me anyway because she just wanted me to be happy.

Thinking about mum made me think about Dad and how hard he has worked since he could start working. He works in plumbing and has always worked six days a week. When it was getting cold out in the winter, he would do extra hours to bring in extra money for the family and help the elderly people who needed urgent help. He helped the vulnerable.

I remember when he came home really late on the 23rd of December. We were supposed to be going ice skating but because he was really late, we couldn't. Mum wasn't happy, but when Dad told us he was fixing vulnerable people's pipes when it was cold, Mum wasn't mad anymore. She just smiled. David and I were still pissed because we didn't understand why he would want to spend more time with an old lady rather than us. Mum had to explain it to us, and when she did, then we understood.

David. We had a strange relationship. Majority of the time, we would happily kill each other for a Cornetto. Now and then, David would be extra nice or super helpful; it would make my life a lot easier. When we were kids, we got on great, we did a lot of stuff together when he wasn't with his mates. I used to watch him play on his PlayStation all the time, but anytime I asked to play he wouldn't let me. I would have probably broken it, and I think he knew that. As we got older, we both grew apart. When he moves out, when he flies the nest, we will probably never speak to each other, but I will always have the memories. I wouldn't be angry with him if he didn't bother with me, I wouldn't bother with me either.

Thinking of David reminded me of the time David, and I went round my grandparent's house, and my grandma and I made cakes while David and Bampy talked about football. Bampy supported Arsenal, David hated Arsenal, but he would like it for Bampy. They would have debates on what team was the best. Bampy and I never spoke about things like that; we would talk about films or books. We would talk about the things I had made or drawn. God, I miss Bampy. I would give half my life to speak with Bampy again. I miss him.

By the time I had stopped thinking about it so much, I was on my road. It had taken me a little over an hour to get home, and when I got home, I was tired, aching, and cold. I went straight into the bathroom and had a shower. I had hoped the shower would burn away my body and I would go down the drain with the rest of the water, but that didn't happen.

I wanted Tom. I needed Tom. I needed him awake and responsive and asking me stupid questions and being as annoying as possible. Oh, what I would give for Tom to be annoying right now.

With Love,

Maddie x

49 DAYS LEFT

Dear Diary,

The void is back. The thoughts are bad. I haven't slept in two days. Since I wrote last time, everything got so much worse. Nothing happened in my life except Tom, but everything got so much worse.

You've gotten him in that coma.

You're the one responsible for all this.

This is your fault.

You can't even keep your friends alive.

What's the point of you staying alive?

It may be 50 days, but you can do it early.

Why don't you?

Why don't you do everyone a favour and die?

The void is getting worse every day. It's constant thoughts and I don't know what to do. I can't even talk to Dr Goodall about it because I quit sessions. I got an email yesterday to say that if I wanted to officially cancel, I needed to sign a form. I signed it straight away without a question.

I don't have anyone anymore. Tom's in a coma. Becks is with Matt. I have no one else to talk to. I thought the void had already taken everything from me, but it seems to find more to take from me.

I found myself at Bampy's grave, I noticed his headstone was slightly dirty, so I went to my car and got a duster out. I started cleaning it. I cleaned his grave until it looked brand new. It needed to look perfect. It needed to look clean. It must have been an hour because Sophie rang me. That's when I realised, I was late for work. I quickly packed and drove to work. I don't normally drive to work or to Bampy's grave, but I've been driving a lot lately, trying to waste the hours that I spend awake. No matter how hard I try, I still don't find myself wanting sleep.

When I got to work, I kept apologising to Sophie. I was only 10 minutes late, but I have never been late to work, not once. I chucked my stuff in my locker and put my apron on. I headed out the front and started making drinks. I couldn't even make good drinks. I was struggling to concentrate at all. I knew the lack of sleep had something to do with it, but I've struggled to sleep for years and never been this bad before. My hands were shaking. My vision was blurry. I didn't panic, but I felt horrible. I felt like I was going to throw up. I asked Sophie to change positions so I could serve customers because I couldn't make a drink without spilling it everywhere. Serving was easier. I didn't need as much concentration, but I was still messing up. Sophie asked me if I was okay, and I just nodded and explained I was probably just tired. Which wasn't a lie.

As the shop got quieter, I turned to Sophie and asked: "Did you know about Tom?" Without turning around, Sophie said "What about Tom?" She continued making the drinks, so I slid across to her. "About him being in a coma?" I said.

She finished making the drinks, sighed, not an angry sigh but a sad one. "Yeah. I did." She turned back around and started cleaning the machines. "So why did you tell me to visit him?" I asked her. Sophie stopped cleaning abruptly and turned to me "Because research shows that talking to people in a coma can help. They can hear you so I thought if you went in, the person he was closest to, and spoke to him then maybe it would help. Also, he's your friend, you should visit him" She told me and resumed her cleaning. I felt guilty at the answer she gave. It was an obvious one. I liked him so of course I should go see him; I just didn't understand why she hadn't told me in the first place.

Sophie and I didn't speak after that. We weren't annoyed at each other.

We just had nothing to talk about. Work couldn't finish soon enough. For the first time in ages, I just wanted to go home and sleep. I needed to sleep. But when I got home, I wasn't tired, and I couldn't sleep. I laid in bed for ages, but all I did was think. I wasn't annoyed with Sophie. I just wish she had told me before I went. It was a shock to me.

Seeing as I couldn't sleep, I got up and got dressed. It was 11 pm, and everyone in my house was happily in their slumber. I put a few films on but eventually got bored with them. I left my house and started walking, I didn't know where my final destination might be, I just allowed my feet to guide me. It must have been about an hour because I ended up in the middle of town. I never went to town at night. There's a lot of drunk or drugged homeless people about. I walked through the rough parts of town quickly and then went to the secret spot.

I remember when I was 15, I had just been allowed out at night. I had a curfew of 11 pm. Becks and I went into town to check out the areas at night and see if we could find a secret spot for us. We found the harbour and by the harbour was an old lighthouse left as decoration. You could never get into the lighthouse because the bottom was boarded up, but the window about 7 feet up was open. I would lift Becks up and then she would help me up. It was our secret spot, inside was creepy but staying on the outside was nice because we could see all down the river. One day we were on our way back from there, and this homeless guy stopped Becks in her tracks. He took her arm and wouldn't let go. We were screaming because of how scared we were. He eventually loosened our arms, and we legged it. We didn't stop running until we hit the bus station and we were safe. Becks never went back. She refused too because she was too scared. I stopped going as well for a while. I started going back two years ago when I realised the guy had probably died already. It was different now because it wasn't our secret spot, it was mine.

Heading to the secret spot, I noticed there was an array of different people out at night. You had the homeless, who would sleep in the day and be awake at night, this was because security guards from local clubs would move them on at night.

You had the skater kids, the ones who skate the entire time, pass around one joint to five people, the ones that were there because they were night owls.

You had the security guards, who would keep an eye on everyone and make sure no no-gooders would get into their bar.

You had the troublemakers, the ones starting fights, the ones graffitiing, the ones making a nuisance. And then you had people like me.

The ones on their own, the ones who didn't have a gang to hang out with, the ones who don't fit into a gang.

The ones who couldn't sleep thought it would be a good idea to come to a busy area and pretend they were in the gang. Maybe even hoping someone would ask them to join.

While I was at the spot, I noticed a few things that might go unseen by most. I didn't have many friends, but I knew people's signs, I could look at people and see what they were really like when their friends weren't around. In the skater gang, there were five people. Two of them seemed like the group leader, the ones making the jokes, the ones rolling the spliffs, the ones who were the main attention. If it was a movie, they would be the main characters (the protagonists). Then you had one guy who would try to be loud but spent most of the time listening, chiming in now and again with good jokes. This person would be the Static Character (the one who doesn't say much but still has a big impact). Then there's one girl who seems to be against it all. She shouts now and then telling the skaters to go careful. She shakes her head firmly when someone offers her the joint. She would be the antagonist (the one that's against the main characters), but they invite her because despite being against all beliefs, she's still one of them. Then there's another girl; she seems to quickly change emotions or feelings depending on who's talking. She seems to be a bit fake and tries to be involved with the gang and know what they're on about. She would be the dynamic character (a character that changes depending on the story.) Finally, is the stock character; he is the stereotypical character. The one who you look at and what you see is exactly what you get. There's no difference. Each of the skaters are a character, and without knowing it, they're in their movie.

I spent about an hour just staring at the life below, but as it got colder, the more I wanted to leave. I jumped off the lighthouse and started walkinghome. It was now 5 am, I didn't have work, so I didn't need to worry about being home. I did, however, worry about whether I'd be home before mum got up. She got agitated when I would leave the house by myself and be gone a long time. She got nervous when I wouldn't be home when she got up, especially if I wasn't doing anything. She got agitated because she was protective of me. It wasn't a bad thing, it was annoying, but she's a mum, so I understand. She's always going to be worried. She's always going to worry, and I can't do anything about that. I'll just tell her that I went for a morning walk. I made sure to keep my speed up. I didn't run because I was too cold and thought I would break into pieces like ice. Before I got home, I went past Bampy's Grave. I stopped for a second, wondering whether to go in or not. I headed in and went to his grave. I sat down next to it

"I wonder what it's like up there." I said in hopes to have a vision somehow, and he would tell me it's great and to come join. "God, I hope there's something after this... because this... this fucking sucks." A tear rolled down my cheek. I stood up and patted Bampy's grave, the way he would pat my shoulder every time he left.

When I came down my drive, I noticed mum's curtains were still drawn, which is a good sign. I walked into the house quietly in hopes of not waking anyone up. As I took my shoes off and headed upstairs, mum came out of her room. Great, she saw me. "What are you doing?" She asked me, still dazed. "Oh, I couldn't sleep, so I went for a walk." Mum nodded her head and walked into the bathroom. I got into my room, got into my pyjamas, and got into bed. I managed to sleep for a couple of hours until I woke up to mum shouting. I got dressed and headed downstairs.

"Fucking useless twats!" Mum shouted. "What's going on?" I asked her, still dazed. "This bloody computer isn't working. I'm only trying to print off a piece of paper." Mum continued to shout. "Move over." I told her and went to the computer. I printed the piece of paper out in two minutes. "Done." Mum looked at me. "Thank you. I don't understand why it never works for me."

"Because you never turn the actual printer on." I smiled and walked back upstairs. I chuckled to myself. It's always funny when mum gets annoyed at an inanimate object. She always calls it names and shouts at it until I come and help. Most of the time it does revolve around the computer and how to print things off or how to download images etc. All she needs to do is ask me to do it in the first place but she's too independent (I call it stubborn) and needs to do it herself.

I headed upstairs and got my phone. Despite knowing he couldn't, I still waited for Tom to text me. Every time I looked at my phone, I would get excited in case he had messaged me miraculously. I sat down on my bed, staring out of the window. I checked my phone. Nothing. I unlocked my phone and went to Becks number. I paused for a second. Did I really want to message her? She hadn't bothered with me for ages. Why should I bother with her? Truth is, I'm really lonely. The last time I felt this lonely was when I had no friends. She may not be as close to me as I am to her, but I really need to talk to someone. I need to get out of this house and not be by myself. I can't deal with being by myself, day after day, waiting to visit Tom or thinking about him 24/7.

I feel like I'm on fire.

I can't concentrate.

I need to get out of this house.

I grab my shoes and coat and walk out of the house. I don't know where I'm headed, but the cold air is helping to calm me down. I look at my phone and call Becks. She doesn't answer. "Umm hey Becks... when you get this, can you call me back? I need someone right now." I put the phone down and continue walking. I get to a bus stop and jump on the bus. I know where I'm going now. I have a destination in mind. Who's the one person who makes me feel so much better when I feel so down?

****

When I got to the hospital, I headed straight to Tom. After seeing him the first time, it was less of a shock to see him this time. I peeked through the window, making sure no one else was there, and when I saw it was clear, I walked in. I took the chair and moved it closer to the bed, angling it towards the door, so we were side by side.

I sat in the chair, then took his hand, slowly stroking it with my thumb, when I looked at him it looked like for a moment, he had a little smirk on his face. I adjusted my body to face him, still holding his hand. "It's not quite the lookout, but we can still be nosey, I guess." I spoke allowed. "Hey, there's a lady in the room opposite you with a huge bouquet of flowers, like it's bigger than her. I should have bought you some flowers. Do you like flowers Tom? You seem like the type of person that likes flowers" I glanced at Tom expecting him to answer but there was nothing.

I didn't know what to say.

If Sophie was right and from doing my research she was, then talking would be the best option, but I had no idea what to say. I'm not exactly the most talkative person out there, especially in awkward situations. I sat there and observed for a second. I changed between looking at the window and Tom's face. I was unsure whether anything I was saying was helping.

"Okay, I'll play 100 questions and then answer them as well." I rearranged myself in the chair, it was un-comfy, and I was trying to not think about how many people had already sat their butt in this seat. I didn't want to spiral.

"Okay, question 1. Weather outside. It's alright. It was a brisk morning, and the sun's trying to break through, but I don't think it will." "Question 2, favourite film. At the moment, I've been rewatching all of the Harry Potter's, and I love the third one. It used to be the scariest one for me, but it's my favourite." I went on and on.

"Question 20, a desert island with three tools. I would have a knife, one of them flints for fire, and I would have a water bottle."

"Question 66, if you could transform into an animal, which one would it be? For me, it would be a lion because I could run really fast and also climb trees."

"Question 100, what would I do to hear your voice? I would do anything right now, Tom. In all honesty, I would do anything to see you get up and walk out of this bed. Even just to turn around and ask me about the shark vs lion debate. I'll agree with you if you just wake up. Please.Tom... Just wake up." I squeezed his hand trying to hold back the tears.

I sat there for a while longer until the nurse came up to me and told me I had to leave as visiting time was over. I stood up, moved the chair back to the original space and before I left, I walked over to Tom, moved his hair to the side and kissed him on the cheek.

****

I decided to walk home again. I needed to get some energy out. I needed to sleep. I think it had been about four days now that I hadn't slept properly, and everything was becoming blurry. The bags under my eyes were massive, and my migraine was growing as big as the bags. I just wanted a good couple of hours of sleep at a regular time. As I was walking home, I checked my phone to see if Becks had rung. She hadn't, but she did text me.

B: Can't talk right now

M: Okay, I need to talk to you, feeling shit atm.

I continued walking. I didn't mind the walk back from the hospital, it was a long one, but there were no hills which was good. It meant a nice, stable walk home. The sun came out as I was halfway through my walk, Tom was constantly on my mind but now Becks had suddenly entered, she had told me to always contact her if I needed her and now, she was nowhere to be seen.

My heart was racing and not just because of the walking, I felt panicked so thought the best way to beat it would be to try the senses game.

Sight - The mixture of blue and green together create a calming summer sky. The clouds' added texture, which made it evident that it was due to rain, but the sun shining down indicated it wouldn't rain for long.

Sound - The cars driving past create a wind that hits me far after they've left my sight. The faster they go; the more wind is created. In the distance, you can hear the screams of a baby, who is either hungry, tired or needs to be changed. The fact the noise goes on longer than anticipated suggests that the mother is ignoring the baby.

Smell - Except for the petroleum scent, the only other smell is coming from back at the ward. The cleanliness of Tom's room, the strong, pungent stink of bleach and other chemicals are stuck in my nose.

Touch - The wind intertwines my fingers as if it's trying to hold my hand and walk with me. Now and then, someone will nudge into me as if the path isn't big enough for both of us to walk on.

Taste – Unfortunately, the cleaning products have also affected my taste as both senses feel the same thing. I even tried sticking my tongue out to find different tastes, but not only did I look like a lunatic sticking my tongue out in public, I also couldn't taste anything different.

It didn't help.

Normally it would ground me, but I feel like I'm as high as the clouds that look ominously grey now. The trouble was, I wasn't high. I hadn't smoked since I was with Tom. It felt like something that only we did together now. I didn't enjoy it as much on my own. I tried to bring myself back down to Earth, I tried to remember where I was and who I was, but this time it wasn't working. I felt like I was watching myself from a metre away like I was outside of my body.

Thinking.

Too much thinking.

Always too much thinking.

Breath

Breath Maddie.

COME ON!

BREATH!

You are so useless; look at you.

Panicking over nothing, freaking out over nothing.

You are so pathetic.

YOU asked Tom to do your shift.

YOU'RE the reason he's in a coma.

That should be you in the hospital. It's all YOUR fault.

This is why you need to complete your mission.

To finish that stupid diary no one will ever read.

You are a waste of oxygen. You are nothing!

You will always be nothing!

Just DO IT!

Nobody will miss you!

Just DIE!

What happened next was a bit of a blur. I don't remember the next hour. Apparently, some women found me freaking out on the side of the road, she said I was clutching my head and hyperventilating. She tried to ask if I was okay but all I kept saying was "it's all my fault" and called an ambulance.

When the paramedics came, they helped me massively. They were concerned that I had just tried to hurt myself or was having a psychotic episode, but when I got my breath back, I explained that it was a panic attack and nothing else. They kept asking me all these questions, typical mental health assessment questions, ones I've had to answer before at the Doctors, and then they tried to get me to go to the hospital. They wanted me to be checked out, but I kept declining so very gratefully dropped me home.

Well, they dropped me to my nan's flat. I didn't want my family to find out what had happened. I didn't want them to think I had gotten worse after all these years. I didn't want anyone to worry. I had told the paramedics to go to my nans block of flats. They waited until I went in, which I was able to because I had a spare key. I remember going into my nans. It was always so bright in her flat. She had photos everywhere of her grandkids, myself included. As I walked in, I shouted out, so she knew I was there. This wasn't completely out of the ordinary as I would often visit my nan at random times of the day. She was in the kitchen, making a cup of tea. I walked into the kitchen to find her there.

"Hello, I didn't expect to see you."

"Yeah, I thought I would pop round." I replied, trying to make out nothing was wrong.

"Do you want a drink?" She asked, and I shook my head.

"No thanks." "What about some food? I have biscuits, crisps. I have a sandwich in there I was going to have for lunch, but you can have it if you want it." She went on while going through the cupboards. "I'm fine, honestly." I smiled back.

We walked into her living room, which was a bit bigger than her kitchen, my nan sat in her chair, and I took the chair next to her. She told me about my cousins and updated me on what she's been doing. "I need ideas for your dad's birthday." She asked. "He likes gardening. Maybe get him some nice gardening gloves and a kneeling pad?" I never knew what to get dad. I've bought him a gift card for the local garden centre the last 3 years. He always seems grateful and ends up buying a load of garden flowers that the caterpillars like eating.

"How's work going?" Nan asked after taking her sip of tea. I thought of Tom and Sophie and everything that had happened and how I didn't want to talk about any of that in case of another blackout. "It's all good. Boring at the moment. Although my manager asked me to do a painting for the shop and paid me for it." My nan seemed chuffed to hear the news and wanted to know everything about the painting and how the conversation went down with Sophie. She had a beaming smile from one side of her face to the other. "My granddaughters an artist." She said enthusiastically. "Well, it's only one painting so not quite" I tried to add in, but she was too excited to listen. "You have your art hanging in work. That's amazing!"

I stayed round my nans for just over an hour, she kept telling me the same stories, but I didn't mind, it kept my mind off Tom. When it got to dinner time I headed out. I decided to get a Taxi home, my nan's house was a 40-minute walk away, and I had exhausted myself out.

I spent my time at my nans acting as if everything was normal, but I wasn't normal.

What had happened? All of a sudden, everything had done a 180 and completely flipped around. Everything was back to before I knew Tom.

I don't know what's happening and why so much of it is connected to Tom, but there's one thing. I'm sticking to the plan.

The void is right. I'm nobody. I don't have friends. I don't have anybody. I'm on my own.

With Love,
Maddie x

46 DAYS LEFT

Dear Diary,

I called in sick to work. I haven't got out of bed in 2 days. Mum came in and told me to get out of bed, that I was being lazy and wasting my days off. I told her I had taken a holiday because I knew it meant no questions. I couldn't deal with mum asking too many questions.

I haven't seen Tom since the public panic attack, I've not felt like myself. I know Sophie would be disappointed but right now she has to join the queue of 'people disappointed with Maddie' because she's not the only one.

Becks did end up messaging me. It wasn't the texts I wanted, she waited 2 days after I messaged to text me. 'I can't always be there for you. Talk to your shrink.' Which was a complete 360 from what she had told me a couple of weeks ago.

I responded, 'I'm sorry for being a pain, but you said I could speak to you anytime.' To which she gut-wrenchingly put, 'That was when I didn't have a boyfriend. I'm too busy, atm.' Since then, I haven't spoken to her, and since then I've been in bed. I know that message isn't from her, it's from her boyfriend, but I thought there would be some form of humanity left in him. I didn't realise he could be so mean. I thought he would just tell me he hates me rather than trying to screw with our friendship.

My mind has gone blank. I can't think of anything, like even basic things. I don't feel anything right now, and no matter how hard I try to think of something that will make me feel, I feel numb. I tried thinking about people and how they make me feel, but I felt nothing, and then when I did, I felt it all.

I felt guilty about how much of their time I had wasted. I felt bad because I knew they would never get to relive those moments and make them better. I knew that I was a waste of space, and I didn't need anyone to tell me that. I laid in bed, dropping in and out of consciousness. I didn't realise that two days had passed until Mum came into my room to talk to me.

"Right, you are not sleeping all day. You need to get out of the house, you've been lounging around for two days, and your room is starting to smell." I groaned. But mum didn't even give me enough of a chance to turn around in my sheets. She ripped the sheets off me and opened the curtains.

I moaned and tried to pretend to be asleep so she would leave, but she didn't go. She decided to annoy me. She started tickling me, trying to help, it did make me laugh but not enough to make me feel better. Once she stopped, I stopped laughing. Then there was an awkward silence. Mum stood in my room just staring at me. I stood up and went over to my wardrobe to get a change of clothes. I looked round and mum was smiling at me. "Go away then. I'm getting changed." I told her and she walked out of my room and shut the door on her way out. I did in fact get changed, I didn't have much of a choice; she took the sheets with her when she left, so I couldn't jump back in them.

I slowly walked down the stairs. I realised that I hadn't washed in three days, I hadn't changed my pyjamas in three days, and I really did smell, but I didn't want to shower. All the energy I had, had been taken out by walking down the stairs. I was exhausted, and I wanted to go back to sleep. When I got downstairs, I noticed mum had a massive grin on her face. She was so happy it actually drained even more of my energy, which despite thinking I had no more, she managed to find some energy and drain that out of me.

"So, I'm going to see your grandma today. Do you wanna come?" Mum asked. I shrugged "Sure." She smiled and finished drying the dishes. I suddenly felt guilty because I hadn't helped her with any housework in days. Yet, she hadn't asked either, which was strange. I wonder if she knows I skipped work. What if she thinks I've gotten bad again and calls up the doctor? They would know that I didn't go to counselling.

Calm down. She doesn't know

Oh, God, listen to you. You're acting as if she cares. She probably already knows but doesn't care. Nobody cares about you. You don't matter.

I try to focus on the five senses, but I don't even know what they are at the moment. I can't focus. I've lost control, but it's okay because we both want the same thing in the end. I walked back upstairs, shut my door, and sat against it. My hands are shaking, and I'm starting to freak out. I try to think, but my mind is blank. Think.

Think of Becks.

Nope, bad idea. She left you like everyone does.

Think of Sophie.

Nope even worse, you're making her worse than she needs to be.

Think of Tom.

Sweet, funny, conventionally handsome. A great friend. Someone I cared deeply about even though I knew him for 2 months.

And like that, I was able to start calming down. I felt a lot better. I sorted myself out, washed my face, so I didn't seem so flushed. My face was red, but I quickly applied some makeup, so it didn't seem like it.

Once I was all set. I walked downstairs, and mum was waiting with her shoes already on "You ready to go?" She asked. "I guess." I said through gritted teeth. I had a splitting headache from hardly eating or drinking.

We spent a couple of hours with my grandma. Mum mentioned the artwork I've been doing, and she congratulated me on it. She gave us all the latest gossip, including talking about what the neighbours have been up to. We had a drink and then left. It was nice to get out of the house, it was a different setting, but I was so tired. I was ready to go back to bed.

This whole life thing is incredibly draining. I wish I could get out of bed and actually want to be part of this world, but right now, I don't care. I just need to stay alive for 45 more days, and then I no longer have to be part of this world. I'm ready. I know Tom will be fine without me.

With love,

Maddie x

44 DAYS LEFT

Dear Diary,

I decided to go to work yesterday. I had already had three days off, so I thought that I should make an effort. I was not feeling it at all. I wanted to stay in my cocoon and sleep yet another day away, but I also knew I wasn't making any money when I was at home, and the savings pot won't fill up on its own. Sophie was not happy. She asked to see me in her office, which means one of two things, I'm either getting fired or I'm in trouble.

I didn't have much time to think because as soon as I was in the office, Sophie told me to sit down. I knew it wouldn't be good. "So, you've been off for a while, and as a company policy, we need to go through some forms." Sophie sat down next to me. I nodded.

"So, there's a few questions. The first one is the reason for sick leave?" I sat there for a few seconds, wondering what to say, trying to remember what I actually said when I did call in sick.

"I was throwing up. I think I had a bug." I told her.

"Okay, next question, how are you feeling now?" She asked.

"I feel fine now." I replied.

"Okay, do you feel like you are able to do your job without any problems?"

"Yes."

"Do you need any assistance with your day-to-day job?"

"No."

"Final question. How are you doing?"

"You've already asked me that." I told her, confused.

"Yeah, this is off the record." Sophie told me while putting the paper down and turning her chair to face me.

"Maddie, in the whole time you've worked here, there's only been one other time that you've been off, and that's when you were really depressed. That's why I'm asking. I know you Mads, and I want you to know I'm always here if you need a chat. What's happened with Tom is affecting you, I can see it in your eyes, in fact I can see it in your whole body. Your aura has changed and I'm worried."

Last year I had a really bad depressive episode and spent five days off work. Sophie knew about it because my parents told her. My parents spoke to my doctor, who prescribed stronger meds for me. I spent those five days in my room, laying there emotionless. I couldn't physically get out of bed. My body didn't want to work. At one point, my parents wanted to call the ambulance on me because they thought I was dead. After five days, I felt strong enough to shower, but that was different from this time. I'm not as bad now as I was then. I only spent three days in bed this time, so that's two days shorter.

I wanted to be honest with Sophie, I knew I could be but my whole body was pushing down the truth.

Come on, she doesn't actually care.

She just wants to make sure you don't go mad, so she doesn't have to get a replacement last minute.

She doesn't care about you.

No-one does.

"I'm fine, Sophie. I was ill." I repeated, and Sophie sighed. "Okay, if it is the other reason, I want you to know I'm here. I just want you to be okay." She told me. She readjusted herself, picked up the paper and tapped it on the table. "I'm fine, Soph. Honestly." I told her as I stood up. "I just... I need you to be okay." "I will be." I half smiled at her and walked out the door.

Nobody needs you. She's trying to keep you in the job since Tom isn't here.

I went out to the front of the shop to start work. I was hoping for a quiet day, but the world doesn't work that way, so of course, every Tom, Dick and Harry came in. Most of them wanted the most difficult drinks, semi-skimmed mocha with orange or a standard cappuccino with mint. The most random things that took up more time than needed. There were a lot of kids in the shop today, which meant I had to repeat a lot like "don't touch the food" or "don't put your hands on that." You'd think the parents would tell them those kinds of things, but apparently, it's also my job to do.

I thought being busy constantly would make the day go faster, but it did not. It went as slow as it felt, and I was exhausted by the time it was lunch. I can't imagine how Sophie does it every day. She works every day and hardly ever takes a holiday. Maybe it's different if this is all she does. She must really love her job to come in six days a week and do 8–10-hour shifts. I can't imagine a job where I would be happy to come in for six days. I guess it doesn't really matter because I haven't got long left. Should I hand in my notice so at least then Sophie knows to start looking for someone straight away? I don't really know what to do with the whole work thing. I have everything planned out with family, and I guess I don't have to bother with friends because Becks isn't speaking to me, and Tom can't. I never thought about work. I always assumed Sophie would be fine, but maybe I should try to figure something out to help.

could hand in my notice the day that I do it, so then at least she'll get some form of a note. I mean, the note will be my resignation letter, but at least she's not completely left out. She will still get something. Maybe I should get her some chocolates or something to make her feel appreciated? It's weird to think about, but when someone leaves a job, it's kind to give a thank you letter, so maybe I can one-up myself and get her some chocolate?

You're an idiot.

Thank you, void.

I'm only saying what everyone thinks.

I know.

What do I do about Tom? Should I leave him a letter for when he wakes up? I haven't visited him in ages. I wonder how he's doing. He must be doing fine. Otherwise, Sophie would have mentioned something at work. I should probably go see him, but I don't really know what to say or do. I feel useless sitting there, but Tom was the only person that I enjoyed talking to, and now I can't even do that.

What am I doing? I'm going to kill myself, and I'm thinking about everybody else? Why do I do that?

Sympathy, probably. You always were a drama queen.

Thank you, again, void.

I'm only saying what everyone thinks.

I know.

While I'm at home, I write out two letters, one to Tom and one to Sophie.

Dear Sophie,

I'm writing this letter as my formal resignation. My notice period will start from today 24th September. The notice period is the 4 weeks' notice as per the company policy.

I have learnt a lot working here, and I'm so thankful for everything you've taught me in the industry. I look forward to taking my knowledge elsewhere. You've been one of the best managers that I've ever had, and I am extremely grateful for the opportunity of working for you.

Thank you for being the best boss anyone could ask for. Thank you for always being there for me and others. Thank you for helping in any way possible and thank you for always making me smile.

With love, Maddie x

Once I finished writing Sophies, I started on Tom's. Tom's was harder than I thought it would be because I knew I could be more honest with Tom. I could tell him everything, and I knew he wouldn't share with anybody else. I was just stuck on what to write. I couldn't verbalise it.

Dear Tom,

Trust me when I say I'm in a happy place.

Nope. Scratch that.

Dear Tom,

Some people aren't made to be saved.

Nope. Even worse.

Dear Tom,

We had the best time.

Not fancying that one either. It took me about 20 separate pieces of paper to finally get it right.

Dear Tom,

You were the best thing that happened to me. In my whole life, I have never met someone with so much energy and spark as you. You make me smile even when I'm not with you. You make me want to get up in the morning.

It worked well for a while, and then the void came back. You know how we spoke about whether I was happy, and I never gave you a definite answer? Well, that's because I didn't want you to think I was a freak. I didn't want to tell you that I get up some mornings not wanting to exist. I didn't want to say how I can be fine and then suddenly feel nothing. I didn't want to tell you about how for the last 60 days I've been keeping a diary counting down my days.

I didn't want you to get closer to me and realise that I'm not what you signed up for because people do that. When people realise, I'm not okay, they run because they don't want to deal with a girl who can go cold on them for a couple of days because she can't get out of bed. I would never want that for you. You deserve so much better, something I could never give you.

Truth is Tom, I am so tired, not of you, never of you, but of me.

It's not just the lack of sleep. It's the thoughts running in my mind all the time. It's the ones telling me I'd be better off dead. The ones that tell me I'm deemed to fail. The ones that make me struggle to get out of bed. The ones that make me hate myself even more, every day. I want to stop being so tired of it all. I'm exhausted by the battle that I have going on, and I have nobody to talk to about it. Because people are only interested in mental health when it's too late, then they'll claim to have loved me, to have wished I had spoken to them, but in reality, they don't give a shit. They couldn't care less unless the attention is on them.

And that's me, and I don't want anybody to have to go through that. I'm sorry. I really did like you. I think if it were different circumstances maybe we could have both been happy together, maybe get a farm like you mentioned. I'm sorry.

With love, Maddie x

After I finished writing, I put it in an envelope, put Tom's name on it

and slid it between some books, so nobody in my house could find it. I had all of the letters in between different books. Tom's letter was placed in between Sherlock Holmes because Tom reminds me of him. Sophie's letter was placed between Harry Potter books because she has a Harry Potter tattoo behind her ear. My family's letter, which currently only has the words 'Dear Family,' in it is between some Disney books. It makes it easier for me to remember where they are if they have reasons to be there.

I don't have long left. I'm starting to accept what's going to happen. 44 days to go.

With love,

Maddie x

40 DAYS LEFT

Dear Diary,

I saw Tom. I decided I would go to the hospital to visit him. Maybe it would help, or maybe it would make things worse. I didn't take the note because I planned to see him on the last day. I didn't want to rush things. I've gone through 60 days. I can wait another 40.

When I got to the hospital, I walked straight to his ward. I noticed that a woman in her mid-40's with bright blonde hair was in his room, so I waited outside. When she came out, I realised it was his mum. I hadn't seen her before, but she looked so much like Tom it had to be her. I got up out of the chair and walked over to her as she was leaving.

"Hi, I'm Maddie. I worked with Tom."

Tom's mum looked at me. The bags under her eyes and the messy clothes indicated she had stayed the night.

"Hi, I'm Tom's mum, Maeve. Tom talked about you all the time." She said, which made me smile.

"He's great." I said.

"Yeah, he really is." She said softly, her eyes filled with tears. "He hasn't made any movement at all. Doctors have told me to hope for the best, but I see it in their eyes." Maeve continued.

I held my head down, not knowing how to reply to what she had just said. After a moment of silence, I asked: "Do you wanna get a drink? They have a coffee shop down the corridor."

I wanted her to know how deeply sorry I was for what I did to him. She stood there for a minute, looking into the room where Tom laid.

"I've been here since yesterday. It might be nice to go for a walk."

We walked mostly in silence. The only noise that came off the two of us was the sound of our shoes against the squeaky, clean floor. When we got to the coffee shop, I got both of our drinks, Maeve had a cappuccino, and I had a mocha.

"What's Tom like with you?" She asked as we sat down.

"He's sweet, very talkative, he likes the 100 questions game, which we often play." While talking, I found myself smiling, which Maeve caught on too.

"A friend of his taught him, they used to play it all the time, and he loved it so much we played it when there was nothing to watch on TV." She smiled thoughtfully. "He's a gem. He has helped me so many times with so many different things, especially the girls. They can be a handful, but he knew exactly what to do to help out, I wouldn't even need to ask him, he would just do it."

I listened to Maeve as she spoke about Tom. In her eyes, he was the man of the house, and he did a great job.

"Tom and I got into quite a few arguments the week before. I just want to apologise and know he'll understand. You know? I just want him to know how much I love him." Maeve confessed. She was like Tom. She spoke a lot. Maybe she missed having him around because they would talk to each other, and now she doesn't have that person, even if some of that speaking was arguing.

"I just wished I hadn't asked him to change shifts. If I had just worked my usual shift, he wouldn't be here." I told her, which in hindsight, I think was a bad idea.

"Wait what?" She questioned.

"I asked Tom to come in early because I wasn't feeling well." I answered honestly. Maeve's expression turned from sad to angry.

"So, if you had done your normal shift, he wouldn't be in this situation." She raised her voice, which got the attention of the customers in the coffee shop. I didn't have time to answer before she began shouting "I hope you're happy with yourself. You've basically killed my boy. Even if he does wake up, we don't know the problems he'll face, and that's on YOU!"

With that, she walked out of the shop. I looked around to see people staring at me, which made me turn as red as a tomato.

I got up from the shop and headed towards Tom's room. As I got closer, I stared in through the tiny window in the door. Maeve wasn't there. My attention turned to Tom. He looked peaceful, but Maeve was right. It should be me there, not him. I held onto the handle, hesitating. I didn't know whether or not to enter. I didn't want Maeve to come back and shout at me again, but I also didn't want to leave, I wanted to talk to Tom. I wanted to hold his hand and plead for him to wake up.

I stepped into the room and sat down on the chair nearest to Tom. I didn't move it closer to him. I made sure to keep a distance. I needed to distance myself from him.

"Hey Tom, it's Maddie. Sorry I haven't visited in ages. I've had a few things going on." I stopped for a second, looking at the door, and then continued. "I mean, I guess you're in a coma, and you won't remember what I told you, sorry that was insensitive. But I guess right now you're the only person I can be honest with—my life's shit at the moment. I know yours isn't great either, so I shouldn't moan because at least I'm still able to, but I'm struggling. I'm really struggling at the moment. I think I've decided to do it. I'm going to end my life, Tom. I'm going to do it on my birthday. I'm not fighting anymore. I'm too tired. I just want to sleep. I want to sleep forever."

I stopped talking because, for the first time in ages, the reality of it hit me. I mean, I've never told anyone about my plan. Tom's the first person to hear about it, and he's not going to remember when he wakes up. It felt good to tell someone, but it made me sad. I don't mean the usual depressed that I am where I feel nothing. Tears rolled down my face, my top lip quivered. I looked at Tom, who was still motionless and soon the sound of the heart monitors and UV lines took effect.

I stayed with Tom for a while. I took a comb out from the drawer and restyled his hair like how he would have it at work. I wanted him to still look his best. He should still look his best despite being in the hospital. I could give him that, at least.

When I got home, mum had food ready for me. I didn't feel like eating, but I forced myself to have a few bites. I hadn't eaten properly in almost a week, which wasn't like me at all. Mum asked me questions, but they all sounded jumbled. I excused myself telling her I wasn't hungry and placed my leftovers (which was everything) into a container and into the fridge. I walked upstairs, each one feeling like I was being pulled into the stairs. I felt heavy. I felt tired.

I looked around my room, and it didn't feel safe anymore. It didn't feel like a den I could go to and pretend the outside world didn't exist. My room wasn't MY room anymore; it was just a room. I looked around at the posters hanging on the wall, the boxes that were under the bed filled with random things I never wanted to throw away. I had a sudden urge to get rid of it all, so I walked downstairs, grabbed a few black bags, and started taking the posters down on my wall and chucking them in the black bags. I then got the boxes from under the bed and sifted through them. I chucked away most of the clutter that was in the boxes. Most of the boxes had things like receipts, cinema tickets, photos of old, fake friends, teddy bears and old perfume bottles. I chucked all of this away. I didn't need photos of myself with someone who remained friends with me until their birthday and then never spoke to me again. I didn't need cinema tickets for movies I watched four years ago. I didn't need any of this. From the boxes and posters alone, I had filled up three black bags. I moved on to my clothes. I had so many clothes I never used, or I kept in case I fitted into them again but never did because I failed my diets four weeks after starting them. I chucked away another two black bags worth of clothes.

I didn't want my family to have to do this when I was gone. If I can make it easier for them, then it wouldn't be as hard. When I was finished, my room looked completely different. There were no boxes under the bed; the wardrobe door could shut because I had the right amount of clothes in, and the walls looked clear. I took the black bags downstairs and chucked them into my car. I'm going to take a trip to the Waste Centre a couple of days beforehand.

When I was finished with that, I decided to shower and go to bed. I slept better that night than most. I don't know whether it was because I had had so little sleep for the last couple of weeks that I passed out, or I had finally accepted what was happening and the void was content.

The next morning, I got up and got ready for work. I didn't want to go to work; all my life had been drained out of me, and if I could have it my way, I would stay at home and turn into my bed. Unfortunately, I couldn't do that. I had to remind myself that I'm not working for myself. I'm working for my family. I'm working to give them some money. When I got to work, I noticed Sophie was acting differently than she usually does. She wasn't her usual happy self, and I couldn't figure out why. When I came in and got my apron on, I headed out the front to help.

"What's up?" I asked.

"Vikki handed in her notice, which means we will go from having six members of staff a couple of weeks ago to only four." She told me. I now understood why she wasn't herself. She was stressed. I'm not great with feelings or emotions when the void has taken over, I seem to forget what that is, so comforting Sophie wasn't going to help. It would be like a robot comforting her. Instead, I decided to make her favourite drink and before she could say anything, I tapped the machine and paid for the drink. This made her smile.

"I'll help out, Soph. I can pick up more shifts."

Sophie hugged me. "I knew I could count on you, Maddie."

I stayed on for a couple of hours as Tom would have been in after me, and the hours needed to be sorted out. I continued to serve customers trying to be as happy as I could possibly be while feeling like I was melting into the floor. Doris even came in wanting my favourite drink order, and that didn't even cheer me up. My signing had gotten a tiny bit better as I had picked up a few things from Doris, which I did use to her delight, but even doing this, which would generally make me smile and feel good, didn't help. I didn't know what to do. Throughout the shift, I found that my welcoming smile was getting lower and lower to the point where I hardly bothered. I needed seven energy drinks to make me feel more alive, and I had higher chances of suffering a caffeine overdose than I did of feeling better.

When I finished work, I checked the time - 5:30 pm; the hospital visiting hours stopped at 8:00 pm. I quickly ran to the bus stop and hopped on the bus. When I got to Tom's room, a nurse was in there taking vitals.

"How's he doing?" I asked.

The nurse put the stethoscope around her neck. "He's doing better." She said and walked out the door. I took a seat next to Tom.

"Hey Tom, it's Maddie." I said. If coma victims can hear us, then I want him to know that it's me.

"I know I'm later than usual. It was a last-minute decision," I explained, then quickly added, "not that I don't want to visit you." I stuttered. I don't know why I was so nervous because even if he could hear me, he wouldn't remember what I said. He wouldn't be judging me, so I don't know why I was so nervous.

"Maybe coming later is better, so I don't see your mother. Who hates me, by the way." I chuckled nervously. "...the new series of Doctor Who is out, so you need to wake up... you need to wake up to watch it." I tried a laugh but failed miserably. I sat there motionless, not knowing what to say. I wanted to grab Tom by his arms and beg for him to wake up. I wanted to pray to a god I don't believe in to turn back time and put me in this hospital bed instead. I wanted to shout and scream so loud that the aliens in outer space could hear me. I did none of these things, I wanted to, but I sat there and stayed quiet. I tried thinking of what to tell Tom, anything new that happened but all that came out was silence. I only sat there for twenty minutes, but the time passed so slowly, and the more I focused on the monitors, the more they would seem to get faster, which would freak me out. I had to constantly look up at the screen to check whether it was happening or if it was my imagination.

I sat there for another 20 minutes, and just as I went to leave, the door opened. I expected it to be a nurse telling me that visiting hours had finished, but when I looked around, it was Maeve. We both locked eyes and stood there in silence. It felt like an eternity before one of us spoke up. It was Maeve.

"Look, I'm sorry about yesterday. It's very stressful at the moment." She said with her head down. "It's just Tom was a massive help around the house. I've got twin girls, 6, and they are little nightmares, but Tom always knew how to sort them out. He knew what to do. I just miss him so much!" She sobbed. I walked over and gave her a hug. I thought this was the best thing to do. It was what I imagined Tom doing when he saw someone cry. It must have helped because she hugged me back, and then a couple of minutes later, she pulled away, drying her eyes in her jumper.

"Thank you." she whispered. I walked out the door, but before I left, I handed her my number. "Maeve, if you need any help with anything. Let me know." She smiled and I walked out and headed to the bus stop.

I thought about Maeve and Tom. I thought about how Tom was the way he was because of his mother. I feel like Maeve, despite good intentions, doesn't always get things right. I thought about how Tom was this caring, gentle creature who seemed to understand everyone without them needing to explain themselves. He was the type of person who would walk into a room and talk to the person on their own because he didn't want them to be lonely. He's the type of person who would do anything to make you feel more comfortable—the kind of person who made everyone feel at ease around him. I couldn't think of anyone who I thought was as great as Tom. He was like an angel down here on earth. Judging from Tom's way, Maeve's parenting must have been wildly different from what I received. Was she overly sensitive? Did she hug too much? Did she say love you way too many times? Or was she completely the opposite? Did she hate him? Did she make him look after his sisters? Was he the sole breadwinner? Is that why he has become such a loyal and caring person? Because he never had it growing up.

I thought seeing Tom would make me feel better, but when I got home, I didn't feel better, every time I saw him, I felt utter guilt, I felt terrible for what happened, it's all my fault. I'm such an asshole. I should have been there instead.

It's true. You finally understand my point of view.

I know, I finally understand.

Well, now you understand you have to finish what we started.

I will. I only have 41 days to go.

I have my list of things to do before I die.

- Go through my room and throw away anything I don't need or use.

- Sell items that can give my family some money.

- Make amends with Becks

- Try to make amends with Becks boyfriend

- Spend the day with my grandma

- Spend the day with my nan

- Get leaving presents for the family

- Tell everyone I love them one last time.

****

I tried to make amends with Becks, but I haven't spoken to her since her last text. Make amends with Beck's boyfriend... haha... never going to happen. I might leave a special note for him telling him to go fuck himself. I've tidied my room and thrown away the majority of my clothes. I have yet to find any items I can sell, but I have a computer that I could get rid of. It might be worth a couple of hundred.

I'll spend time with my grandma and nan a couple of days before, and I will find some presents for my family. I have no idea what I'll get yet. I haven't done that much on my list, but most of it is things I will do at the end, mainly for my family's sake. I want them to know that they aren't the reason that I've taken my own life. I want them to know that nothing they did made this happen. I do not want them to blame themselves for a decision that was my own.

*DISCLAIMER: Mum, Dad, and David. I'm talking to you specifically if you're reading this. I didn't kill myself because of you. I didn't do any of this because of you. You were the best during the worst times. You tried to help, you really did, and I recognise that, but I can't be helped. I hope this makes things clearer for you.

I will probably write them a letter closer to the time, but I'm writing this to give them peace of mind. Something more substantial. I want to help them when I'm not here and writing this diary should do that. I also know the common miscommunication about suicide and how it's selfish. I know that, in one way, I am selfish. I'm taking my future into my own hands, but that's why I'm doing all of these things before the day because I want to make sure I do not leave a trail of carnage behind me. I want everyone to accept it. In the end, it will be better for everyone.

I did not sleep much. I tossed and turned. I couldn't stop thinking about Tom or Becks and her boyfriend or my family. In every dream I had, they were happier without me. They didn't have this gloomy cloud hanging around them because I wasn't in the picture. I couldn't stop thinking about the plan and how I should think of a schedule for how I will do this. It needs to be planned and precise. I can't have a messy end. I got up from my bed and wrote down the dates.

21st September - I will buy presents for my family, which I will then wrap and hide until the day.

22nd September - I will visit my nan, take her out for a meal, give her some flowers and then say goodbye (I will make sure it's not too teary because I can't raise suspicion).

23rd September - I will visit my grandma and do the same as I did with my nan. I will then give Tom my letter.

24th September - The last day. This one's a busy one. First, I'll hide each of my family's gifts in their room. Then I'll walk to the coffee shop and hand in my resignation letter to Sophie and thank her for everything. Then, after all my goodbyes are done, I'll walk to Bennetts castle with nothing but my special bag and one last spliff. I'll smoke it, and then when the time comes, I'll do the one thing that will set me free from this life. And that's it. The End.

When I finally had it straight in my mind, I was able to rest a little better. I knew what needed to happen, and now I just had to wait for the day. I was not excited. I was not looking forward to it. I was petrified and scared, but I had to do it. I had no other choice. I've tried everything, and nothing is working. I just want to feel good for once in my life. I want to be able to smile and for that smile to be a real one. I want to feel warm inside. I want to feel loved and be able to love without bad thoughts. I want to be able to walk down the road and not feel like I should jump in front of a car. I want to be able to be free of these chains. I want to feel something positive again, but that's not going to happen. I'm one of those that can't be fixed no matter how hard you try.

With love,

Maddie x

37 DAYS LEFT

Dear Diary,

Not much has happened since my last entry. I've been working and doing a lot of overtime to give more money to my family. I sold my computer. Mum asked me why I was selling it. I told her it was because I didn't use it and it took up too much space. I told her I was thinking of getting a tablet instead. She believed me. That was an extra £200 that went straight to savings.

I went to see Tom yesterday. When I got there, his mum was just leaving but before she did, she turned to me and said, "I'm glad he has someone else who visits. His friends visited once, and then gave me some stupid excuse for why they couldn't come, so I'm glad you're here."

To my surprise, she gave me a hug before leaving. I didn't think she liked me much, but it was nice to hear that she appreciated my visits.

I sat in the chair across from Tom and took his hand.

"Tom, if you can hear me, I'd really love for you to wake up.... Please just try for me," I wiped the tear from my face and looked at Tom, who looked exactly the same from the first time I ever visited him. "If you die, Tom, I will kill you, you hear me."

I rested my hand on top of his and put my head back. I spoke aloud "Tom, you are an amazing person. You have this brightness that I have never seen in anyone else before. Your smile is contagious, and when you wake up, you are going to do amazing things. You'll be the writer that you wanted to be, and you'll become famous and mega-rich, and you won't even think about me because you'll have this amazing new life. You'll get everything you deserve."

At some point, I must have fallen asleep (exhaustion had really hit lately) because I awoke to a nurse softly shaking my shoulder.

"Excuse me, visiting time is over."

I apologised and left; I told Tom I would see him again soon.

****

've decided that it's over between Becks and me. I've come to the conclusion that we're no longer friends, I mean I'm unsure if we were truly friends to begin with. Maybe when we were in Primary school but the last couple of years, we've only been friends under her conditions, but it only took a couple of weeks out with Tom for me to realise what true friendship was about.

Not only has Becks not apologised for what Matt said, she also hasn't apologised for the many horrible things she's said. If she doesn't miss me already, she won't miss me when I'm gone.

On a separate note, I've been staying out of the house as much as I can. I want my family to get used to me not being there. I haven't got long left. Truth be told I am petrified, I am so scared about what will happen, but I'm also ready. I have nothing left to live for.

With love,

Maddie x

35 DAYS LEFT

Dear Diary,

I still have 35 days left.

I'm ready to go now.

I don't know what to do, should I do it early? No. I have to wait. I have to stick to the plan. It will be better for everyone if I go now, but I have to wait for only 35 days to go.

The last two days have been hell on earth. It all started on Wednesday.

I woke up on Wednesday, and I felt different, it wasn't a good or bad difference, but I felt different. I got up, got into the shower, and got dressed, all of which was easier to do that day compared to all of the others previously. I thought at the time that it was slightly strange how I felt lighter, but I didn't think anything of it. I went downstairs and ate some BREAKFAST, which I don't think I've done in ages, and left to go to work. I had a spring in my step, which I wasn't used to. I felt like a puppet being held up by strings.

As I got to work, I noticed the shop was already open and incredibly busy. I wasted no time in getting into my apron and serving the customers. I even thanked some of the nasty businessmen and women who stuck their nose up at me. I went through the day absolutely fine. The people coming in and out weren't as bad as expected, and I didn't need Sophie to help, which was a plus.

On my break, I noticed a missed call from an unknown number. I thought nothing of it because I get spam calls all the time. I headed back out onto the shop floor, and surprisingly, it was completely empty.

"Has everyone vanished?" I jokingly asked, but Sophie didn't laugh. She silently stared at the phone in her hand.

"Sophie, what's wrong?" I asked, panic starting to seep in.

"Take a seat, Maddie." She pointed towards one of the chairs, and we both sat down.

"What's is it, Soph?" I asked again, anxiety in full swing.

"Maddie...I have some bad news." She began.

"Tom... passed away this morning."

NO. NO. NO. NO.

She can't be right.

I only saw him yesterday.

"The doctors were concerned he wouldn't come out of the coma because of how long he'd already been unresponsive..." Sophie continued, but I didn't listen.

Everything went numb. I stared at the table.

"Maddie, it's not your fault..."

Why him? Why did it have to be him? He was so good. It should have been me.

"Maddie listen..."

It should have been me.

"Maddie!"

No matter how much Sophie tried, I couldn't hear her. All I could do was think about Tom. It's all my fault. If I had just worked that shift, then I would be gone, not him. I wanted to die, I was practically begging for it, so why was Tom gone and not me?

It is all your fault.

You killed the only person that actually liked you.

This is why I'm always right.

You screw everything up!

And now that young man is dead because of your selfishness.

I was in shock. Just yesterday, I had imagined the life that Tom would have. I saw it so clearly. He was not supposed to die. Not now. Not while he was still so young and full of life. I wish it were me. At least I wanted to die. Tom deserved to live. Above anyone, he deserved a chance.

All the thoughts were rushing through my mind at once. I thought about Maeve and how she's going to cope without him. I thought about how she has the twins to look after and a full-time job. How is she going to manage to do everything without his help? I thought about Sophie and how she would have to carry on working at the shop while trying to hold down the emotions because work carries on. I thought about how she's going to have to put up new job applications right away and how she won't have time to mourn the loss of Tom. I thought about me, I thought about how Tom was the only person who understood me, he was the only one who was able to calm me down even if he didn't know I was freaking out. He was the only one to talk to me even when I was in a bad mood and wanted everyone to leave me alone, and he was the one and the only person to make the void disappear. Now that he was gone, everyone's world would become darker. He was the small ray of light in this world.

Sophie and I sat in silence for the next hour. At one point, she stood up and made us both a drink but remained silent. We didn't know what to say, we were both devastated.

"So, the shop's shutting for renovations. We both need to go home. I'll call Maeve later and let her know if there's anything she needs then she can call me anytime." Sophie said.

"I told her a couple of days ago to call me if she needed anything. I think she called me today, but I didn't answer it." I told Sophie, who moved her chair closer to mine and took my hand.

"Maddie, whatever you're thinking, this isn't your fault."

I felt nothing. I felt as if my whole world had caved in, and now there was a big hole that couldn't merely be re-filled.

This feeling was familiar to me. It was the same as when I lost Bampy. It was like I had no soul. I didn't cry, not initially anyway. I was in too much shock to cry. It was the single-handedly worst thing that has ever happened to me. When Bampy passed away, he was in the hospital, he had cancer, and we all knew that he may not come out again. Of course, I was still distraught when he did pass away despite us knowing it was coming. With Tom, it was different. I expected him to be coming out of the hospital, all guns blazing and ready to go on another adventure, but that didn't happen. It's times like this where I wish I believed in a god, so I would think that Tom was going to heaven and that he would be in a better place. But I don't believe in God, and Tom's better place would be to be alive, happy, healthy and with me.

He would be asking me 100 questions, most of which he's already asked, and then when I reply differently, he would turn to me and say, "well, last time you said this..." and I would tell him, "Well, last time I was a different person" and we would laugh. Oh, how he would make me laugh. He was the first person to make me laugh in ages, and I mean a proper, real laugh. And now he's gone. Forever.

Sophie and I both left at the same time. As she was locking up, she put a sign on the door that explained we would be shut for renovations until the 15th of September.

"When I hear about Tom's funeral, I'll let you know. Also, we do have a number for a counsellor on company money, so free of charge. If you want to talk to them, here's their number."

Sophie handed me a piece of paper.

"He really liked you; you know that don't you?" She said as she hugged me. Tears had begun to roll down her face.

"I liked him too." I admitted, and at that moment, I realised how true it was. I liked Tom. I really did like him, and now he was gone.

I didn't know what to do when I got home. I didn't want to explain what had happened to my family because I didn't want them to think I'd get bad again. I didn't want them calling my doctor and for them to finally realise I hadn't collected my med's for a couple of months. I didn't want them to be affected by this, but I also didn't want to keep it a secret. The person who was my closest friend, someone who I liked romantically had just died, and I didn't know what to do. I was completely lost.

I sat in my room, but it didn't help; all I did was think about Tom. I tried to think of him as he was, not the guy in the hospital for two weeks being kept alive by machines. I wanted to remember him as the bubbly guy with the big personality. I tried to think of his face and remember his features; his brown hair that would be in a quiff at the beginning of the shift and then would flop down to his eyebrows by the end of the shift. His eyes were like a galaxy. They were a portal to his soul and the brightest blue you could ever see, as blue as the ocean. And his smile, the smile of a saint, the smile that would cut you if you stood too close, the one that would make your world feel better when you thought it wasn't possible.

Thinking about Tom made it worse. It made everything darker. It made the void louder. I got up from my bed, and I put my shoes on. I left the house and went for a walk. I ended up walking to Bampy's grave. I sat next to his grave and took off some leaves that had fallen on top of it.

"This is one of the times that I want you back here, Bampy. You would know exactly what to say right now to make everything better," I spoke aloud, "I told you about Tom, do you remember? Well, he passed away this morning." I allowed a tear to drop from my eye. "I don't know what to do. If I think about him, I'm sad. If I don't think about him, I feel guilty, or I feel like a false friend. I don't want to talk to Sophie about it because she's in the same boat as I am and I don't want to talk to Maeve, his mum, because well, it's his mum, she's going to be devastated, and the last thing she needs is for me to be in her way and acting like I'm the sad one." I looked around, making sure that no one was listening to me. "I don't know what to do, Bampy, I'm getting bad again, and I can't stop it anymore." I held my head down and prayed to a god I don't believe in.

"God, if you exist and if you're listening, I need your help. Can you please put Tom back on earth and take me instead."

I waited for 10 minutes, hoping for some sort of miracle, but of course, nothing happened.

"Fuck you, God." I shouted out. Then I left the cemetery, feeling worse than when I arrived.

I didn't go home, I walked to the lookout, it is Tom's favourite place, and I wanted to remember the day we came here and talked for ages. I headed up, which took less time than expected, and by the time I got to the lookout, my legs were burning. I went to the area where Tom and I had gone and stood on top of the rock, looking down at the city. The city looked quiet for once. It wasn't as busy as it usually was, and I wondered if Tom had anything to do with it. I wonder if people out there who didn't know Tom woke up today feeling sad without knowing why. It wouldn't surprise me, Tom was the sunshine in this world, and it's cold and dark without him. So, I wouldn't be shocked if everyone in the world was feeling sad today.

I stood up there for about 40 minutes when a familiar voice called out my name.

"Maddie?"

I turned around to see who it was. "Maeve. What are you doing here?" I asked, surprised to see her.

"It's Tom's favourite place. We used to come up here every Sunday and watch the sunset. He used to say it was the most beautiful thing he'd ever seen...and then he would turn to me and say, actually it's the second most beautiful thing he'd ever seen" This made Maeve smile, and her eyes filled with tears.

I got down from the rock and hugged her. She began sobbing violently and began to shake. I didn't say a word. I just held her.

"I can see why Tom liked you so much." She said after a while. I didn't answer as I didn't want my voice to betray the way I felt inside. I just smiled in reply.

We walked over to the cliff edge, and after a moment, I spoke.

"To have someone like Tom as a friend meant more than anything in the world. He gave me a chance; not many people do." I told her.

"He is... was so special, no matter what he did, I was so proud of him." She replied.

We spent a while just talking about our memories of him. Maeve told me that when Tom was little, he packed his bags and moved to his friend's house for a day because she wouldn't give him a brownie for breakfast. After he stayed there for a day, Maeve and his friend's mum convinced Tom to go home by saying they would call the police on him for running away. She said it was quite scary at the time, but she wanted to teach him that she was the boss of the house and wouldn't back down. She told me how much they would laugh about it as he grew up. I wished I had stories of Tom like Maeve had but hearing the stories made me think about Tom in a different light. He had a rebellious side that, from what Maeve said, I was lucky I didn't see, but overall, Tom was as sweet and kind and caring as he showed to me.

Apparently, when he was 15, he had to do work experience, and he chose to work in a care home because he wanted to help those that couldn't help themselves. He originally worked there for the week, but the manager told him that when he turned 16, he could have a part-time job alongside college. He ended up working at the care home for a year, and he loved every minute of it. Maeve told me there were moments which weren't as nice, like when an elderly person was ill, and he needed to change bedding while they were still in bed, or when one of the people passed away, but she told me about how happy he was to work there.

Maeve and I stayed at the lookout until it was dark.

"Thank you, I know it was a coincidence that we were both here, but I think you were my angel today. Tom must have wanted us to be together." She hugged me and left.

I stood rooted to the spot. Maeve's words stunned me, and before I knew it, the tears were uncontrollable. I wasn't an angel; I was the person that killed her son. How can I be an angel? If it wasn't for me, Tom would be here. I didn't feel like an angel. I felt guilty. I walked home, and for the first time in forever, I could not stop the tears. I fought my hardest to control myself before getting home, but I couldn't.

When I eventually got back, I went straight upstairs to bed. I didn't want to get up for anything. Even when mum came in to ask how my day was, I kept it brief. "Long and tiring." which wasn't a lie. I'm exhausted.

****

I slept for the rest of that evening. It was not restful sleep. My dreams were disturbing. I had a dream where instead of Alice stabbing Tom, it was me at the last minute instead. Anytime I would try to run away, I couldn't. The knife was attached to my hand, and he was moving closer to me like he was on a conveyor belt. I woke up dripping in sweat, it was pitch black. I went to the toilet, washed my face, and tried to go back to sleep, but I was too scared. I didn't want a repeat of the dream. I didn't want to dream at all. I laid in bed on my phone, watching videos until my body finally succumbed to sleep. I didn't dream this time, it felt more like I had shut my eyes and opened them a few seconds later, but it was bright outside when I did open my eyes. I looked at my phone. It was 11 am. I'm surprised my mum hadn't come upstairs to check on me. She normally would have by now.

I went downstairs to find a note left on the fridge by a magnet.

> I'm working early. Washing needs to go in. The dishwasher needs to be done and vacuuming needs to be done. Be home at 4 pm. Mum x

I groaned loudly. The last thing I wanted to do today was chores. I did them without complaining, knowing that I was helping mum.

I usually forget about chores, which makes mum angry, but she doesn't realise that a symptom of depression is memory loss. She thinks I'm lazy when actually I just can't remember much.

I had completed the chores and headed straight back to bed. As I got into my bed, I checked my phone—one text from Becks.

B: Can we talk?

I didn't respond. I didn't want to respond. She had hurt me badly. She hadn't talked to me in weeks, and now she wants to talk. Why? Because she and Matt probably broke up, that's why.

Two minutes later, my phone rang. It was Sophie.

"Hey Maddie, how are you doing?" She asked.

"I'm alright," I lied. "How are you doing?"

Sophie kept a brief "I'm fine" She sighed. We were both lying.

"I called to let you know that Maeve has a date for Tom's funeral,"

"When is it?" I asked her. I knew I was going to go. I had to go.

"It's September 9th at 11 am." Sophie sniffled, which made me think she was crying.

"Thank you." I whispered and hung up the phone, and I cried.

I led on my bed on my own, and I cried as loud as I could. I knew my neighbours would be able to hear, but I didn't care. I cried so loud that my chest began to hurt, and I struggled to breathe. I had never cried like this before, and now it was all coming out. I cried until there were no tears left, and I gave myself a migraine. I cried until my shirt was wet, my pillow was wet, and my blanket was wet. I cried until there was nothing left, and then I sat there in silence.

I wanted to cry until I died because that's what I deserved. That's what I did to Tom, and that's what I deserved for myself.

After a fair amount of time had passed, I managed to stop crying long enough to check my phone... one missed call from Becks and one text from her.

B: Please text me. I need to talk to you.

I ignored it, I can't believe it after everything, now she wants to talk to me. She only wants me when she hasn't got anyone left. Unfortunately, I know how this ends up, she'll call me again, I'll answer, she'll explain Matt was a dick, I'll apologise, we'll meet up chat, she'll tell me they're finished, a week later they get back together, then she ignores me and it all repeats.

I can't help myself sometimes, sometimes I think it's better to have one non-friend friend than to have no one. Sometimes I just get so lonely that I'd rather hang out with someone who was being fake and call me up last rather than no one at all.

Becks used to be that true friend until Matt came along, and then she changed. She didn't want anything to do with me unless it suited her.

That's not a real friend, and I know that, but when you have no other friends than the one person who shows up once a month, you take the friend that only shows up once a month. It gets to a certain point where going out on your own becomes depressing. You watched the people around you laughing with their friends or their partners, and you're there on your own talking to yourself. It gets lonely sometimes, or it did before Tom came along. But Tom's gone now, and I'm alone again.

When mum came home, she came upstairs and knocked on my door.

"Yeah?"

"I'm thinking of ordering something tonight. Work has been a nightmare, so think about what you want." Mum smiled.

"Okay, what kind of food are you thinking?" I asked.

"Probably a Chinese from Sensations."

We spent most of the time in silence while eating food. Mum occasionally would stop eating to talk about Work or how proud she was of her kids and how we turned out. I know she was only adding me in on it because I haven't done anything to make her proud, but she would feel bad by just saying she was proud of David.

I hadn't done anything to make her proud.

David had gone through years of apprenticeship and is now an engineer for one of the biggest train services in the UK. He travels all around the UK fixing trains that have broken down, and he's now applying to be the next assistant manager. He was clever, and I'm not surprised that Mum was proud of David. I mean, I'm his sister, and despite us as siblings having to hate each other, I was proud of him. He did something, he worked his ass off, he stuck to it, and now he's going to be a manager. It was amazing.

Then there was me. I did college, got my diploma in art, and then worked at a coffee shop. I had no artwork until recently when I had two, which made me £40 in total. I turned down the option for a management position, and then only two weeks ago, I killed someone.

David and I are completely opposite. He's going to be super rich, with loads of cars and dogs and probably even a maid. In comparison, I will be six feet under.

As soon as I finished eating, I went upstairs and changed into my pyjamas. I tried to sleep, but the thoughts of Tom became stronger.

You killed him. How could you?

You kill anything good in this world.

You need to finish it before you hurt anyone else.

The void was right, I did, but I have to wait 35 days.

I have to do it on my birthday.

With Love,
Maddie x

30 DAYS LEFT

Dear Diary,

Today, I had no idea what to do. I was so drained of all my energy that I couldn't move. I tried to stay in my room, but the void started taunting me. Luckily, just before the tornado of bad thoughts could completely overtake me, my phone started ringing. It was Maeve. I looked at it for a second, trying to compose myself before answering.

"Hi, Maddie."

"Hi Maeve. Are you okay?" I asked.

"I'm...I'm trying to sort stuff out for Tom's remembrance, but I'm struggling to do it on my own..." She stopped for a second. All I could hear on the other end was sniffling where she was crying. "...I was wondering if you could come over and help. He would want you to."

I didn't know what to say. I didn't want to turn her down because I promised I would be there for her, but I also didn't want to think about Tom for another minute longer; otherwise, Hurricane Void would come and eat me up. In the end, my conscience got the better of me.

"I'll be round in half an hour." I finally replied and hung the phone up. I couldn't let her down, she was going through the hardest thing, and she called me. She wanted my help. I had to help her, for Tom.

I got changed into some better clothes, brushed my hair, and put some light makeup on. I went downstairs, picked up my car keys and left the house. I knew where the house was, but a strange feeling came over me as I was heading to it. It felt like I had swallowed a bowling ball, and my whole body was weighed down. As I got closer and closer, that sinking feeling was getting stronger, and by the time I was outside the house, I couldn't concentrate. My breathing was becoming faster. My heart felt like it was going to leap out of my chest and into the road. I tried using my senses to calm me down.

Sight - The house, the house where my only friend used to live. It looked darker now. It looked more depressing. It was as if the house itself was mourning the loss of Tom.

Sound - The silence, the silence of the road, the lack of cars driving and only now and then hearing the cries of a child.

Touch - The cold steering wheel and the rumbling of the car that I had yet to turn off in case I needed a quick getaway.

Smell - The car had a stale cigarette stench with a hint of added Weed and a drop of car freshener that clearly needed to be changed.

Taste - I couldn't taste, my mouth was as dry as the Saharan desert, and anytime I would take a sip of water from the old bottle that I had leftover in my car, my mouth would suck the moisture, and my mouth would remain dry.

The senses allowed me to focus this time, but it didn't remove the bowling ball feeling in my stomach. I had been sitting in my car for five minutes until I decided it would be a good idea to get out and go in. I just needed to do it, like how you would rip a plaster off. I stepped out of the car and shut the door behind me. I locked my car and slowly edged towards the house, taking in all of the details of the house that I had been unable to beforehand. The house had plants going down the entire side of the house. The door was red but showed visible fade from the sun. The windows were immaculate, with a blind in each of the windows. I edged towards the door and rang the doorbell. Within 2 seconds, a small child opened the door.

"Can I help you?" the girl asked.

"I'm here to see Maeve. Your mum?" I told the girl, who I'm assuming was one of the twins. She ran inside, and a minute later, Maeve came out the door.

"Sorry, Elise likes to answer the door, which isn't always a good thing."

Maeve laughed while gesturing for me to come in. I entered the home where Tom had lived. It was so clean, Maeve took me into the living room, which had glitter wallpaper, a Tokyo photo hung up, a tv, a big corner sofa and a chest. On top of the chest were photos and a laptop. Maeve sat down and got right into the subject itself.

"I'm trying to figure out what to do for Tom's remembrance. I was speaking to Sophie earlier, and she told me we could use the coffee shop as the reception. She told me she would speak to someone about getting it for free," she began, "the problem I'm having is making it personal. Tom was an extraordinary person. I just don't know what he would want."

I stayed quiet for a moment, thinking of something that could be helpful to her.

"Well, Tom likes Harry Potter, Doctor Who, those kinds of things, why don't you mention that?" I told her, Maeve wrote down the suggestion, "I can write something for him if you like."

Maeve's face didn't change, but she gave me a small smile. "Thank you. I know Tom would like that."

Maeve and I went through the music, the images to use and discussed things he would like. We chose "You'll never walk alone." by Gerry and the Pacemakers for the first song because he was a big Liverpool fan, which I was unaware of. We then chose "Spirit in the Sky" by Norman Greenbaum for the leaving song. Maeve told me that they would sing that all the time with a Western American accent. She told me she didn't know why they did it but that it made them laugh uncontrollably. We then chose a couple of photos of Tom for the pamphlets. One was of Tom, about 12 years old, eating an ice-cream, one was of his whole family at a Christmas dinner, and one was of Tom when he graduated from his A-levels. Maeve talked through every photo she had of Tom, which I didn't mind. I liked learning more about him, even if it was too late.

"Do you want a drink?" She asked.

"Can I have some water?" I asked her, and without even answering, she disappeared. I looked around the room, which I'm now noticing had many photos on the walls. It looked like she had pictures of Tom through Nursery right up until he was 16, and it was the same for the twins. Maeve came back in with a bottle of water and some biscuits.

"Help yourself," she said, but I politely declined. "Those are Tom up there. He was such a cute baby." She must have seen me looking at them. "He was such a good boy. He would do anything for me." Maeve continued.

"For me as well," I replied.

"He kicked out my ex for me not too long ago."

"What happened?" I asked her.

"My ex wasn't nice, although I didn't know that when we were together. We broke up ages ago because I'd found out he'd been lying. He kept asking me to take him back, but I wouldn't. A couple months back he came round trying to make amends. He was clearly drunk and when I refused to get back with him, we tried to hit me. Tom swooped in front, took the hit, and then kicked him out, but my ex didn't have it. He tried kicking the door down, and when Tom went out to see what was happening, my ex threw a brick at him." That explained why Tom wasn't in for a couple of days. "Tom was fine, we took him to hospital, and my ex isn't allowed anywhere near us now. I didn't want Tom or any of my kids to get hurt, I just thought I loved him because he was nice, but he had a dark past." Maeve stopped talking, and all that came out of me was:

"Shit." which Maeve seemed to understand.

"Yeah." is all she replied back.

I must have spent hours at Maeve's, but it didn't seem like that long. When it was time to leave, Maeve thanked me, and I drove home. By the time I got home, I was starving from not having eaten all day, but I didn't want to eat. I wanted to start writing a eulogy for Tom. I wanted to make him the best one that anyone could have thought of. I wanted to write one so well that Tom would be happy with it. I wanted one to show off how good of a person Tom was, but I knew I wasn't that good at writing. I would need a miracle to write something nearly as good as what he deserved. I thought about what I could write about the first day Tom worked at the shop. I thought about writing about our little adventures and the wild words he would speak. Anytime I thought about Tom, it made me smile, which then made me sad. It made me think about how we would no longer have moments as we did and how I wish we could have so many more.

Once I had completed the first version, I stopped. I didn't want to read through it. Writing it was hard enough. I went to bed that night but couldn't sleep. I haven't slept properly since the news about Tom being in the hospital, but it's getting harder. I don't want to sleep and have the same dream. The dream about Tom is a recurring one that wakes me up sweating.

I must have dozed off because I suddenly awoke to my phone going off. It was Maeve again.

"Hey Maddie, I was going through Tom's things looking for some photos or something he might want with him, and I found a letter addressed to you."

Did Tom write me a note? When did he do that?

"Oh, wow, okay, can I pick it up later?" I asked, shocked.

"Of course, what time are you thinking, as the twins have a ballet class at 3 pm."

"11 am?" I asked. It was only 7 am now, giving me a good couple of hours to sort myself out.

"Yeah, that sounds great." Maeve put the phone down.

My mind raced. What would Tom have to say to me? I was anxious to get my hands on that letter.

After Maeve called me, I couldn't sleep. I was somewhat excited to see what Tom had written for me. The in-between time of me getting dressed and waiting to leave to go to Maeve's seemed like an eternity. When it was eventually time for me to leave, I got into my car and drove there. I didn't wait in my car this time. I got straight out and rang the doorbell. Elise answered the door again.

"I'm here to see your mum." I told her, and she walked inside shouting after Maeve.

Maeve came to the door. "Oh hey, sorry I lost track of time, so the letter is still in his room." She gestured for me to come in. "You can go up and get the letter if you want. Tom's room is up the stairs, the second door on the left."

I hesitated for a second. I had my hand on the railing. I slowly walked up the stairs. I could hear the twins in their room, playing with toys. As I got to the door, I saw a sign that read 'Tom's Room.' I was hesitant, but I opened the door. There were so many questions I had. I opened the door and stood outside. His room was pretty empty. He had grey walls, with a solar system poster neatly placed in the centre of one of his walls. He had a desk that had one photo of him, his sisters and mum. He had grey curtains that were neatly placed in a curtain hook, and his bed was made perfectly. I looked around. His room was bare. It looked more like a University Students apartment than it did a bedroom. The note was on the desk. It was the only item that seemed out of place. I picked it up and put it in my pocket.

"What you doing in Tom's room? No one is allowed in Tom's room, it's his rule." A squeaky voice asked from behind me. I turned to see one of the twins standing outside of the room looking in.

"I'm picking up a letter Tom wrote to me." I told Tom's sister, which I was sure was Callie, because Elise wore something different.

"Are you Tom's girlfriend?" she asked.

"No, I was just his friend."

"Tom talked about you all the time. I'm sure he wanted to kiss you."

I laughed, and it made her laugh as well, and then Elise came out and started making kiss sounds with her mouth, which made Callie laugh and soon the both of them were kissing the air and laughing at each other. It made me smile. I walked out of the room while they were both still making the noise and laughing,

I headed downstairs and down into the hallway. Maeve was in the kitchen.

"I have the letter, thanks." I told Maeve, who looked flustered with a burnt omelette on the oven top.

"Oh, that's good." Maeve said.

"If you don't mind me asking, was his room always that tidy?" I asked Maeve, assuming she would tell me she chucked his stuff out.

"Yes, Tom suffered from OCD. He had to keep things a certain way. Otherwise, his brain would tell him that something bad would happen. Like if the photo frame was on the left side of his desk instead of the right then his sister would fall down the stairs. It consumed his life, it made him depressed, he wouldn't leave his room but with the help of Dr Sanford, Dr Goodall and some medication he was able to control it, well somewhat anyway, and he was able to get the job at the coffee shop" I stood there stunned, I had no idea that Tom suffered from mental health problems or the fact that he was seeing the same therapist as me. I wondered if Dr Goodall ever realised that I was talking about his patient when I mentioned Tom.

"I used to see Dr Goodall as well. I never knew any of this about Tom, he never said."

Maeve turned around and looked me in the eyes "He didn't want to scare you away. He told me that himself."

Tom and I really were not that different. I met someone who I thought was my saviour, and now I'm wondering if he thought I was his.

I left not long after that. I drove all the way home and went into my room before taking the letter out of my hand. I held it like it was a priceless jewel. I turned it around and carefully opened it up. Inside were two pieces of paper, one had a note on the inside, and one had what looked like a story.

Dear Maddie,

I don't know if you'll ever receive this letter, I know you may think of me as this cool guy who could speak a thousand words a minute, but when it comes to feelings, I'm a typical bloke. From the first minute I laid my eyes on you, this electricity went straight through me. I wanted to get to know you. I wanted you to get to know me. I'm a difficult person to understand. I make these connections with things that aren't connected at all. I say words, but I never actually speak. I'm trying to get better, I'm writing this just after you dropped me off and I kissed you, I can't stop smiling. Like right now writing this letter I'm so happy. I want you to know how much you mean to me, how much better my life became when you came into it. I like to think that the world brought us together because it knew how much we would mean to each other. I think about the fact that if I wasn't walking past the coffee shop on the exact day that Sophie had put the signs up for new staff, then none of this would have happened, and I may not be here writing this letter to you.

I thought about our conversation about my love of writing, and I've written a story that I hope you will love. Maybe you could do the illustrations for it, and it could become a book. The story is mine, and I understand if that puts you off. The last thing I would want to do would be to scare you away.

With Love,

Tom

P.S. I know you always thought I was gay, but I can assure you I am not. It was just that I wasn't interested in any other girl except you.

I opened up the second paper, and on it was Tom's story. Although it looked more like a poem than a story.

There once was a young man who needed to face all his demons,

He couldn't live happily until each one had been slain.

At first, he allowed the demons in without any reason,

Until there was a princess, he couldn't get out of his brain.

He wanted to show how much he appreciated her wisdom,

How this one princess had shown him a better path.

And without her realising, she gave him his optimism,

So, he fought off the demons even if it was a bloodbath.

Because his Princess was the reason he wanted to heal,

He wanted to show her the Beautiful world that was around them.

However, the Demons wouldn't give in. They didn't want him to feel,

They wanted him to themselves. They wanted him to be numb.

So, he battled the demons every day until the demons left him alone,

And when they did, he got down on one knee and told the Princess.

'I love you more than words can say. Will you be the Queen on my Throne?'

I thought about Tom and what he would have been like while writing this letter, I remember what I was like writing Tom's letter, and then I think about why he wrote it. Did he write it for the same reason as to why I wrote him one? Was this going to be his final letter to me? His dying words. The thought of Tom writing a suicide letter to me seemed out of the ordinary, but I also didn't know until today that Tom suffered from depression. Maybe it was his letter, and he was waiting like me. He was waiting for the right day or time to give it to me, one that wouldn't raise suspicion, and then I think about the fact that he never had time to give it to me. He passed away with so many open questions.

After I read Tom's letter, I placed it back into the envelope and hid it in between my books. I didn't know how to feel, I felt all of these emotions coming into play, I felt happy that he both felt the same way for each other, I felt sad that I wasn't able to express those feelings to him and potentially have my prince charming and happy ever after. I felt angry at myself for being the one that made him change shifts and for that being the reason he's dead. I had so many emotions and I didn't know what to do with them.

****

Maeve called me every day after that visit. I think she wanted someone to talk to, and seeing as the twins were only 6, they didn't exactly have deep, meaningful conversations. I think Maeve was lonely, so I answered her calls every time, sometimes she would call up to ask me for photos, which I never had, sometimes she would call to see how my speech was coming on, but without fail, every day, she called. I wondered how she was feeling. She just lost her son, who was her life, he helped her in so many ways, and she has to try and continue on and be strong for the twins. I wondered whether or not she was depressed, whether the stress of new everyday life had affected her. I thought about how at least she had a reason to feel that way, and I did not. I may have lost a friend, but I only knew him for two months. She knew him for 24 years. I couldn't imagine the kind of toll that would take on someone.

I have this urge to want to help Maeve, she's a nice woman, and she reminds me so much of Tom. I like her, but I can't get close, not again. If she wants my help, I will help her, but I won't get emotionally attached. That doesn't end well for anyone.

With love,
Maddie x

25 DAYS LEFT

Dear Diary,

It was my dad's birthday a couple of days ago. I gave him his presents, and as always, he seemed grateful for them. I feel like you could give my dad a scratch card and he would be happy with it. He had a good day, and honestly, so did I. It made me glad to see him happy.

On Dad's birthday, Maeve called up to ask some questions. She didn't have time to ask them as I told her that it was my dad's birthday and that I'd call her tomorrow. She seemed sad, but she didn't complain. She said she hoped we had a good day and hung the phone up. I did feel guilty, but at the same time, it was my dad's birthday, and we were spending it together.

On the night of Dad's birthday, there wasn't much to do, and I didn't want to stay in all night. I knew the dreams would be worse if I did. I got my shoes and jacket on and went for a walk. I knew where I was heading, I didn't have high hopes, but I thought I could give it a try. I walked for about half an hour until I came to Maeve's Street. I walked down the road and stopped outside Maeve's house. There were lights on inside so I knew someone was there, but I didn't know if she would answer. I walked up to the door, making sure I didn't trip on the step. I rang the doorbell. Elise answered.

"What you doing here?" she asked.

"I was wondering if I could speak to your mum." I told her.

She closed the door. I didn't know whether or not she was going to get someone or if she just closed the door because she wanted to. I waited for a couple of minutes, and then Maeve opened the door again.

"What are you doing here?" She asked me.

"I'm sorry if I sounded rude earlier. If you have questions, you can always text me, and I'll answer when I can." I paused for a second as Maeve's face now held a frown. "Or if you're calling because you want to talk to someone, that's fine too." I then added.

Maeve looked at me. I couldn't tell if she was happy or sad, she was smiling, but her eyes were filling up with tears.

"Are you okay?"

"No, I really miss him." She only just managed to get out before sobbing uncontrollably.

I went inside, and she made us a cup of tea. We sat and spoke about Tom for hours.

"Tom changed lives, anyone's life that he came into he changed massively. He changed my life in so many ways, and I don't know who I would be without him." This made her smile. She told me it made her feel like she had succeeded with one thing. She had raised a kind, charming young man. It's like Maeve had made a diamond. She was the carbon, her love was the fire, and her lessons were the pressure. If you put all of these things together at the end, you create a diamond. Tom was a diamond, he was one of the most prized gemstones, but he didn't know it. While Maeve and I were talking, Elise asked Maeve to read her a bedtime story. She specifically wanted the Dr Seuss Book 'Green Eggs and Ham.' Maeve told her to go upstairs and read it herself as I was there, and they were busy talking.

"I can read it to you if you want?" I asked Elise, who suddenly beamed with the thought of someone reading her a book.

"Are you sure? You don't have to. She can read herself." Maeve told me, but I insisted. I had never read a book to a child before, and I might not get the chance too. I walked upstairs with Elise, she handed me the book that was at the top of the stairs, and we walked into her and Callie's room. Callie was already in bed. She had the duvet over her mouth with only her eyes showing. I read the book to the twins. I made sure to add funny noises for each character and to add in dramatic music at points, the music which was me humming or going 'dun dun dun' but they loved it. By the time I finished the story, they wanted more, but I told them that if they went to sleep, I might be able to read more another time. I knew children remembered things like that, so I made sure to add in that I only 'might' be able to do it. I walked out of their rooms and headed back downstairs. Maeve had fallen asleep on the sofa, so I headed out.

As I headed back home, I thought about reading the book to the twins and how I had a good feeling inside for the first time since Tom passed away. It was a weird feeling but seeing them laughing at the voices did make me feel good. When I got home, everyone in my family had gone to bed. I wasn't home that late, but I guess everyone was tired and had work the next day. I headed upstairs as well, still thinking about Maeve and the girls. I wanted to help her out. I really did, I have less than 30 days to go, but I wanted to help her as much as I can before I pop off. She was Tom's mum, and Tom was my friend, and I killed Tom, so it was the least I could do for the terrible thing I did to her. I went to bed that night in a weird mood, I felt somewhat good about what had happened and how I made the girls laugh, but I also felt bad because I knew if it wasn't for me, then their brother would be able to be reading them bedtime stories right now and not me. I wouldn't be comforting Maeve because I wouldn't need to. Tom would still be alive, and everyone's life would be so much happier, but I had to ruin it by asking him to swap shifts. No matter who tells me it wasn't my fault, I know it was. Nobody can make me think otherwise.

The next day started off pretty boring. I did the housework, watched some movies, and thought it would be a quiet day until my phone started ringing. It was Becks. I paused for a second. I didn't want to answer, but I also did, I wanted to tell her to fuck off and hang up. I didn't care. I wanted her to know how she made me feel. I wanted her to feel like shit for falling for Matt again and doing the one thing she said she wouldn't do. I answered the phone.

"Maddie?" Becks said softly.

"What?" I grunted.

"Did you want to meet? I haven't seen you in ages." She would never apologise for the way she treated me. She would just want to carry on like it was nothing.

"I'm busy." I told her.

"What's wrong? Are you pissy with me?" She asked. I couldn't believe she was asking such a stupid question. She never knows what she does wrong.

"No shit Sherlock, but you know what, if you don't know what you've done wrong, then I'm done." I was ready to hang the phone up but also waiting to see if she'd fight for this.

"What, because I was spending time with Matt and didn't see you that much, you're not the only person in my life. Unlike you I do have more going on." Becks raised her voice.

"You know what, Becks? Fuck you." I said and hung up.

I was seething. I wanted to smash everything in my room up. I was so angry. I wanted to go to her house and beat her up. I knew. Luckily, I'm not a violent person. So, I did the one thing that I always do when I'm angry, I self-harmed. I went straight to my drawer with my blades and released all the anger out onto myself. After a couple of minutes, I started calming down, I felt more in control of my body, and it made me wonder if that's why I was freaking out so much because I wasn't using my normal techniques to calm down. I cleaned myself up, got on some plasters and continued watching the film, but my mind was in other places. I couldn't help but think about Becks, and how in all the time we've been friends, it really was a one-way thing. She knew I had no other friends. She knew I had nothing else, so she would make sure that we did the things she wanted. We would always go watch films she wanted to watch or go to the restaurants that she liked. We never did anything that I wanted. We never watched Harry Potter together because she told me it was shite, but I remember when her and Matt got together, and he made her watch it, and she told me she didn't actually mind it. It was always about her until Matt came along. They suit each other. Matt treated her like shit, and she treated me like shit.

I always wondered why I didn't have any friends. I would have been the best friend to someone, I would have made an extra special effort on their birthday, I would have noticed small signs and I would have made sure they were happy. All I wanted was a friend, and I don't understand why I never got one. I knew I was different, but I didn't think I was a bad person. I mean I must be if I don't have friends because everyone should have friends. I would have liked at least one friend, one honest, decent friend. One that wanted to know what I wanted to do, one that remembered my birthday, and even if they couldn't afford a card made one instead. That would have meant more to me than anything because at least they would have bothered, even if they didn't have money.

Becks never did that; she knew when my birthday was, but she wouldn't even get me a card. On my last couple of birthdays, I've asked her to come to a restaurant with me for my birthday and she cancelled at the last minute.

If Becks was my real friend, she would know about Tom because I would have told her. I'm not bothered about talking every day because we have our own lives, but I wish she could at least spare some time for me. When we do meet it's all about her and when she does eventually ask about me, I get two sentences in and then it's all about her again.

Maybe I'm one of those people that was born to be alone.

****

Maeve called me again today. It has become a daily thing, not that I am complaining.

"Hi, Maeve, what's up?" I answered.

"Hey, sorry to call. It's just the twins are asking if you could read them a bedtime story. I wouldn't normally call but it's all they're asking for so I told them I would see if you were free." She asked. "You can say no." She added in a hushed voice so the twins wouldn't hear.

"Well, I'm just about to eat my tea…" I could hear the twins as they sulked in the background "…but if they're allowed to stay up, I can make it in about 40 minutes." I heard loud cheering in the background. Maeve quietly thanked me and then hung up.

What on earth am I doing? I'm planning on ending my own life in less than 30 days and I'm going around Maeve's to read a bedtime story. I must have truly lost it because not only am I not a fan of kids, but I also am getting way too involved in their life. I should be taking a step back by now otherwise I won't want to do it.

I finished my tea, put on a jumper, and got into my car. It didn't take long to get to Maeve's and as I got out of the car, Elise already had the door wide open with a smile as wide as her face. "Maddie!" She shouted as she ran towards me and gave me a big hug, I tapped her on the shoulder and entered the house with her, shutting the door behind me.

"Thank you for this." Maeve said, looking slightly embarrassed.

"It's alright, if it carries on, I'll charge." I smiled, joking.

I walked upstairs and sat on a chair that had been placed in the middle of the twin's bed's. There was a selection of books led out on the floor.

"Which one is it tonight then?" I asked.

"It's your choice, we chose our favourites."

There was a choice of Green, Eggs, and Ham by Dr. Seuss, Snow White and the Seven Dwarfs by The Brothers Grimm, A Bear Called Paddington by Michael Bond, or The Story of Robin Hood by Rob Lloyd Jones. I chose Robin Hood.

While I was reading the twins' story, I thought about when Bampy and I would watch Robin Hood and how he would know all of the words and how excited he got when the bow and arrow tournament would be on. He loved watching Disney films. I enjoyed reading the book to the twins, I used different voices, and I acted out parts and by the time I got to the final part I noticed they were settling down, and by the time I finished they were asleep. I walked downstairs and saw Maeve on the sofa watching TV.

"They're both asleep." I told her while standing at the door.

Maeve stood up. "Thank you again, all they went on about was how they wanted you to read a bedtime story again. They really like you. I think you remind them of Tom, he used to do the voices just like you."

It made sense, kids had different ways of dealing with grief than adults do.

"As long as it helps them, I don't mind helping. I like seeing them smile, they're so young to deal with loss so to see them happy and smiling and laughing it's a good thing."

"That's all Tom would have wanted, he wouldn't want us moping around the house all day. He would be so happy to know you were making the twins smile."

Once I got home, I couldn't stop thinking about the things Maeve had told me about Tom. He had such a beautiful outlook on life, even though he was suffering greatly. "Every day is a gift, that's why we call it 'the present'." Okay, it was a cheesy line, from a cheesy film, but it resonated with me. Tom was consumed by his OCD and depression, but he never let that get in the way of his optimism that there was good out there. He was, ironically, the most optimistic, happy, depressed person I knew.

I wish I could look on my life as Tom did, like it was a precious gift, but when I think about mine, I see a broken gift that has been forgotten about. I am broken and I wish I could find the strength and determination that he had, but it seems I was born without it.

****

Every day since then I have gone to Maeve's house to read the twins a bedtime story. One day was Snow White, one day was The Jolly Green Giant and yesterday's was The Gruffalo, which was my request. I have enjoyed reading the twins a bedtime story, they always get really excited at the beginning of the book, at the middle of the book they've calmed down and by the end of the book, they're always asleep. After I finish reading a bedtime story to the twins I always go downstairs and talk to Maeve. Only we don't just talk about Tom now. We talk about me, which is something I'm new at. She asks me about my art because apparently,

Tom wouldn't shut up about it. She asks me about my life and my family and work. She asks me questions just like Tom would. It was nice to have someone that would listen to me and ask questions about me like she was interested in who I was. It was a shame she was 30 years older than me otherwise I feel like we'd be best friends, which is something I told her. She replied that when you hit adulthood, you realise having friends isn't about having them for the small moments like going clubbing or food etc, but for the deep moments. She told me friendship wasn't based on age, but on the idea that two people form a deep connection. Which, thanks to Tom, we had.

We always started a conversation on happy notes but halfway through Maeve would always cry. I didn't mind, I just never knew what to do, I would do my best to be comforting, but that wasn't second nature to me. She'd try to insist she was okay, but it would happen every night which made me think otherwise. I wish I could mourn as Maeve does, I wish I could cry like that, but I either don't cry at all or I don't stop crying.

Maeve and I talk to each other every day and it has been nice to have a friend with whom I can really connect with. I don't know if it's because she's bashed it into my head every day for a week or so but I'm starting to understand her when she says that life is important, and you only get it one chance. The question is am I important enough to continue living?

With love,
Maddie

16 DAYS LEFT

Dear Diary,

The days seem to be slipping away faster and faster as I get closer to my birthday. I've gone to Maeve's every night to read the twins a bedtime story, each night was a different story. It's been a way of distraction for the twins, and I think it's been a good distraction from me. For the first time in ages, I've had some sort of purpose. Once the twins were in bed I would then go downstairs and talk to Maeve. We would talk for an hour or so before I would head home. Maeve and I spoke about so many things, we spoke mainly about Tom, but we would also talk about Maeve and her life and her ex's and for once we spoke about Me and my life and things I've done. I remember when she asked me about what I wanted to do in the future or what I wanted out of the future, and I couldn't answer. I'd spent so much of my time thinking about my birthday and planning that out, but I couldn't tell her that. I couldn't tell someone who'd just lost their son that for the last 80 days I had been planning my own death. I couldn't tell anyone about my plan. I didn't want to. Things have changed in my life, I looked forward to seeing the twins all the time, but my plan still stands. I only have 16 days left.

Wow, you are a homewrecker.

You come into a family's life after a heartbreak and then just like that a month later you're going to top yourself?

How selfish are you?

Wait? So, you want me to stay?

I want you to suffer

I want to make sure you suffer, you deserve everything you get but this, doing this to those poor children, this is the worst thing you've ever done. You see them every day and soon Maeve has to tell her children that you can't visit because you're dead as well.

You're stupid.

You got yourself into this mess, so you need to sort it out.

I think you need to be quiet, when my time is up you win. You always win. There's no point in arguing with you.

I'm always right.

We've been preparing a lot for 'Tom's remembrance.' Maeve doesn't want to call it a funeral because it sounds too depressing.

"Although Tom suffered from depression, he tried to see the happiness in things. He didn't wish it on others. He would prefer us to celebrate him"

Of course, we both knew that was probably a performance, but it was best to remember him in the positive light that he showed us. We wanted to remember Tom the way he would want to be remembered, we made sure there was Doctor Who, and Harry Potter references splashed in. Maeve even gave me suggestions for what to write in my speech. I had about a page of things to say about Tom. I wanted to keep it short because I wanted the sentimental moments to remain between the two of us, I wanted them for myself.

I would get such a high from hanging out with Maeve and the twins for a couple of hours, they gave me such a feeling of warmth. One that I wasn't used to. I could tell despite Tom's loss killing them on the inside they would still laugh and joke, they would carry on. They knew that was what Tom wanted. I felt like Tom deserved for the world to stop altogether, to remember him.

Maeve and the Twins had this connection that I only wish I had with my family. Every night before I read a bedtime story, Maeve and the Twins come together in a massive hug, and they tell each other how much they love and cherish each other. It was the best thing I had ever seen. The love they showed to one another was unlike anything I had ever seen. It was amazing. Every single night they would do it without fail. I'd like to think about what Tom would say, about what he was grateful for. I asked Maeve why they did that, and she told me that the girls learnt it in pre-school while Tom was in hospital and wouldn't stop, when he came out, he started doing it as a joke and now it's a daily thing.

She explained that their real dad had left after the girls were born and then he never returned. She also told me that Tom decided to step up and try to be the father-figure for the girls. He switched his college to part-time instead of full time to help out around the house and with the twins. When he finished his course, he then took a job to try to help with money but was let go when he was in hospital.

Maeve told me about Tom and how he would do anything for the twins and even Maeve. She told me about the time that she was struggling to buy presents for everyone because money was tight, so Tom bought all of the twins presents and pretended Santa and Maeve had got them. He didn't take one bit of glory for that moment. She told me that he even bought his own present as Maeve couldn't buy him what he wanted, so he bought the present and then she paid him back month by month. It always surprised me how kind they were despite not having a lot.

Maeve and Tom's dad were teenage sweethearts, they had been together since they were 14. She told me she had Tom when she was only 18. Apparently, Tom's Dad didn't have a big bond with Tom because he preferred science fiction rather than football and apparently that made Tom 'gay.' He used to be horrible to Tom, he would call him 'useless' for not knowing the Leeds Striker's name or a 'faggot' for playing with Lego's instead of going outside and playing football. From what I've heard Tom's dad was horrible.

When the twins were born, Maeve was working two part-time jobs, which gave her very little maternity leave. Tom's Dad was working full-time at £8 an hour and Tom was 18 so he did a couple of hours in a shop for extra cash. Maeve and Tom's dad used to argue all the time, to the point where his dad would accuse Maeve of cheating and wouldn't pay for the twins because they weren't his. One day she woke up and there was a note that read "I'm done. You can keep the house." and that was it. That's how he ended a 20-year relationship.

It always made me wonder about my life. I mean I always knew my life was easy, I had two parents who were both still together. I had gotten through school and college with high grades. I didn't have to work; I chose to work. I was lucky and yet I was still depressed. I had everything a human being could want, and I still wanted to kill myself. I had what some people would call the perfect family and I still wanted to get rid of it completely. Maybe I am luckier than I realise.

It's Tom's remembrance tomorrow. I've been putting off thinking about it. Thankfully, the twin's and Maeve have provided a welcome distraction. I've been trying to ignore it completely but tomorrow is the day. I hope I can keep it together. I need to be strong, not just for Maeve but for Elise and Callie as well.

With love,
Maddie x

15 DAYS LEFT

Dear Diary,

It was Tom's funeral today.

I woke up stupidly early, and once I was up, I couldn't go back to sleep. I kept thinking about how this was the 'big' day. It was the day Maeve and I have been organising and talking about for weeks. I laid in bed looking at the outfit mum had picked out for me. She had chosen a black floral shirt with black skinny trousers; she also got me some shoes that had a slight platform on. The outfit wasn't too bad, but I never dressed up like that, so it made me incredibly uncomfortable.

The funeral wasn't until 11 am, and it was only a fifteen-minute drive, so I had plenty of time. I had three hours to waste. Which meant that I had plenty of time to sit and dread the day ahead. I hated funerals, I mean no one likes them, but it made me think of my own. I wondered how my family would feel about mine. Would they cry? Or would they hide their emotions like usual? Would many people turn up? Or would the stalls be empty? I'm just glad that I will never know the reaction to my death. I will never be weighed down by the people who do not care.

When I got to the funeral service, I was still early but I wasn't the earliest one there. I stayed in my car until I saw Sophie.

"Hey, Soph."

"Hi Maddie, how are you doing?" She asked.

I shrugged my shoulders. "Same old, how about you?"

"Ya knows. This sucks."

We stood around for a couple of minutes until we saw the hearse slowly driving up the road and into the cemetery.

We watched as they slowly came up and stopped. The hearse that carried Tom looked beautiful. His name had been formed with red and pink roses, as chosen by the girls, and son was written in dyed blue flowers. The coffin was glossy and had a photo of Tom placed in a frame at the top.

The car behind had Maeve and the twins in it as well as Tom's grandparents (Maeve's parents). As they left their car and followed Tom's coffin into the church, Elise looked around and as we locked eyes, I could see she had been crying. I didn't realise that the twins would know exactly what was going on. I didn't think they had the same understanding as adults, but I was wrong. They felt their brothers' loss as deeply as everyone else.

She tried to smile at me through the tears but the pain in her eyes was clear. I smiled back hoping to give her some small comfort.

"We're going to carry the coffin in, if the pallbearers could step up" The funeral minister (the person who conducts the funeral) took a couple of minutes as Tom's grandad stepped up. Maeve and some other family members also joined. Maeve turned and looked at me.

"Maddie, would you?" She asked.

I was honoured that she had thought of me, I just hadn't prepared myself for this moment. I awkwardly made my way to take hold of the coffin.

"Once the coffin has been taken in, the immediate family will go first and then everyone else will follow." The Minister said. We slowly walked in, I kept my eyes to the ground making sure I was copying the person in front of me, I didn't want to go too fast or too slow.

We put the coffin down and sat down. Maeve dragged me to sit with her, I looked at Sophie who was saving me a seat and mimed 'Sorry' to which she smiled and waved her hand like it was nothing.

The remembrance started, the Minister started talking about Tom, his life, his accomplishments, and there were even a few funny stories added in. Maeve and I had gone through the speech so many times I knew what he was going to say. After we had a minute of silence, the celebrant spoke again, "Maddie was a friend of Tom's and she's written a few words that she would like to share." I got up from the bench and walked over to the podium where the mic was, I looked around at everyone, there were a lot of people there, some people my age, some older. It shows how many people cared about him.

> "I only knew Tom for a couple of months, but in those couple of months, he taught me more than the school system did in 16 years, he cared more about everything than anyone I had met before him, and he learned how to make a cappuccino quicker than I had taught anyone previously..."

A few people chuckled at this.

> "Tom was, no, still is, the one person that made me realise there's more to life, and I'm not on about going to different countries or learning new hobbies, I'm talking about the simple things in life. For example, I remember the time he told me the story about The Dog and the Shadow.

It goes something like a Dog is walking home with a piece of meat in his mouth. On his way home he crosses a river and looks into the water. He mistakes his reflection for another Dog and wants this dog's meat. As he opens his mouth, the meat falls into the river and is never seen again. He would then say 'We have to be happy with what we've got because if we are constantly thinking about the things we don't have, we miss the wonderful things we do. He would say 'one day we might have nothing worth money, but we can always have something more, we can have love and that, that's the most valuable item anyone could own..."

I took a breath before continuing.

> "Tom is one of the only people that affected my life, he came running into it at 100mph, and he left the same way. I wish I could have 40 more years with Tom, I wish we could grow old and still have conversations about the constellations and how celebrities are actually aliens. Conversations that I did not cherish at the time. I'm glad I had

the pleasure of spending 2 months with Tom, I had the privilege of coming into his life and now being a part of Maeve, Elise, and Callie's life as well." The tears subtly rolled down my face, I sniffled, and looked towards the casket "Thank you Tom, for not only making my working day easier but for brightening up my life. I will miss you, forever."

I looked down at the piece of paper and folded it neatly, placing it back into my pocket and sitting back down. Maeve was in floods of tears, and Elise who was sitting next to me held onto my arm.

The tears fell down my face for the rest of the service. I just cried, I cried because even though Tom wasn't blood, in that short time he became my family.

When the service finished, we headed out to where the flowers had been placed. There were a lot of people at the funeral and most of them came with flowers. Slowly everyone dispersed and headed to the coffee shop. Sophie was able to get permission from the company to be able to use it a couple of days before it was due to open.

When I walked in, most of the shop was still covered in white sheets so I couldn't see much of the new designs. Sophie had laid out some food and drinks for the wake and it looked pretty good. I wasn't hungry but everyone else seemed to enjoy what Sophie had put out.

Sophie and I were able to meet up again at the coffee shop, I stayed with her most of the time. We spoke about the coffee shop and how it should be open in a couple of days. She told me that she really wished Tom could have seen the final product as he helped just as much with ideas as the rest of us did.

"I asked the corporate if we could remember Tom somehow in the shop, but they said that unfortunately they couldn't." Apparently, they didn't give her a reason as to why, which means there were either too many reasons or no reason whatsoever except they didn't want us to.

Maeve went around talking to everyone that was at the wake, she thanked them all for coming and talked to each person for a couple of minutes before moving onto the next person. The twins sat in some chairs and played on their video games. They were tired from the service and kept asking to go home, so their grandparents ended up taking them home.

Sophie and I stayed for 2 hours, she then headed out the back and I headed home. Maeve was so busy talking to everyone that I didn't have a chance to say goodbye. I just left thinking she wouldn't mind at all.

With love,

Maddie x

12 DAYS LEFT

Dear Diary,

Over the last few days, I have been consumed by thoughts about Tom. About how if I had never asked him to swap shifts, it would be me in a coffin and not him. How Maeve would still have her son and the twins would still have a brother. By doing something so small, I have robbed them all of the chance to see what kind of man Tom would become. I should have been the one to serve Alice and I should have been the one to end up in the hospital. Tom should not be dead. I should be. I can't comprehend in my mind or my heart what has actually happened. I know that Tom is never coming back but every time my phone goes off or someone walks into the shop, expect it to be him. No matter how hard I wish, it doesn't happen. It never will.

I cannot live with the guilt of it all. I will go to my grave with one massive regret; that I could not save him. That I unknowingly put him in danger when it should have been me. I am relieved in one way that I will not have to carry this burden with me forever, it will surely kill me eventually. If anyone deserves to live it's him, not me.

Christ. I don't even want to live. How can life be so cruel as to take someone who has given up completely. I am wasted in this life, but Tom? He had a real chance. A chance to be better. A chance to succeed. I know it and Maeve knows it, Tom lost his life in my place, and I will do nothing but waste it.

I already miss him. Sure, we knew each for a short time, but in that time, he became my closest friend and I wanted so much more than friendship from him. Knowing that Tom felt the same way makes it worse. I keep thinking about all the what if's. What if we dated? What if we grew old and lived in that old house Tom always dreamed of? What if he didn't get killed? What if I didn't kill him?

****

The shop opened three days after Tom's funeral. So, to some extent, life returned to normal.

On the Saturday before, I headed to work. As soon as I turned the corner and looked at the shop it was completely different. The outside was now a light grey instead of a white, the sign was now in front of the door in big writing and had led lights around the outside. As I stepped into the building the whole atmosphere had changed, there were 2 lots of sofa seating which consisted of windows with a table with two seats on either side, opposite the window on the wall side was a quote in big cursive writing it was the company's motto 'An extra shot helps the day go away' which I always thought was quite depressing. Underneath the writing was a piece of wood used as a table with bar stools. Then there were two circular tables, one was in the middle of the shop, and one was closer to the door. It looked great, flowers were hanging from the ceiling, the lights were natural white LED's, and my picture was framed right next to the till. I walked round to the door and headed to the machines, the cash register was new and so were the machines, and there were two instead of one! There were also now two mixers, and the cake stand now had a protective glass (just like Tom asked). Sophie came out of the back of the shop

"What do you think?" She asked.

"This looks amazing Sophie! Did you design all this?" I looked at her gobsmacked. It looked completely different.

"Well yeah, a few things the head office chimed in on but yeah, I designed most of it. With your guy's help obviously." Sophie smiled.

I took in the whole room. It was amazing how different the coffee shop looked and how it went from a tiny coffee shop to this. It used to look old and worn. Now it was fresh and looked like it belonged in the 21st century.

Sophie showed me the new menu, the old drinks all stayed the same, but we added in some extras. Sophie told me that with the new items it would take a while to get used to, but if enough was sold and we went above and beyond for our targets, the store would get a bonus.

Once Sophie finished showing me everything, I was free to go, I picked up my bag and went to head out.

"Oh Maddie, I almost forgot," Sophie said as I was leaving. "This is the new uniform, it's more than just an apron now." She told me while handing me a bag. The new uniform was a dark blue shirt with the shop's logo on the side. I thanked her and turned around but before I could continue walking Sophie asked, "Do you think about him?" I didn't need to ask her who she was talking about because I knew.

"All the time." I told her without turning back around.

"Does it make it easier?"

"No." I sighed and walked out.

As I walked home, I realised that I hadn't been thinking about Tom all this time, that since I've been seeing Maeve and the twins, I haven't thought about him as much, it made me feel bad because I should be thinking about Tom 24/7. I should always be thinking about Tom and how because I couldn't be bothered to wake up early in the morning to go to work, he died. I should think about him when I'm awake, I should think about him when I'm asleep. I shouldn't be playing best friends with his mum or be the babysitter for the twins. I should be the friend, the friend who made a stupid error and got someone killed.

12 days. In only 12 days I won't have to worry about any of this. In 12 days, I can walk to my favourite spot, and I can meet Tom again. I don't believe in life after death, but I'd rather be nowhere with Tom than anywhere with someone else.

With love,
Maddie x

7 DAYS LEFT

Dear Diary,

1 week left until the big day.

Today was not good. The void came back. I thought I was finally finding some peace, but it came back. I tried to not think anything of it, but I had a big fight with my family. They asked me why I kept going over to Maeve's because Tom was gone, and the funeral was over. They couldn't understand why I was still seeing them. They didn't get it. They thought it was weird that a 22-year-old was hanging out with a 42-year-old and two 6-year-olds. I tried explaining that it started as one bedtime story, but the twins love it and Maeve, and I talk about Tom, but they didn't understand. Mum got angry, which meant Dad got angry. We called each other all the names under the sun, I went upstairs to my room and packed a bag. I wasn't staying here. I don't get angry often so when I do it's all this built-up anger that seems to implode. It's like I'm a volcano that is filled with lava and one day it just explodes, and it burns everything near it. That's what I am, I'm an erupting volcano.

For a while I was getting somewhere, I thought the void was just nonsense, that whatever it said it was making up, but my parents said a few things, things I couldn't shake. You know how sometimes you get thoughts about how useless you are or how the way you said something was mean and hurtful, and sometimes you can swipe them away. You can get rid of them and make yourself believe it's just thoughts until someone says something that your thoughts told you all along. Then you believe everything that your thoughts tell you, you believe your thoughts when they say you're useless or you're fat or you're a horrible bitch. You believe them because someone's stated that thought in their mind and verbalised it. That's me. The voids right, if the void has started all of that and my parents have just said 10% of those things to me then the other 90% is right as well. I'm ready. The void's ready and it seems that my parents are ready as well. They want me gone. I'm gone.

Maeve didn't call today either, every day for the last 3 weeks she's called to ask me to come round. I would hear the kids talking in the background asking for me, begging Maeve to put them on the phone and ask them but she never would. She would always ask politely and try to tell them to be quiet, which obviously didn't work. I would always laugh; I thought it was funny how they would be annoying Maeve so much she would call me. She would always start with "I tried talking to them for 40 minutes, but they only want a story from you. They say you're the best." It made me laugh, also made me feel a bit sad because Tom used to be their favourite and now, I've replaced him. I didn't want to replace him. I just wanted them to find some normality during the hard times. Maybe they've found normality now, maybe they don't need me anymore. It's always the way, people move on from me, when they get their own better life, they don't need me anymore, my use is over with. I should have seen it coming, they are 6, and even though I don't know a lot about kids, I know I was reading on my own at 6, so they probably read to themselves as well.

I sat in my car all day, I spent most of the time just staring at my phone waiting for it to go off. It didn't, of course. I didn't drive far, I spent most of the time driving around the village, I wanted to stay close, so I drove to Bampy, I sat in my car for a while just staring into the cemetery and when I was ready, I slowly walked over to the cemetery and made my way through to Bampy's grave. Despite it being September, it was a colder day than usual, the slight wind caught into my jacket and made me shiver. I sat down in front of his grave. "I need your help, Bampy. I know I haven't visited in a while, and I'm sorry about that but I could do with some wise words right about now." I waited as if I would hear something as if Bampy would turn up all of a sudden. He didn't, obviously. "I don't know what to do, I'm so alone, I have no one. Everyone leaves."

"It's easy to stand in the crowd but it takes courage to stand alone."

I turn around suddenly to see an elderly gentleman standing behind me. He's wearing a dark grey suit that looks a bit too baggy on him, and he's carrying flowers.

"I'm sorry?" I asked him.

"It's easy to stand in the crowd but it takes courage to stand alone. It's a quote from Mahatma Gandhi." He smiled.

"Thanks." I smiled back.

"Just because you're alone it doesn't mean you're lonely. You just have to find the right person." He added. I looked around again and he was now at a grave not far from Bampy's.

"I found the right person, but he's gone now." I stood up, patted Bampy's grave and went to head off.

"They're never truly gone, you know." He continued. "Even when they've passed on, they never truly leave you. If they meant so much to you, a piece of them is within you. You may not even realise it, but you might find yourself doing something different or thinking something different because of them. For example, do you ever do something and think, would they approve?"

I nodded

"That's because they've had that impact on you. Someone isn't truly gone when they pass away, they live in your heart forever." The gentleman smiled at me and put the flowers down.

"I hope that's true." I say as tears begin to sting my eyes.

"I believe so. My wife's been gone for nearly twenty years, and I still feel her every day." He blew a kiss at the grave he stood in front of.

"Thank you." Is all I manage to say.

"You're welcome. Just remember, you are never truly alone." The man patted me on the shoulder and then made his way out of the cemetery.

After that, I couldn't help but think about what the old man said. I don't have anyone anymore, everyone's moved on.

Becks is off somewhere with her stupid boyfriend, Tom is gone, Bampy is gone, Sophie is my manager, so I have to stay professional, and my family don't even like me anymore. I thought I was lonely before but now, now I truly know what it means to be alone. I may have Tom in my heart, but I need him in real life right now.

With love,

Maddie x

6 DAYS LEFT

Dear Diary,

I assumed the void would be quieter the closer I got to my D date; however, I was wrong.

In the last couple of days, it's been a voice that's taunted me. It's called me stupid and fat and lazy and ugly. It's told me to kill myself in so many different ways, it's laughed at me when I dropped a cup or when I got some toilet paper stuck on my shoe.

It's becoming one sentient being in my mind and I can't stop it. I can't stop it and I shouldn't. I've realised that the voice is right and has always been.

The first thoughts I got from the void was at age 10, it called me fat and told me nobody liked me, and everyone took the mick out of me. It was true, I remember being in class and a group of girls started throwing things at me while making pig noises.

I started believing the void because I thought it was some sort of psychic ability. I thought I was able to read people's minds, as I got older and the void became stronger, I believed less in the fact that I was psychic and knew that it was just my brain.

I will always remember when the void started because it came out of nowhere, nothing massive had happened in my life at that point, Bampy was still alive, Becks and I were good friends, and I was a kid.

I thought the worst thing to happen to me was when my mum wouldn't let me stay up past 7 on a weekday to watch Doctor Who repeats.

Then like a light switch the void came into my life, it started as a whisper now and then, and then it turned into what it is today. The void was sly, it would be quiet for a couple of days, weeks or even months and then all of a sudden it would turn up again, and it would knock me off my feet.

I thought about how I used to feel when the void would whisper things to me. At that age I was so self-conscious of everything. I didn't want to go up and sharpen my pencil because my anxiety had taken over control. I would wait to use the bathroom because I didn't want to stand up and walk out of the classroom in case something embarrassing happened and everyone laughed at me.

I thought about that feeling of fear, the fear of rational things that people shouldn't be afraid about and how that all derived from the void feeding thoughts into my head.

I thought about how I feel now, and it doesn't compare. I get moments of complete heartbreak, there are times when I feel my heart shattering into millions of tiny pieces because of how much guilt I feel over Tom and how much I loved and adored him and how I will never be able to tell him that.

I get moments of disassociation where I feel like I'm in somebody else's body watching over my own, looking at myself and thinking 'is that really who I am, wow the void is right.'

There are moments where I am on top of the world and nobody, not even the worst villain in the world could stop me and then there are moments where I'm ringing out my pillow cases because I've cried the same volume as the Niagara Falls in under 12 hours. But the worst moments are the moments where I sit there, and I feel nothing.

I feel like I'm a robot who's computer software hasn't yet allowed them to feel. I know what sadness, happiness, fear, and anger all should feel like. I know what facial expressions people make when they are either one of those or when each one of those emotions should be expressed depending on the situation, but I just don't feel them.

When I say I feel nothing, I'm not trying to make a joke, I'm being deadly serious, it's like my emotional receptors turn off.

I've learnt the void doesn't stop; it just teases me. It wants me to think

I'm getting better so that when I get bad again it feels like ten steps back. I just don't know what to do anymore.

I don't know who I am, and I don't think I can keep on going.

With love,

Maddie x

4 DAYS LEFT

Dear Diary,

Only a couple more days to go. I can't believe in 4 days my whole plan will come to life. The thing I've been working on for 96 days will be here.

Getting up yesterday to the sound of my alarm confused me a lot, I was so used to waking up naturally that the alarm shocked me. I didn't have to get up mega early, I set my alarm for 6:50 am as I was opening the shop at 8:00 am. I would also be the only one the entire shift unless it got busy so Sophie would help out. I got out the new outfit from my wardrobe, I put the shirt on which was a bit baggy on me, but I didn't mind that. I put the apron in my bag and headed to work. I got to work 10 minutes early so I could set everything up and start the coffee machine. Sophie came down to try to help me out so I could have 5 minutes for a drink.

"Are you excited to be back?" she asked. "I guess, it's better than being at home doing nothing, I was so bored." I told her.

"You could have always messaged me; you could have helped with the renovation."

Sophie looked different, she styled her hair differently, she had a new uniform that was a different colour to my shirt, and she looked different. She looked sadder but was still smiling massively, she was hiding something.

"I'm not a huge renovator, I'd only get in the way." I replied but continued starting the machine and taking the plastic off the cakes. At 8:00 am we opened the shop. It was quiet to start with especially for a Monday, loads of businessmen or women come in to get a coffee before they head off to their very important business meeting. Maybe they didn't know we were open, although the huge board outside the door should be an obvious sign.

I finished work around 6:00 pm. When I finished, I went straight home and to my room, I wasn't hungry all I wanted to do was write the letters. I didn't want to put it off any longer, I had to write letters to mum, dad and David. I had to get them over and done with, I didn't want to wait any longer. I started with David, I thought it would be the easiest one because I wasn't as close to him as I was mum and dad.

Dear David,

We never really saw eye-to-eye, growing up I didn't have friends, but you did, so I would always try to join in playing with you and your friends. You would always tell me to leave you alone, you didn't want your lame, younger sister joining in playing tag with you and your friends. It would always make me sad when you wouldn't let me play because I'd see other siblings who would play together but we didn't have that. On the small occasion that I would annoy mum into making you play with me, you'd always give me the worst job, like if we played tag, I'd be the one running trying to tag people and because I was a fat kid, and you and your mates were skinny and fast, I would never catch you guys. So, I would give up. I think you always wanted that; you knew if I had the worst job in the games then I wouldn't be there long. I know you didn't do it to be mean, I know that if it was the other way round then I would do the same. I'm not angry about what you did, you've always been the popular one. You've always had loads of friends; you've always had someone to hang out with. I was never that lucky, even in our neighbourhood the kids were all boys and all around your age. I'm not holding a grudge, we were kids, kids do stupid things. If anything, I'm jealous, I wish I had the guts like you did to make friends or I wish I wasn't such a freak that people would want to be my friend. I wish I could have been more like you.

If you ever have kids, I want you to make sure they get along. I want you to make sure they play happily together, that they are friends as well as siblings. I would love it if they were so close that they could confide in each other. I know it's not always possible especially with different genders but it's possible.

Live every day like it is a new day. Live like there's a tomorrow because I didn't get the chance.

With love, Maddie x

Once I had finished David's letter, I placed it in an envelope and put it with his photo frame. Next, I did mum and dad's. I thought about writing a separate letter for both of them but what I wanted to say was basically the same. There were a few things that would have been different but apart from that the letters would be the same.

Dear Mum & Dad,

I don't know when you're reading this, you could be reading this a day after I've gone or a month. It depends on how long it's taken you to go through my room. As you will find I've taken the liberty of clearing out most of my things for you already, which will make it easier to sort the rest.

I'm sorry I couldn't be a better daughter, mum you always taught me to have a career and not a job and I wasn't able to do that. I'm sorry that most of the time I would be moody or miserable or a damn right pain in the ass but that was me. I wish I could change that, but the more I tried the worse the thoughts took over. I spent so much of my life trying to be happy, but it didn't happen.

Do you remember the time when we went to the beach and the puppet show was on? I must have been about 8 years old. David had gone off to play on one of the games they had set up, but I watched the puppet show. Do you remember how you had to drag me away from the puppet show because we had to go on the pier before it shut? I remember we got to the pier, and we found David and Dad playing a shooting game, so we went to the claw machine. It was the first time you allowed me to properly go on the claw machine and I won! I won a tiny teddy bear; you told me how proud you were of me that I had won. We went and got ice cream and sat out on the pier and watched the sunset, and you listened to me talk about the new episode of Doctor Who I had just watched. I know you never wanted to hear about it, I know you didn't care about it, but you let me talk. That was the last time I remember being happy. My last happy memory was at 8 years old, going to the beach unplanned and it was the best day I had ever had.

It all went downhill from there. I had started year 4 and I was always alone. I had no-one and that basically continued on for the rest of school, I had Becks of course but we grew apart. There's always been this cloud over me, one that changes so quickly. I don't feel happy anymore, I feel nothing.

As much as you can be a pain in my ass, don't think for one second, you're the cause of this. You aren't. You tried, you tried to help me, you tried to get me help but it didn't work and that's fine. I've come to peace with my demons, I want you guys too as well.

With love, Maddie x

Writing mum and dad's letter made everything more real. It wasn't soppy like Tom's, but we weren't a soppy family, and they still had this diary that they could read for more clearance. Once I finished the letter, I put it with the frames and hid them in my wardrobe. On the day I would put them in a more obvious place, my family wouldn't come into my room, so they won't find it for a while.

****

I woke up this morning in pain, it was strange, my body was aching all over. It couldn't have been because of work because when I wasn't at work I did a lot of walking, it was a different kind of ache. It was a numbing ache. I had a quick shower, stuck my hair up in a half bun and headed to work. Tomorrow I'm going to see my nan, I'm going to pop over and take her out for some food. I think it will be good to see her one last time.

With love,

Maddie x

3 DAYS LEFT

Dear Diary,

I saw my nan today. I was only at work for a couple of hours as I needed to make up a couple of hours on my contract. It worked out perfectly, finished work at 2 pm, and headed straight to my nans. My nan lives about 20/30 minutes away, it's the other side of the city so I drive there. When I get to my nans, I have my own key, so I let myself in but before I head in, I ring the doorbell and shout hello, so she doesn't get scared when I just walk in. She seemed happy to see me, as when I got in, she gave me a massive hug. It felt refreshing. I'm not a massive hugger but getting a hug off my nan was always nice.

"Get your shoes on." I told her

"Where we going?" She asked.

"I'm taking you on an all-inclusive trip to the pub for some classic pub grub."

"Ooo' how lush." My nan smiled brightly.

15 minutes later and she was still in the bedroom, I went over and knocked on the door

"Come in," she shouted, which gave me a sigh of relief. "I just thought I'd put on some makeup."

I walked in and she was adding blush. I smiled; it was sweet that she wanted to get glammed up for us to go to the pub.

"All done," She exclaimed and looked at me "how do I look?" she asked with a gleaming smile.

"You look great." I told her.

We headed out to the local pub, nan decided to have one of the classic cheeseburgers and I went with a panini and chips. As I sat there, I took in all of her features, I looked at her face, I looked at how despite not being a makeup artist she had taken her time and had come up with a look that turned out good. She had this blue eyeshadow that went well with her top, she hadn't put too much eyeshadow on, so it looked subtle. She did have a nude lipstick on, but it had rubbed off. I looked at her laugh, nan always found everything funny, I assume that's where dad gets it from.

I knew this was my last day with my nan, I knew that I wouldn't ever see her again and the thought of that kept spinning around in my mind. While we were eating, I could hardly talk, I knew what to talk about, I could talk to her about Tom, or the family but anytime I tried to it just wouldn't come out. I wanted to say everything and nothing at the same time.

"How's the family?" I finally managed to ask.

"Yeah, they're okay, Joe came up the other day to see me so that was nice. Oh, Sarah is expecting another child! She told me a couple of weeks ago. How's the family at your end?"

"Yeah, they're all good. David might be getting a promotion at work." I told her, I didn't add that in three days I wouldn't be here.

Once we finished our food we headed back to my nans. I knew I needed to make the most of my last visit, I needed to talk to her as much as possible and let her have as many memories as she can. However, when I imagined this 97 days ago, it wasn't how I imagined it would be. I thought I would be hugging her, saying goodbye, making conversation and having a laugh but at the moment, as it's happening now, I'm in shock. It's become reality, this is the last time I will see my nan.

My Nan and I sat in the chairs for a while watching tv, I wanted to make conversation, I wanted to ask her all about her life and find out anything and everything, but this sudden anxiety hit me. I wondered if she would know what my plan was or if she would just think I was being weird. After a couple of minutes of total silence, I asked her "how did you and grandad meet?" I've always wanted to know, but never actually asked her.

"Well, I was down at our local pub, I was with Janice and Susan, and we were having a few drinks to celebrate Susan getting a new job. I went up to the bar as it was my turn for rounds, when a young man approached me. He asked me if I wanted a drink which I politely declined at first. However, every time I went to the bar, he asked me if he could buy me a drink and eventually, I caved in. We started talking and he made me laugh, oh, how he made me laugh." I looked at my nan who's eyes were filled with tears, I smiled and soon my eyes were filled with tears.

"So that's how you met granddad?" I asked her with a tear rolling down my face.

"Yeah, he was such a looker back then, a year later we were married with our first home." Nan got up from her chair and started digging through an old shoe box. From the shoebox she pulled a photo of her and grandad on their wedding day, they both looked amazing. Grandad had a tux with a top hat and Nan wore a white dress with lace at the bottom. It was simple but they looked amazing, and I told her that.

"Nan, how did you know when you fell in love?" I asked her, still holding the photo in my hand.

"Oh, that's easy, I knew I was in love when the thought of being without him crushed me. I remember when he would go to work and I would just wait for him to come home, all I wanted was for him to come home."

Nan and I sat in silence for another couple of minutes until I spoke up again. "I think I fell in love." My nan looked at me with the biggest grin on her face and I continued talking "he was amazing, he made me laugh just like grandad did with you, every time I spent with him it was magical. We could spend 4 hours talking and it would feel like 40 seconds." I looked down at the photo, my tears were running down my face, the thought of no longer having it made me really fucking sad. Nan came and sat next to me on the sofa and pulled me into a massive bear hug, I went in and hugged her back, and the tears wouldn't stop. I went from crying over Tom to crying over my nan, I knew that when the hug stopped, and I went home that I wouldn't see her again and the thought of that broke me.

Once I had calmed down, nan got us both a drink, she tried to make me laugh by talking about how she accidentally farted on the bus, she explained that she bent down to get some change that fell from her purse, and it just happened. It did make me laugh and automatically I felt sad again. Nothing could make me feel better because this was it when I walked out that door, I'm gone.

When it was time to leave, nan came to the door to wave me goodbye, she has always done it since I was young, at the door we hugged goodbye, I kissed her on the cheek and I told her "I love you so bloody much, you wouldn't believe" and I pulled her into another hug "oh darling, I love you even more than you can think" she replied. I stayed strong while I was in her eye-view, I didn't want to cry again but once I got in the car and started driving the tears flowed out of me. I had to stop twice on my way home to try and compose myself, but it didn't work. The realisation that that was the last time I would see my nan finally hit me and it broke me.

****

When I got home, everything was going through my mind. I had only 3 days left, and all of the thoughts were getting stronger, the void had completely taken over and now I didn't know what my thoughts were and what the voids thoughts were. I didn't need to ignore the thoughts anymore, I just needed to hold on for 3 more days.

I was led in bed when my phone went off, it was Maeve. I answered the phone a bit too quickly.

"Hello?"

"Hi, Maddie, how you doing?" Maeve asked.

"I'm good, how are you?"

"Yeah, I'm good. Elise is asking for you again. I've tried telling her that you can't always come round but she wouldn't stop until I rang you." I could hear Elise in the background begging me to come round.

"Umm, I'm free if you want me to come round I can." I told Maeve.

"That would be lovely."

I headed over to Maeve's and read the twins a bedtime story, this time I read Alice in Wonderland to them. I made sure that my characters were stronger than they had ever been before, I even stood up once in a while to dramatize the story. When I had finished reading them a story I headed downstairs to Maeve. I popped my head into the living room where Maeve was sitting reading a book.

"They're asleep. Look if you don't want me to read stories to them just let me know. I don't want to overstep." I told her.

She looked up from the book and rested it on her knee "I don't mind Maddie, it's good to see them getting excited over reading. Tom was the only one ever to get them interested." I nodded and thanked her for letting me read to the girls.

Maybe they were away for the last couple of days, or maybe the twins didn't want a story, I'm unsure, but I didn't want to ask either, it's not my place to ask, I'm not family I'm basically just a babysitter. The void didn't stop while I was at Maeve's, it hasn't stopped in the last week, it still told me how useless I am. It told me how I'm selfish for going round when in 3 days I won't be able to. I should have detached myself; I don't know why I didn't.

With love,
Maddie x

1 DAY LEFT

Dear Diary,

Yesterday I spent the afternoon with my grandma. I wanted to make sure I said goodbye to her, she wasn't quite feeling like going out for food, so I took a few things from the coffee shop. I thought it might be nice to have afternoon tea at her house. When I arrived at her house I sat in my car for a bit. I kept thinking about how everything on my list was almost completed, and tomorrow was the day. I thought about how after today I wouldn't see any of my family or friends again. I thought about how I wouldn't be able to hear their voices again, how I wouldn't be able to go to work and make coffee for a variety of different people, how I wouldn't be able to progress in sign language and have an actual conversation with Doris. A million thoughts were running through my head when all a sudden there was a knock on the window. I jumped out of my skin and turned to see my grandma standing by the window looking at me. I quickly got out and brought in the bags of food. The first thing my grandma said to me when I got in was.

"Sorry for not being able to go out, I've not been feeling too well." She told me. I knew Grandma had been ill as mum told me. So, I didn't mind at all, I wanted to make her feel better before saying goodbye for the last time.

"That's fine, I'd rather stay here and know you feel comfortable than to make you go out. I did get some things for an afternoon tea." I held up the bag of food, which made her smile. I headed through to the kitchen to put things on plates. We sat down at the table and my grandma spent a lot of time talking about her being ill and not being able to go out. She told me "it's not like I even drive, it wouldn't be so bad then." I looked at her and replied, "you're never too old to start." This made my grandma laugh, which then made me smile. I thought about how when I go tomorrow, my grandma will have one less visitor. My mum and I are the two main visitors so now it would be only my mum. That thought made me go from smiling because I brought my grandma joy and made her laugh to being deflated because I realised my grandma won't have many visitors after I go.

After we had finished our mini afternoon tea, I cleared up and then sat on the armchair with my grandma. Unlike yesterday I didn't struggle as much in making conversation with my grandma. I asked her to tell me about how her and grandad met. I have heard it before, but I loved it so much that I wanted to hear it again.

"Well, my friends and I used to go dancing in town, we always had one place we would go, every week we would go, Bampy would also be there, I was too nervous to go up to him and ask him to dance but one day he came up to me. We danced all night and then he walked me home, and that was when we realised, we lived a couple of houses apart from each other. After that we went out another couple of times. On the fifth time we went out he asked me to court him. He was so handsome that of course, I said yes. Two years later we got married."

I always loved hearing that story mainly because of the fact that they lived a couple of houses down from each other and didn't meet until that dance. I loved hearing about my grandma and Bampy especially when she talks about Bampy specifically. We always got a bit teary talking about him, but it also made us laugh, Bampy was a character, and he did a lot of things to make his grandkids happy, like letting me be a hairdresser and combing his hair and trying to perm it. He absolutely adored us and I'm so glad I have so many amazing memories with him before he passed away.

****

Once at home I went straight to my room. My family were home, on one hand I didn't want to get too close because tomorrow was the day. I wanted to isolate myself, prepare myself but on the other hand, I wanted to spend my last night with my family because I wouldn't ever see them again.

You're pathetic, you had to do a 100-day diary because you couldn't just die you had to be dramatic. Why does it matter what you choose to do, your family doesn't care about you.

The void was right, nobody cares about me. Nobody likes me. I'm useless and a waste of space. Maeve hasn't called. Becks hasn't bothered. My only ever love was gone forever. Everything I touch turns to shit. That's why everyone leaves me because I'm well and truly messed up in the head.

Although I bet when I'm dead, people will come and say how much they loved me and miss me but in reality, they didn't even drop me a text or call me. It's amazing isn't it how people pretend to care when you're dead, they go on about wishing you'd called out or asked for help, but you did, and they didn't hear you or they chose to ignore you. They only want people to ask for help when it makes them look like a good person when it helps them sleep at night knowing they shared a link on Facebook about suicide prevention, yet they do nothing in the moment. These people are leeches sucking everything out of you until there's nothing left and then pretending, they were there for you the entire time.

****

When I woke up today, I realised I didn't have work. I had asked Sophie for today off as my leverage for doing the artwork. It took me a moment to realise I had 1 day left. It was my birthday tomorrow. Time had gone by so quickly; things had happened in the last 100 days that I didn't think would ever happen. I decided it was the best opportunity to go out and see everything for one last time.

I started by walking to the lookout; this was Tom's favourite place and I wanted to feel his presence. I don't believe in anything spiritual like that but for Tom I would believe anything if it meant one more second spent with him. I focused on my five senses, taking it all in slowly and photographing everything in my mind.

After about an hour at the lookout I walked to Bampy's grave. It was a 40-minute walk that took me an hour and a half. I stopped to let every person pass me, I felt the leaves on the trees, and I petted every cat I saw. I took everything in, I appreciated everything because tomorrow would be the end.

When I arrived at the grave it was evening and the wind had picked up. I walked straight up to Bampy's grave and sat crossed legged. "I miss you Bampy, but if the believers are right, I may be reunited with you tomorrow, we can see each other again."

"I wouldn't take the chance" a voice from a distance spoke. I turned around to see the old man from a couple of nights ago. He was walking up to his wife's grave with an identical bunch of flowers. "Pardon?" I asked, confused if he was even talking to me.

"Your death is something that happens to everybody else. Your life is not your own, so keep your hands off it." He spoke in a monotone voice.

"Mahatma Gandhi?" I questioned.

"Actually Sherlock, the BBC version, but I think it speaks volume." The old man placed his flowers onto his wife's grave then turned and started walking towards me, I too stood up.

"I lost my grandson to suicide, he killed himself last year. He never left a note, in the shows and movies they always left a note, but he didn't. My daughter couldn't understand why he did it. He seemed happy, he had everything going for him. She tried to find a reason, she spent months trying to find out why he did it, she was so set on finding a reason that she forgot she had two other children who were also mourning. They not only lost their brother that day, but they lost their mother too, and I lost my grandson and daughter."

I didn't know what to say, the old man pulled out a hanky and wiped his tears. "I just wish he told us; you know. We could have worked it out together." "I'm sorry" I whispered to him, a tear falling down my cheek. He walked away not saying another word, and all of a sudden, I felt terrible. I knew my parents would be upset; I knew they would mourn me, but I also thought it would be easier for everyone if I just disappeared. I don't know what's right anymore.

I stood motionless in the graveyard, allowing the wind to move me from side to side. All of a sudden, my phone rang, it was Maeve. I hesitated before answering.

"hello?"

"Code red, I repeat code red." Maeve shouted and then laughed at the end.

"I'll be there in an hour." I told her and hung the phone up.

I walked to Maeve's; it was a short distance from the graveyard, but I had to walk through a field. As I walked, for the first time in ages, I appreciated the sun that shone brightly in the sky. I stopped to smell the flowers, and to touch the grass. I stroked every dog that passed me by. All the things that I will never do again. I felt the breeze on my face for the last time and smiled at every person that passed. They smiled back, having no idea that they were the last people who would ever see me smile.

I rang the doorbell and immediately heard thudding coming down the stairs, Elise answered the door.

"You're here! I missed you!" She screamed and threw her arms around me.

"I saw you the other day." I told her while laughing.

"Yeah, but I still missed you! You always tell the best stories."

Maeve came downstairs with a towel on her head, I'm guessing she had just got out of the shower.

"Oh hey, sorry I didn't expect you for another 15 minutes" She told me while towel drying her hair. "Come on in."

I stood in the living room looking around, I noticed Tom's pictures had been put into a different place compared to last time and there were more of them. Maeve came downstairs, she had something different on now and her hair was slightly damp but not completely soaking.

"The kids are very excited." She told me.

"Thanks."

"Sorry about not calling recently. The twins have been with their grandparents quite a bit, just so I can go through Tom's things. I don't want to change his room, but the twins will want their own room someday so it's better to have it now." Maeve tried to smile but it wasn't convincing, and I think she knew that, so she stopped.

"I can't imagine what you're going through Maeve, I have no idea, I lost my grandad, and we were really close but losing a child must be a thousand times worse. Why do you think I always offer to come round?"

Maeve smiled and hugged me. I turned around and headed upstairs. I heard the twins giggling from halfway down the stairs, as I got into the room the twins were wiggling around in their bed waiting for me.

"So what story is it today?" I asked them.

"We want you to tell us a story." Callie shouted out, which made both the twins laugh.

"You want one of my stories?" I asked, and they both shouted "Yes!"

"Okay, buckle up because this story is going to be crazy." I told them when in reality I no idea had what I was actually going to say.

I thought for a second until I came up with the great idea of telling them the story Bampy used to tell me.

"Once upon a time there was a princess, she lived in the perfect world, she had everything she wanted, she lived in a giant fairy castle, with everything she could imagine but the princess was still not happy. The King couldn't figure out why the princess was unhappy so would give her more gifts to try and cheer her up, but it wouldn't work. One day the princess was walking in her garden when she heard screaming, she followed the noise to try to figure out what the noise was. When she got closer, she found a group of children with worn-down clothes playing together..." I continued telling the story of the Princess and how she played with the children even though the King didn't want her too. Every now and then the twins would interrupt to ask questions.

When I finished the story, the twins were still up. "I don't get it." Callie said.

"Well, the point of the story is that you can have everything you want but it doesn't mean you'll be happy. Sometimes the poorer people are the happiest because anything they have, they cherish, and they know the true meaning of happiness isn't bought."

Callie and Elise both looked at me and smiled "I know what I cherish." Elise shouted out "What do you cherish Elise?" I asked her expecting her to say family. "I cherish you; I love it when you come round and tell us stories. You're the best!" She exclaimed. I stood back for a second. "We love you, Maddie!" The twins told me as they jumped out of their beds, ran over to me, and gave me the biggest hug. I couldn't believe what I was hearing. Tears formed in my eyes, my nose was running, and I was trying so hard not to cry in front of the girls. Nobody has ever said they cherish me; no-one has ever made such a heart-warming comment as these girls did and for the first time in ages, I felt warm inside. It was also the first time since Tom that someone's comment had quietened the void.

"I cherish you too." I told them and tucked them back into bed. I couldn't stop thinking about their comment and how happy that made me.

"They're both asleep." I told Maeve.

"Thank you, they honestly don't stop going on about you. You took over from Tom, he used to be their favourite storyteller."

"That's the last thing I wanted to do." I told her.

"It's not a bad thing, you've been the best thing to happen to this family. Everything you've done for the twins and me, and I can't thank you enough, although I feel like I should pay you." Maeve laughed and so did I, but my laughter quickly turned to tears. Maeve hugged me and I hugged her back. "If he could see us now, he would be so happy. Maddie, he loved you and you have become family to me and the girls. We love you."

"You think of me as family?" I asked through tears.

"Family is made up of the people that mean something to you. Not the people who share the same blood."

"Thank you, Maeve." I said simply.

"What for?"

"For giving me something to be thankful for."

As I walked home, the sky now dark, I thought about all the things Maeve had said. I was a part of something, and not because I had to be, but because someone wanted me to be a part of it. Maeve had no reason to be loyal to me and yet she thought of me as family. The girls had no reason to love me and yet they did. I had never experienced this kind of free love before. Love I didn't have to work for. I just had to be me.

And now tomorrow has just been made so much harder for me.

With love,
Maddie x

HAPPY BIRTHDAY TO ME

Dear Diary,

Today's the day. My whole family decided to stay home even though I specifically told them not to, which has already ruined my plan because now I have to extend the plan until the end of the day. I know they mean well, they want to celebrate my birthday. It's a big thing to them but with them being home it's making it harder to say goodbye. I wanted it to be done the easy way with them, I thought if they were at work, it wouldn't be as hard on me or them. I have a mix of emotions. I feel angry they didn't listen and annoyed that they don't want to leave my side, but I do also feel grateful because not a lot of people get this kind of opportunity. I think about how Maeve won't be able to do this with Tom anymore, and then that makes me feel sad.

My family wanted to spend the entire day with me. When I got up, they surprised me. I asked them what they were doing at home, and they told me that they wanted to be here with me, even David had pulled a sicky. I was surprised that David had decided to stay home, I was unsure if it was for his own benefit or if the family knew something that I didn't, or they shouldn't. I know I should have been happy that they all took time off to spend with me on my birthday, but I felt annoyed that they didn't listen to what I said. I told them to go to work and they stayed off, it's so typical of them to do that. I know I should be grateful but today is the day, I've been planning it for 100 days and the one thing I wanted them to do was to go to work and they didn't do it.

I went into the living room and saw a few presents hanging around, I didn't want to sound ungrateful but again it was something I specifically didn't ask for, it's going to make it so much harder for them to return them now. I opened the presents hesitantly and tried to pull the best smiley face I could, I thanked them after I opened each one, I didn't want to come across as rude. I knew they were trying to make me feel better, but it was making me feel worse, because I knew that when I went to Bennetts Castle that would be it, and it was making it so much harder. It was making me doubt if I wanted to go but I knew I had to. It's day 0, this is what I've been waiting for and even though they stayed home my mind can't be changed, the plan must go on.

My family got me perfume, some makeup, and some sweets. I wasn't ungrateful but I knew that I would have no need for these presents after today. Once I opened the presents, we had some breakfast, got ourselves ready and then headed out. Mum thought it might be nice to go into town, do some shopping and then get some food. I didn't want anything in town, but I looked around and pretended to be interested. We went into a few shops and mum was trying to get me to try on clothes and shoes, I was able to convince her that I either don't need it or I didn't like it. I tried to look like I was interested but I was honestly just thinking about my plan. My mind was in complete meltdown mode and all my thoughts and feelings were spilling out. I didn't know if I would be able to handle being out for much longer.

Luckily after an hour of me saying no to everything we got some food at a BBQ place. It was nice but I wasn't interested in eating, I didn't want to eat anything at all. I was feeling sick to my stomach, so I ordered the smallest meal on the menu. Even with that meal I was struggling to eat it, I was swallowing it quickly so that I didn't puke it back up. My stomach was turning, and I was feeling more anxious than ever. It felt like I was holding onto this massive secret that nobody else knew of and that secret would change the lives of the people around me. Oh wait, that is exactly what's going on here.

Once we finished in town we headed back, mum got me a caterpillar cake, which I did think was pretty cute, and was my favourite kind of cake when I was younger. Everyone sang me happy birthday and then we all split up. David went upstairs, mum and Dad went into the living room, and I went into my room. I stood by my drawer for a while looking at the bag, I picked it up and looked inside making sure everything was still there, which it was. As I was looking at the bag I had a life moment, I thought about everything that I've done (and haven't done), I thought about how my life was turned upside down by Tom and how he showed me how beautiful life could be. I thought about how despite having a lack of emotions and feelings for so many years, I was able to feel things for Tom that I had never. I thought about the loss of my two favourite humans in the world and how if I believed in Heaven, they would be up there getting to know each other.

Before I had a chance to put the bag into my pocket my phone rang, it was Maeve. I answered and all of a sudden, a load of shouting came from the phone.

"HAPPY BIRTHDAY TO YOU. HAPPY BIRTHDAY TO YOU. HAPPY BIRTHDAY TO MADDIEEEEE. HAPPY BIRTHDAY TO YOU!!"

Once they finished singing, they all cheered, I heard Elise and Callie getting excited in the background. "Thank you." I said as my eyes filled with tears. The thought that this could be the last time that I hear their voice or see them filled me with utter sadness, and with all the emotions and feelings that were spilling out of me, I broke. I fell to the ground and started crying my eyes out. At one point I had to put myself on mute because the twins were asking if I was okay. When I finally sorted myself out and cleared my throat, I unmuted the call.

"Will you read us a birthday story later?" Elise asked through the phone.

"A birthday story?" I questioned, and now more tears were coming from my face.

"Yeah, it's a special story told only on birthdays by the birthday girl." Elise explained. I heard the excitement in the girl's voice when they told me about what a birthday story was.

"Hmmm, I'll have to think about it." I chuckled.

Maeve put the phone to her ear now and told the girls to leave.

"Hey, I have a present for you, so if you can come round later just let me know and you can have it then, maybe we can have a celebratory drink." She asked.

I couldn't believe she had gotten me a present. "That would be lovely," I said and hung up the phone. I didn't know what to do. I didn't know how to react or what to think. I don't think I've ever been as welcomed into a family and treated like family as I had with this one. From the first day,

Tom and I met at the coffee shop he made me feel welcome, and right up until today when I got a song and a present from his family. I never knew that one family could possess such kindness.

****

Looking back on the 100 days, I didn't realise how much my life has changed. So many good things have happened but along with that so many terrible things too. Not only have I lost and gained friends, but I've changed as a person, I can feel it. It makes this day the hardest day it could be. It makes the choice I have to make nearly impossible. At the beginning of this I felt like I knew exactly what was happening, I knew my purpose and I knew my end but then Tom came along, and his family and I realised my worth with Becks and it changed my perspective on everything. Dare I say it but I'm more optimistic about life and the things that it throws me. The void tells me things that for so long I listened to religiously, but I've found that I'm able to tune it out if I try to.

It's strange that out of nowhere, there is this small glimmer of hope. It could be a person you meet, the perfect stranger standing in a coffee shop, with a goofy smile and messy hair or perhaps you finally find the place where you fit. The place that has needed you all along. Maybe there's a place that I do fit in, where I can be me and I can finally understand what happiness is. I may never find someone as amazing and loving as Tom was but maybe one day, I would find someone else I fit with... Maybe I could become a manager of the coffee shop or be able to live off my artwork. I don't know but what I do know is that if I die today then all of my achievements will stop. I won't be able to succeed at anything else and make a name for myself. I won't be able to do any of that, and at the beginning of this diary that seemed fine, I was okay with that, but now I'm not.

So, I could continue on with my life, I could make something of myself even if it is something small or I can finish what I started. I could take the short walk to Bennetts Castle and end my life there. Say goodbye to all the pain and anguish that I feel in this life. Or I could wake up and realise that life isn't all that bad. Sure, there are times where it is unbearable. When it hardly seems worth the effort. When it feels like despite trying my hardest nothing good happens. When the void is so busy overtaking my mind that I forget who I am and what life is all about. The void is still there, it eats away at me every day and I know there will be days that are worse than anything I've ever experienced. Perhaps, if I do not do this today, I am just prolonging the inevitable?

Sometimes it feels like I'm taking two steps forward and one step back, but I have to remember that two steps forward and one step back is still one step forward. I think in times of peril, when there's no other end in sight it's easy to overlook all the small things that make for an amazing life. Just because I'm not a famous artist it doesn't mean that I'm not good at art, it just means that I haven't found my style yet. I could still find a job based around art and do something good. I could be a great person or even a good one.

I think I know what my decision is. It's a pretty easy one when I think about it. I've known my answer for a while, but I wanted to be sure. I knew that I had to wait until today so that I could fulfil my diary and complete the 100 days. I knew that if I felt the same way I did a month ago then that would be my only choice.

As I'm writing this, I'm realising how far I've come. I look at the person I was 100 days ago and it's completely different to the person writing this now. I've grown as a person not just in knowledge but with emotions too. When I started, I wouldn't be able to explain what was going on in my head and yet now it's so much easier. It's as if my eyes have been widened and I guess the only real person that I can thank for that is Tom. He made me a better person; he helped me express my feelings and emotions in a way that I didn't even realise I was doing. He brought me into a family that I cherish and adore, and he's helped me do all of that. He was my guardian angel in a time when I needed one the most.

No matter the choice I make today my goal for this diary has been well and truly met. This has been the self-portrayal and confessions of Maddie Miller.

With love,

Maddie x

About the Author

Amber R Cotterell is a Bristol born author. She's always had a keen interest in writing and at 10 years old her first ever piece was published as part of an anthology of poems by people in the UK called "A guiding light". Her second published piece of work was a short story that was submitted when she was 14 that was inserted into a book called "A twist in the tale". Reading was always a great escape for Amber, and she soon found that mental health wasn't written about nearly as much as it should be. She decided to write a book that she wanted to read and in 2021 "With Love Maddie" was published.

Amber has now created the Coffee Shop Collective, a trilogy of books that focus on 3 main characters and their struggles with mental health. Tom suffers with OCD, Maddie suffers from Anxiety, and Sophie suffers with PTSD. All incredibly serious mental health disorders. Each character has their own battle to face, all while working together in the same coffee shop. The Coffee Shop Collective is all about encouraging people to talk about mental health as well as learning to be kinder to those around us, as we never know who may be struggling.

Printed in Great Britain
by Amazon